RUIN ME

FORGIVE ME
BOOK 2

A. NASH

Ruin Me

Ariana Nash

Subscribe to Ariana's mailing list & get the exclusive story 'Sealed with a Kiss' free.

Join the Ariana Nash Facebook group for all the news, as it happens.

Copyright © Dec 2023 Ariana Nash

Edited by No Stone Unturned / Proofread by Marked & Read

Cover design by Trif Book Design

Authors note on languages and content:

In this series, "Mafia" is used as a catch-all term for Italian organized crime. For legal reasons, the author has chosen to use the fictional name "Battaglia" in place of real crime syndicate names.

The opinions and beliefs of any characters within this series are those of fictional characters and are not indicative of the author's personal views.

www.ariananashbooks.com

CHAPTER ONE

Vitari

Rome was all the best parts of Italy. The endless pace, ancient history, and beautiful people, thrust together in a swirling dance of religion, crime, and politics. Vitari walked among it, shoes clipping the uneven cobbled road.

He loved this city.

A deluge had washed the day's heat away, leaving the roads gleaming beneath streetlights. Traffic hummed, horns honked, and the night air buzzed with anticipation.

The doorman outside the piano bar, Buona Sera, nodded him through. Inside, shining glass, glossy black surfaces, and supple leather screamed luxury. Enormous chandeliers hung from fourteen-foot-high ceilings, making the people inside the historic converted convent appear small.

Carving through the crowd, he approached the plain door near the back of the main bar. A second doorman opened it, revealing a spiral metal staircase, and down Vitari went. Whatever the original use of the nuns' underground vault, the Battaglia had repurposed it. Ancient, solid stone walls made great soundproofing.

"Boss," Neo greeted, arms crossed over his silk waistcoat. Neo's real name was Lorenzo Bianchi, but as Bianchi was wanted by the police for smuggling arms and allegedly shooting up a DeSica bar, "Neo" worked just fine. The DeSica shooting had earned him an *in* with Giancarlo. Any enemy of the DeSica was a friend to the Battaglia. It helped that he dressed well and groveled whenever Giancarlo clicked his fingers.

Slumped in a chair beside Neo, a man not much younger than Vitari sweated through his cheap pink shirt. His eyes widened on seeing Vitari, then his gaze bounced to Neo and back again.

His day was about to get a whole lot worse.

Vitari shrugged off his tailored jacket, folded it over the back of a nearby chair, and rolled up his sleeves, taking his time. "Nice shirt."

"Uh... thanks." Mr. Pink Shirt fidgeted, only now beginning to realize the depth of shit he was in.

Vitari gave no warning. He swung, cracked his knuckles across Mr. Pink's cheek, then waited for Neo to right him so Vitari could hit him again.

"Wait, wait!" Mr. Pink blabbered. "Tell me what you want!"

"Right now?" Vitari flicked out his burning knuckles. "I want to beat the shit out of you." He hit him again to drive the point home, then backed off, saving his knuckles.

"Fuck." The idiot dribbled blood. "I'll talk, just tell me what to say!"

"Hold him," Vitari said.

Neo adjusted his stance to stand behind Mr. Pink,

grabbed him by the head and neck, and held him firm.

Vitari dug into Mr. Pink's pockets, grabbed the little bags of coke he'd been handing out like fucking candy in the wrong part of town, and tossed them onto the chair he'd hung his jacket on. He kept one bag back and weighed it in his palm.

A message was necessary, something obvious enough the stupid DeSica understood it.

"Wait!" Mr. Pink wriggled. "Don't." He knew where the bag was headed. "Is this about the priest?"

"What priest?" Vitari asked casually. It probably wasn't *his* priest. You couldn't throw a stone in Rome without hitting a man of the cloth. There were plenty of priests to go around. And besides, Giancarlo had said Francis was *protected*. Whatever the fuck that meant. So this DeSica dick couldn't be talking about *his* priest.

"You're Angel, right?"

Vitari narrowed his eyes. "And you are?"

"Freddy—Frederick—Ricky, it's Ricky." His knee jumped, vibrating from nerves.

"Freddy-Frederick-Ricky. What does you selling blow on my streets have anything to do with a priest?"

"It's just... I thought... I didn't take the job. It's fuckin' nuts, I thought that's what you wanted, what I'm here for?"

"What job?" Vitari snapped.

Ricky's eyes got all twitchy and vague.

Vitari nodded at Neo. Neo flicked a knife from his pocket and pressed the blade under Ricky's chin.

Ricky's gaze stuck to Vitari, his savior, the man who held his life and death in his hands.

"What job?" Vitari asked again.

"The hit. On the priest?"

"What fucking priest?" Vitari asked, fearing he already

knew. It was Francis. It was always fucking Francis.

"Father Scott."

Vitari froze his expression as his heart tried to fight its way out of his chest. He nodded at Neo. "Give us a minute."

Neo removed the blade. "You sure? This guy is a prick. Probably full of lies—" Neo gave him a playful slap around the back of the head. "Can't trust a word he says."

"I'll handle it."

"All right." Neo left Ricky panting in the chair and climbed the clanging metal spiral staircase. Ricky's glare tracked him the whole way. Vitari heard the door open. Thumping music and chatter poured in, then the door closed and all was silent again.

Ricky slumped, letting out a huge sigh, as though Neo were the one he feared. He really was an idiot. "I told the guy, it's nuts. Everyone knows the priest is untouchable. Taking that job is asking for the... for you to hang them by the balls from Ponte Sisto."

Vitari sucked on his teeth in thought. Ricky was right. Nobody would be stupid enough to accept a contract on Francis's life. Which begged the question, who wanted Francis dead so badly that they risked the Battaglia wrath? The last he'd heard, even the DeSica had withdrawn their offer of a million euros to bring Francis in.

"Who issued the hit?"

"No idea." Ricky straightened in the chair and dabbed at his swollen cheek.

"Who told you about it?"

"Big Eddie."

Big Eddie was a low-level piece of scavenger shit who picked up all the little jobs none of the real businessmen wanted to touch. He was also useful for gossip, if you could separate the truth from the stream of bullshit Eddie liked to spew. He could just be swinging his dick and making noise to drum up business. Or, the hit was real. Who the fuck would go to such lengths just to kill Francis? Not even the DeSica were that stupid.

"I mean, I guess I could find out?"

Vitari arched an eyebrow. "You that eager to flip sides, Ricky?"

Ricky had begun to relax, now they were talking like friends. "Man, I just sold a few grams. I didn't even know it was your turf. Let me go, and I'll find out who issued the hit. Nobody needs to know. My guys, your guys. It's just a little deal between you an' me, on the down-low, no?"

The idea wasn't all that bad. Vitari couldn't go asking questions about a hit without raising eyebrows. But nobody cared about this lowlife.

"The DeSica find out you're working for me, they'll be the ones to hang you from a bridge by your balls."

"They won't." He laughed tightly. "I'm just asking around. No harm done, right?"

If Ricky kept his word, then it would save Vitari from having to ask some uncomfortable questions. Questions that could not get back to Giancarlo. All mention of Francis was forbidden, if Vitari wanted to keep his tongue.

Vitari leaned forward and braced his arms on either side of Ricky, trapping him in the chair. They were close now, so close Vitari could smell the fear wafting from him. Sweat beaded on Ricky's top lip and dribbled down his forehead.

Finding out who was bankrolling a hit on Francis was information worth having. "All right. Keep it between you and me, and you've got yourself a deal." He shoved the bag of coke back into Ricky's pocket and backed off. "I'm keeping the rest though," he said, grabbing the other bags.

"Shit, man. That's a few fuckin' grand—"

"Watch your manners. Get me a name for who wants the priest dead, and you'll get it back." Vitari shrugged his jacket on, filled the pockets with coke, and nodded toward the stairs. "Run along, Little Ricky. I'll be in touch."

Ricky stumbled and tripped around Vitari, then hurried up the stairs, vanishing like a rat when the lights went on.

"You let him go?" Neo asked when Vitari joined him at the noisy, packed bar.

Vitari flashed his typical smile and settled on the stool beside him. "Just delayed the inevitable. Any time I can flip a DeSica, I'm game."

Neo smiled and sipped his drink. "What was all that about a priest?"

"Nothing." Vitari signaled the barman and ordered a beer. "Just Big Eddie making noise."

"Are we going to have a word with Eddie?"

Have a word meant break his legs. "It's not important." Vitari scooped up his beer and eyed a group of young women enjoying Rome's nightlife. "You up for getting fucked and high?" If he could distract Neo with drugs, sex, and alcohol, he'd probably forget all about Ricky and any mention of a priest. He also needed to tick the monthly box that made it clear to anyone paying attention that he fucked women. Because there was no doubt in Vitari's mind that Giancarlo was watching. His father had more eyes in Rome than back home in Calabria.

Hopefully, it would all turn out to be Eddie shooting his mouth off, because anyone insane enough to put a hit out on Francis was mad enough to carry it through, and with Vitari's hands tied several thousand miles away, Francis was on his own.

CHAPTER TWO

Francis

Stanmore House slumped in its overgrown gardens behind metal construction fencing, weighed down by decades of ivy and decay. There were no signs to announce the Victorian building had been a children's home in its past life, just a sorry story of abandonment.

He should probably turn the rental car around and go back to Westminster Cathedral, but he hadn't come all this way to balk upon arrival.

He parked the car along the street and walked back toward the grand house, hands in his pockets. Spring leaves had sprouted on the rows of naked trees, signaling warmer days were right around the corner. The air was warmer too, and the quiet suburban street was an idyllic slice of the UK.

Stanmore Boys' Home, with its boarded-up windows and rusted fencing, was a blight on the neighborhood. It should have been sold and bulldozed years ago, replaced by a small estate of eco-homes. Something good in its place, something that erased the past.

Faded posters fluttered on the fencing. Someone had cable-tied a bunch of flowers to one of the fence panels. The flowers had wilted and browned, so all that was left were brown stalks.

Francis peered at the house. He remembered it being huge, like a castle from a fantasy novel. Now, it was just a house, certainly not a castle. Funny, how time and child-hood memories warped the past. Or perhaps Francis's perspective had changed.

Through the brambles, he spotted the old coach house. Its roof had fallen in, and the windows were all smashed. Bored local kids and nature had ravaged it.

He glanced up and down the street. Nobody was about. Driveways were empty and houses quiet. Almost everyone was out at their day jobs. He walked around the side of Stanmore's gardens, where two fence panels had been forced apart, and squeezed through, then made his way around the back. Not much remained of the little yard they'd all kicked a ball in. The asphalt had cracked, turning to loose stone, and grass had grown to waist height.

Maybe he shouldn't go in.

But he needed to. He wasn't even sure why. He needed to see it, to change his memories. He needed to know it was over.

A wooden gate had rotted off its hinges. After shoving it aside, he ventured into the walled courtyard. The old stables had been converted into an outdoor toilet block long before Francis's time, and next to that, an old dairy loomed. He'd always avoided the dairy, sensing a chill around it.

Francis stared at that triple-bolted timber door and a familiar chill trickled down his spine. He didn't want to go near it now either, fourteen years later. His gaze wandered, seeing through all the overgrown brambles into the past. Behind an enormous buddleia that had taken over was the corner where Robbie Johns had fallen and broken his wrist trying to climb over the wall. Beneath all the rotting leaves and overgrown grass, there had been a patterned brick pathway. They'd all run along it, tousling and tumbling. Shoving each other, punching for fun.

There were other things boys had done out here, confusing things, when Francis had been too young to understand what that touching had meant.

He sighed through his nose and pushed through a curtain of ivy, into the back of the house.

A startled pigeon escaped through the hole in the roof. Despite the home's derelict state, much of the interior was as he remembered. The carpet, now rotten, was the same beige flower swirl. He passed under the crucifix on the wall and stopped as glass crunched underfoot. He nudged a shattered framed photo with his shoe, picked it up, and shook off the algae-green glass.

Stanmore Boys' Home. September 2009.

"Good lord." There they all were. All fifteen of them in a line, chins up, shoulders back. Francis stood off to the right, in what should have been a picture of boyish innocence, but he'd known by the age of ten he was broken, and it showed in his eyes. He'd been all arms and legs back then, skinny as a bean pole. Some things hadn't changed.

He plucked the photo from its frame and brushed off the dirt. Strange, how it had survived, all these years. What happened to the other boys?

But more importantly, Vitari wasn't in the picture.

Francis had believed him when he'd said he'd been a victim here, without any doubt. But he'd never seen Vitari during his years at Stanmore, and this photo proved it. There was the Stanmore Francis knew, and then there was another one, in the same house. Hidden from sight.

Francis tucked the photo into his pocket and took a deep, cleansing breath. He was here. And there was more to find.

As children, they'd had the run of the house, but there had been areas kept behind locked doors. He passed through the kitchen to a locked door they'd always been shooed away from. It wasn't locked now. Its bolt had broken, either kicked open by vandals or rotted off its hinges. He stepped through into an oddly shaped dogleg of a corridor, brushed dangling ivy aside, and entered a small dark, narrow room. There wasn't much to see. A high-level window with bars diffused the daylight. A few bare beds were bolted to the concrete floor. Another door opened into a small washroom with a toilet.

The beds seemed strange. Why keep beds off a kitchen?

Then the walls caught his eye. Much of the wallpaper had turned to dust and faded away, but in some places crayon drawings showed through, the wax defiant against weathering. Francis crouched by a bed frame and ran his fingertips over drawings of joyful stickmen with their cartoon sun. The more he looked, the more drawings began to reveal themselves, until they were all around him, on every wall. Faded, but still there.

The beds, the crayon drawings...

The boys had been too small to reach the window, so they'd drawn their own.

Francis covered his mouth.

How many had been kept in that one small room and for how long?

There were initials beside some of the pictures, and

some names, like Tommy and Caleb... Francis hurried along, searching just for names. He fumbled his phone from his pocket and took pictures, using the flash to capture the evidence.

Then he saw two initials he knew, bright under the phone's unforgiving light.

V.A.

It could have been anyone, could be any number of different names, but as Francis touched the initials, he knew. Vitari Angelini.

He stood too fast and stumbled back through the kitchen, down the main corridor, into the front room. The chair was still there—the chair he used to kneel on and wait at the window, watching for Father Charles Montague's little red sports car.

He brushed sweat from his face and gulped air. He couldn't leave, not yet. There had to be more to find, more... proof. An office? Somewhere they kept all the papers and records? He eyed the rotted staircase, then figured if he could survive the Venezuelan jungle, he could survive a rickety staircase, and climbed, careful to avoid the worst of the treads.

The bedrooms were to the left, he remembered that, so he turned right, then maneuvered down another offset, wonky corridor. Old floorboards creaked and groaned. A second staircase emerged, once hidden behind a door that had again been torn free.

He peered up at the narrow space strewn with ivy and cobwebs. He had to go up there. There may not be another opportunity to come back and if he missed something important, he'd never forgive himself. It was fine. Nothing here could hurt him.

He waved the webs away and climbed into an attic space.

Weak sunlight filtered through a filthy skylight. Documents lay strewn about, scattered over two desks and all over the floor. Kids had been in and trashed it all. He rummaged through the papers at the nearest desk. Letters, invoices, reports. Some of it was too faded to read; some had been eaten by mice. It was a mess. He'd be here all night trying to go through every piece of paper. He grabbed a box, swept the papers into it, then moved to the second desk and shoved all that in too. Dust clouded the air. He coughed and grabbed a second box. He'd take it all and rifle through it later.

The first box cradled in his arms was almost wider than the narrow staircase, but he managed to shuffle down it, collecting more spiderwebs on his way, and hurried outside to the car. Unlocking the trunk, he dumped the box inside and returned to grab a second.

On the third trip, a blue Mercedes parked several yards down the street caught his eye.

Had it been there earlier?

Somebody sat behind the wheel, but under the glare of sunlight he couldn't see their face or what they were doing.

It was nothing. Just his paranoia.

It had been months since his return from Venezuela, but he still jumped at shadows.

He slammed the trunk closed and shielded his eyes.

The Mercedes' engine burbled to life. The car pulled from the curb and drove on by.

It probably didn't mean anything.

He climbed behind the wheel of the rental and started the car, then pulled to an idling stop outside Stanmore, giving the house one long, final appraisal. He wasn't the same boy who had stared out of that window in hope.

He still had hope, but now he knew it came at a price.

He was done here.

Dusk had taken hold by the time Francis arrived at the cathedral grounds. Cars weren't permitted beyond the bollards, so he stopped outside and opened the car's trunk.

A dark-colored Mercedes parked across the road, under a broken streetlight, caught his eye. Was it the same? He couldn't tell if the color was blue or black. He kept his head down, and picked up a box from the trunk. He couldn't march over there and demand the driver move or accuse them of following him—he'd look crazy. Perhaps the car just happened to be the same make as the one outside Stanmore. Not everything was a conspiracy.

He carried the box of documents into the old school-house apartment building, unlocked his apartment door, dumped the box, and hurried back outside.

The Mercedes was still there. But without its driver. Nobody lurked nearby. Just rows of terraced houses with their curtains drawn, lights glowing from inside. Not even a barking dog. Was everything *too* quiet?

"It's nothing." He transferred the rest of the boxes inside, made sure to lock the apartment, and then hopped back inside the rental. The car was due back by nine p.m. He had some time to test a theory. He pulled from the curb, checked his mirrors—the Mercedes hadn't moved. After taking a few random turns, he glanced in the rearview mirror again. No Mercedes.

He was a fool. It was nothing. Jumping at ghosts.

He circled all the way around a few one-way streets, came to a T-junction, and there it was, joining traffic farther down the street. The blue Mercedes.

Not a coincidence. Not a crazy conspiracy theory.

He *was* being followed.

His plan had been to drop off the car at the rental lot, then hop on the Tube back to Westminster. However, if someone was following him, wandering around the Tube at night was out of the question.

What would Vitari do?

Lure the stalker into an alley and assault them.

Francis winced. He couldn't do that.

He drove back to the cathedral grounds and parked the car illegally next to the bollards. He'd get a fine, or maybe towed, but he'd rather deal with that than be kidnapped again, or worse. In his apartment, he locked the door and kept the lights off. Should he call the police? What could they do? No crime had been committed. And what if he was wrong?

He grabbed a knife from the block in the galley kitchen and returned to the living area. The stacks of Stanmore boxes loomed like ghosts from the past he'd brought home with him.

It would be all right.

He was safe here. Nobody would do anything untoward on cathedral grounds.

Seconds ticked into minutes, into an hour. He peeked through the drapes at the courtyard, but at the late hour, nobody was around. It probably was nothing. Why would anyone tail him? The entire Mafia fiasco was long over—all of *that* was in the past.

He opened photos on his phone and scrolled to the images of the crayon names:

V.A.

It was real. All of the horror. Everything Vitari had said.

What sin brought you here?

You did.

He'd been kept in that horrible dark room. He'd said, back in Venezuela, that he'd been... lined up outside—probably in the old dairy room with its triple-bolted door. *I'm soiled goods, one of the ones they used to line up at the back and take turns to fuck while you got a one-way ticket to sainthood.*

Harsh words, for a terrible act.

Francis laid the phone on his chest, over his heart. No child should ever have to suffer like that. It wasn't right.

Francis might be the only one who could do something about it.

The abuse had been systematic at Stanmore. Looking back with adult eyes, he understood that now. Vitari and the other boys had been hidden like dirty secrets behind that bolted door. They'd been *ruined.*

What had happened at Stanmore could not be allowed to go unpunished. Francis was going to expose it all.

CHAPTER THREE

Vitari

Rome had gotten noisy outside his window, which meant it was late. Vitari rolled over and squinted at his watch. Ten-thirty. Could have been worse. Shit, what day was it? Where was he supposed to be? He'd been out with Neo, they'd had a few drinks—

Someone shifted in the bed next to him.

He glanced over and followed the smooth curve of a woman's naked shoulder, down her arm. The sheet covered the rest. Fuck, he'd forgotten her name. He'd gotten so goddamned wasted he couldn't even be sure what they'd done, if anything. Although, he was naked too, so...

He dropped his head back and blinked at the apartment's cracked ceiling. His thoughts dragged, weighed down by coke and the weed he'd smoked. Taking product. Bad move. He needed to get a grip or he'd turn into Luca Espinosa.

He groped for his phone on the side table, ignored all

the messages on-screen, and—padding bare-assed from the bed—dialed the number in his contacts for *Frank*. He probably wouldn't answer.

It rang and rang. He wasn't going to answer. Sometimes he did, but lately he hadn't—

"Angel."

God, he loved the way Francis said his name when he wasn't throwing it back at him like an accusation. Vitari savored that sound, let it warm him through, all the way down to his balls. He sauntered into the galley kitchen and leaned both elbows on the countertop, keeping the unknown woman in his sights should she wake.

Francis had sounded gruff this morning. What time was it in the UK?

"Where are you?" Francis asked.

Vitari savored that too, the throaty *late night, morning after* gruffness. What had he been doing that had him so tired? "Rome," Vitari croaked, keeping his voice down so as not to wake *whatever her name* was. "Did I wake you?" *God, please say I did.* He could see him now, all messy haired and sleepy eyed, his lips soft and plump, perfectly bitable.

"No, I... I had an interesting night."

Fuck, he was getting hard behind the counter, and he liked that too. How there was a woman in his bed, but he had Francis on the phone, and he needed the priest—craved his lithe, pale body—more than anything that woman had likely done for him.

He'd had Francis to himself for one night—one perfect night—and all it had done was whet his appetite for more. He needed him in his veins, like a drug. The more time Vitari spent away, the more desperate the need became. And these calls, so forbidden, but worth every risky second. "Fuck, I want you," he whispered, still drunk, high, both.

Maybe he shouldn't say it. It wasn't going to change anything, just make the pain worse. "I dream about you," he admitted, "all the fucking time."

"I..."

Did Francis dream about Vitari? Was he about to say it? Vitari wet his lips, switched his phone to his left hand, and dropped his right to his dick. Should he tell him how he had his cock in his hands, how it made him remember when Francis's fingers had grasped him, how he'd jacked off to Francis's memory more times than he dared count since Venezuela.

"Angel?" *whatever her name* said.

Vitari looked up, into the eyes of his sleepy no-name lover.

"Come back to bed," she said in smooth Italian.

"Is that a woman?" Francis's voice peaked in Vitari's ear.

Vitari heard it, the note of jealousy and something else. Shock, maybe. At least Francis didn't understand enough Italian to know what the woman had said. "No..." He winced. Francis wasn't an idiot. "Yes?"

"I see."

And now he sounded sad, and Vitari's heart got all twisted and tangled in its own restraints. "It's not like that."

"It doesn't matter."

It did matter. Vitari dropped his dick. He felt like shit, like he'd done something wrong, like he'd broken a vow, which was ridiculous. He and Francis weren't anything and would never be anything. It had been a one-night fling, a crazy thing in a faraway world, like a dream.

God, he wished he were dreaming now so he could kick the no-name woman out and tell Francis how he was fucking his own hand just for him. He'd probably hate that too. Shit, Vitari didn't know how to fix this—knew he *shouldn't* fix it. It was better this way. Cut Francis off, like an incurable cancer. But Francis wasn't like cancer at all. He was kind, and occasionally amusing, painfully cute, but mostly a pain in the ass, and fuck, Vitari wanted to go to his knees and beg for forgiveness.

"I'm sorry," Francis said. Why the fuck was he apologizing? "You have your life and I have mine. I don't know what I was thinking picking up. You shouldn't call anymore."

Vitari rubbed his forehead. He couldn't do this with a head full of drugs. He'd say all the wrong things and make it worse. "I'm so fucking high right now. Forget I called. Forget all of this."

"Angel, wait—"

He ended the call and bowed his head, running his hand through his hair. It didn't matter, because at this rate, Francis would stop taking his calls anyway, and then Vitari would be alone again, just like he'd always been.

"Come back to bed, amore."

"Get out," he barked, then felt bad about that too. Where the fuck were all these feelings coming from? Shit, he was an asshole, confirmed by the many varied and imaginative insults the no-name woman was calling him. She threw on her clothes, strutted out, and slammed the door.

Hefting a sigh, he deleted the call to Frank from the call history, like he did every time, then flung the phone across the room. It hit the wall and bounced on the floor.

And rang.

Vitari dashed out from behind the kitchen counter, vaulted the bed, and grabbed the phone. "Yeah?" *Please be Francis, please be Francis, please be—*

"Answer your fucking texts. Giancarlo is coming," Sal said. "Be ready." He hung up.

Vitari slumped against the bed and listened to Rome's chaotic traffic churn outside the window.

Giancarlo was coming to Rome, so he'd better roll out the red carpet, when all he really wanted to do was take a private flight to England, find Francis, throw him against a wall, and kiss him until he came undone in his hands. Even if it meant his father would cut out his tongue.

"Fuck!" he yelled at the empty apartment.

Francis was right. He shouldn't call him again. But he would.

He got to his feet and stumbled toward the bathroom. He had a few hours to sober up and get his shit together, and then he'd be the loyal Angelo della Morte.

Because business always came first.

Giancarlo swept into Rome like royalty, bringing with him his entourage of old Italian blood. Little had changed in the way the Mafia operated in the past fifty years. The don was still the king on his throne, and he had his finger on Italy's pulse.

But the Battaglia would exist long after Giancarlo and Vitari; like a creature of myth and legend, if it lost a head, another would replace it.

Vitari went through the motions of greeting his father at Buona Sera, then disappeared into the background, fulfilling his role as the known secret and the attack dog. Despite everyone knowing he was Giancarlo's son, it didn't garner special attention. If anything, most everyone despised him. Vitari was scrutinized from all angles, from those who wanted to be him and those who wanted him out of the way. There were enemies everywhere—in the bar, out on the street, behind prison bars, in his own home.

Luca Esposito was gone, and his older brother was locked up, doing time for murder, but there were plenty of others, watching and waiting for a moment of weakness. He scanned the crowd. Buona Sera throbbed, wall-to-wall with socialite celebrities, politicians who needed a few palms greased, and anyone else Giancarlo kept under the heel of his boot.

Vitari spotted Sal at the bar and sauntered over. His bearlike embrace crushed Vitari. "Fratello!" Vitari grabbed Sal's shoulder and gave him a welcome shake.

"You good?" Sal grinned, playfully shoving him off. "You look good. Rome air, or is it the women, eh?"

Vitari snorted. "Something like that. You put on weight, Sal?"

Sal barked a laugh. "I told you, this is all muscle. Don't you wish you had some?"

He chuckled and settled at the bar, then spotted Neo by the door and waved him over. "You met Neo?"

Sal turned to get a good look at the man striding toward them. "Heard of him. Heard he's up Giancarlo's ass."

"No more than the rest of us. He's all right." Vitari swooped in, threw an arm around Neo, and dragged him to the bar for introductions.

Sal soon had them laughing. They got comfortable at the bar and fine wine flowed, as did business talk. The Venezuelan gold mine was back under Battaglia control. Vitari feigned disinterest and shut down all the fucked-up memories from that disaster. Sal cast him a few knowing glances, since he'd been the one to find Vitari in a Caracas hospital bed. Everyone knew Vitari had been in the thick of it, but few knew the details. Just that Luca hadn't returned.

Rumor was, Vitari had pulled the trigger, and that rumor suited him fine.

The night wore on and Sal left to meet with his father, Giancarlo's underboss, Little Toni, leaving Neo at the bar.

"Did you see your guy hanging from the bridge?" Neo asked, still chuckling from Sal's parting comments about canned tomatoes being the next big money earner.

"What guy?"

"Shit, you didn't see?" Neo leaned in, eyes sparkling in the bar's twinkling lights. "You need to start watching the news. Ricky, the guy we dealt with, selling coke on our streets? The idiot was hung by his neck with rocks in his pockets."

Vitari's mind raced as he forced a shallow smile. Ricky, who he'd hired to get answers about Francis's hit, had expired in less than forty-eight hours. "No, I didn't see that."

"What? I was sure it was you." Neo grinned as though Ricky's death was some kind of inside joke. "Let him go, then hang him from a bridge later? Seems like the kind of thing L' Angelo della Morte would do."

Vitari laughed, hoping he didn't sound distracted. "Not this time." Someone had worked fast to shut Ricky up. "Guy had it coming though. You don't sell on our streets and walk away for long. Which bridge?"

"Uh, I dunno. Not sure. Sisto, maybe?"

The exact bridge Ricky had mentioned during their meeting. Strange coincidence. Either he'd talked, or someone had been listening to their conversation. Was the room bugged?

Vitari eyed Neo in the corner of his vision. Neo: Lorenzo Bianchi. Smart, brutal, clean. He was exactly the kind of new and eager blood the Battaglia thrived on. And he'd absolutely sell Vitari out to Giancarlo if he thought it would get him a win with the don.

But there was no evidence for that, just Vitari's mind trying to connect the dots to make the picture he was looking for. Neo had been reliable, and loyal. And all he knew was that Ricky had mentioned a priest. There was no reason for Neo to take anything further.

Even so, Vitari had lost his lead on the hit.

Had Ricky asked someone the wrong questions?

The idiot hadn't seemed the brightest. If he'd shot his mouth off about Vitari letting him go, the DeSica themselves might have finished him off.

Were the DeSica trying to grab Francis again? It seemed unlikely. They knew, same as the Battaglia, the priest was *protected*.

A handsome, blue-eyed, blond-haired middled-aged man entered the bar. American, by the sounds of his accent. He said a few loud hellos, appearing to be well-known, then headed toward Giancarlo's corner.

Nobody walked off the street and right up to Giancarlo. Where was security?

Vitari straightened. Something about him felt off. The American's blue eyes fixed on Giancarlo. He reached inside his jacket.

Vitari shoved from the bar, and in three strides blocked the man's path. Vitari placed a hand on his chest and met his cool-blue eyes. "Stop right there."

He wore a priest's collar and Vitari's thoughts tripped on seeing it.

"It's all right, Angel." Giancarlo's deep voice bubbled up from the booth. "Father Davis is a friend."

"Show me your hand," Vitari said, unconvinced he wasn't about to pull a gun.

Father Davis straightened. "Interesting name, *Angel.*" From inside his jacket, he removed a small tin and flicked it open, revealing a row of cigars nestled inside. Not a gun.

Vitari knew people, read them in seconds, and the bullshit charm this priest was giving off sat uneasily in Vitari's gut. He narrowed his eyes, making sure the man knew he was on thin ice.

"Let him through," Giancarlo ordered.

He lowered his hand and backed off, letting the American priest close in on Giancarlo. They shook hands, exchanged pleasantries, and Davis got comfortable among Giancarlo's inner circle as though he'd always belonged.

"You can go," Giancarlo grumbled, sparing Vitari a dismissive wave.

He returned to the bar and Neo, who had watched the whole thing unfold. "Father Davis," Neo said.

"You know him?"

"Know *of* him. He's the flashy face of the American Catholic Church. Likes to come to Rome to throw his weight around. He's in with the Vatican. Didn't know he was friends with your father, though."

Father Davis didn't seem the sort Giancarlo would befriend. People like a handsome, brash American priest were noticed. Giancarlo must have a use for him, perhaps as a middle-man between the Vatican and the Battaglia. The Vatican would never stoop so low as to be associated with organized crime. Not publicly. But this was Rome, where crime and religion were two sides of the same ancient coin.

"There's something about priests," Neo mused. "All that religious baggage, then add the glamor and theatrics." He gestured with his wine glass, encompassing the bar and its illustrious patrons. "When it all mixes, you get some real psychopaths." He laughed at his own assessment, but he wasn't wrong.

The arrival of Father Davis spoiled Vitari's mood, and he couldn't even put his finger on why. Davis seemed charming, likable, and he played Giancarlo's table as though he were the hired entertainment. Maybe he was. But like everything else since Vitari's return from South America, it didn't sit right.

Neo left in search of better company, since Vitari's mood had soured. A little while later, Sal reappeared, beaming his typical grin.

"Hey man, you dropped this." He took Neo's place at the bar and slid Vitari's phone across the bar top.

"Shit." He had no idea and couldn't recall the last time he'd had it. "Thanks. Hey, what do you make of the American priest?"

Sal snorted and followed Vitari's gaze to the man in question. "Father Davis? Wannabe hanger-on. Likes to do lines of coke off Filipino girls' breasts and then claims he's a saint the next day."

Vitari should have asked Sal first. It sounded as though they were acquainted. "You know him?"

"Papá knows him. Hates the fucker. Says he has no integrity."

His papá, Toni, sat at the booth too, and from his thin smiles and dark-eyed glower, he didn't appear too pleased by Father Davis's presence either. Interesting...

If Father Davis had vices, then he would have been caught in some kind of compromising act, which Giancarlo would use as leverage. "Why's he here?"

"Same reason as everyone else—to stroke your father's ego." Sal turned his back on the room and eyed Vitari. "You heard there's a hit out on your priest?"

"He's not my priest," Vitari mumbled. "Someone has a death wish."

"You haven't tried to contact Father Scott, maybe warn him?"

Vitari narrowed his eyes. "No." Why was his friend suddenly so interested in Francis? "Why the fuck would I?" Did he know about the photos of Francis giving him one of the best hand jobs of his life? Giancarlo wouldn't have told anyone, but Luca might have before Francis shot his heart out of his chest. The list of people Luca could have told was endless, including his brother in jail. If his brother knew, then the whole fucking world probably knew.

"Yeah, right, why would you?"

Vitari did not like Sal's tone, or how he said it with that sly, knowing grin. It was all fun and games until Vitari got his tongue cut out for the sin of desiring men.

"I'm just looking out for you, fra," Sal said, his big smile fading.

"Don't. I left all that shit behind in Venezuela." *That shit* encompassed whatever Sal thought he knew and no more needed to be said. Ever.

"Just be careful, Angel."

Vitari shrugged off Sal's concern and grabbed his friend's shoulder. Time to lighten the mood and change the subject. "We're here, on top of the fuckin' world. Nothing can touch us. Another round? Something stronger? Your first night in Rome for a while. Let me show you how it's done."

Giancarlo left the piano bar near dawn, but instead of cutting Vitari loose, he summoned him to ride in his car back to the villa. They traded small talk, but it was as awkward as always. The only time Giancarlo ever seemed to relax was when he threatened Vitari.

The grand villa was made up of sprawling rooms, an army of staff, lavish gardens, and a pool that looked inviting as the sun began to rise.

But it wasn't a home. Too many eyes and ears in the staff.

Vitari retired to his room—a bland, soulless space with no more character than a hotel suite—and lasted all of twenty minutes before wandering through the house. He found his father by the pool, alone, smoking Father Davis's gifted cigar. Stalling in the shadows, Vitari contemplated leaving. If he said good evening, it would be wrong. If he left without speaking to him, that too, would be wrong.

"Come here."

Vitari sauntered over. What the hell kind of threat would he be getting now? He'd probably been too visible, too loud, or not visible enough. He'd learned, long ago, he couldn't do a damn thing right.

"Sit," Giancarlo said, gesturing with the glowing end of the cigar for Vitari to take up the seat at the table beside him. As Vitari sat, Giancarlo asked, "What do you make of Father Davis?"

Vitari sighed and squinted into the rising sun. "Don't know him."

"First impressions?"

"I don't trust him. He's fake, eager to please you. I heard talk he has no integrity."

"Well then, it sounds as though you *do* know him." One of Giancarlo's rare smiles warmed Vitari like the rising sun, and like this, sitting by the pool in the sweet morning air, with the breeze rustling palm trees and the world quiet, it seemed as though Giancarlo were a normal man, a normal *father*. Not a father who put a gun in Vitari's hand at sixteen years old and told him to kill a man.

"Who is Frank?" Giancarlo asked, still smiling.

"Frank?" Vitari echoed, as though his heart hadn't stopped. How the fuck did Giancarlo know that name?

"Yes, Frank." Giancarlo drew on his cigar and puffed smoke toward the sky. "Who is he?"

"I don't... I..."

"His number is in your phone." Giancarlo tilted his head, waiting for the answer.

Vitari's phone. He'd lost it the night before. Sal had given it back to him, then asked about Francis.

Fuck, Sal had taken Vitari's phone and given it to Giancarlo. The backstabbing bastard! Vitari's heart thumped in his throat. "Frank is a contact."

"But you do not call him, and he does not call you? There is no history in your call lists. So why is his name there?"

He'd deleted all the calls, thinking that would wipe any incriminating evidence, but hadn't realized the lack of Frank's number in the call history would be a smoking gun. He had two choices: Be honest, come clean, and hope Giancarlo was in a good mood. Or lie, and hope he didn't know who Frank was. Honesty was always best when it came to Giancarlo, but honesty in this case might see Vitari lose his tongue. Or worse.

But he hadn't *seen* Francis. Just called him.

His father had threatened to cut out his tongue if Vitari sucked dick, which he hadn't.

"I will tell you this now, my son," Giancarlo puffed on his cigar. "Just because we are blood, it does not forgive you your sins."

Vitari winced. There was no doubt Giancarlo knew he'd been calling Francis.

Giancarlo rested his arm on the table and peered at Vitari. "Look at me."

Vitari looked, keeping his chin up, even as he wanted to drop to his knees and beg for forgiveness and vow to never do it again.

Giancarlo jabbed the cigar toward him, punctuating his next words. "I got you out of England." His father paused, carefully selecting his next words. "I brought you into my home, and I made you who you are. Stay away from the priest, and from the past. There are things even I cannot protect you from."

That... wasn't the criticism he'd expected. It almost sounded as though Giancarlo *cared*.

"Understand?"

Vitari nodded. "Yes, Papá."

Giancarlo sat back. Ash rained from the end of the cigar. "Do not disappoint me, Vitari, and one day, all I have built—and my father before me, your grandfather—will be yours."

A strange kind of warmth built within him, a sense of belonging, a sense of pride. He'd never felt its like before. He'd always been shoved in the dark, locked away, the secret nobody wanted to talk about. Giancarlo's words implied there was a place in his life for Vitari. Not just a place, a throne.

"I won't let you down."

"Good boy."

Vitari leaned back, heart pounding, and watched the sunrise alongside his father.

CHAPTER FOUR

Francis

St Andrews Catholic Boys' Academy in Westminster was well-known for its charity events, supported by the cathedral and its beloved Archbishop Montague.

Francis attended today's spring fete in the school playing field at Montague's behest, and it soon became apparent the real intention was to demote Francis to the fetch-and-carry assistant, while the dashing, now beardless, Montague soaked up all the attention of the school governors. Montague radiated harmless charm, the same charm that had first lured Francis, and the longer the day of the fete went on, the more the moms fawned over Montague and the fathers laughed with him, and the more Francis seethed inside.

Montague was quick to kneel in front of the young children, take their hands, and tell them they always had a friend in God.

Francis tried to concentrate on being the exemplary

priest he was supposed to be: a pillar of guidance and understanding, a steadying hand, and a comfort to all those who came to him. And as he had found notoriety, he spent much of the day fending off questions about his kidnapping at the hands of the Mafia. But all the while, he kept Montague in the corner of his eye.

The day wore on without too much strife, until Montague, seated at a picnic table among the cathedral's staff, laid his hand on a boy's thigh with what appeared to be a simple gesture of comfort.

The past came roaring back. Montague had touched him that way. Before things had gotten worse.

Francis excused himself from a group of parents and approached Montague. "May I have a word, Archbishop?"

Montague looked up from his chair. "Oh, Father Scott, what is it? Are you all right? You seem... flustered."

A few of the staff looked over too. "In private, if you will."

"We're rather busy—"

Francis grabbed the archbishop's wrist. Turning him away from prying eyes, he whispered, "Do not touch him."

Montague yanked his arm free and his grey-blue eyes flashed. "Whatever has gotten into you?"

The boy scooted off, gone to find his parents.

Francis held Montague's gaze as the archbishop rose to his feet. He knew damn well what had gotten into him.

"I think perhaps you should leave," Montague advised. "We'll discuss this behavior later."

A few parents had turned to watch. Staff from the church too. This was not the place to argue. Francis hurried from the school grounds and walked the mile along Westminster's streets to the cathedral. Once inside, he shut himself in his office and paced. He'd watched the archbishop and had thought that perhaps everything Montague had done in the past had been a one-off, because of how Francis had encouraged him. But now, seeing the archbishop among children, what if Francis was wrong? What if Montague's predatory desires weren't over?

He opened his desk drawer and from between the pages of his pocket book of psalms, he took the photo of the Stanmore boys. Then, turning on his laptop, he opened a browser and searched for the boys' names. With the staff busy at the charity event, the office was quiet. Montague wouldn't be back for several hours. This was the perfect time to research the others. If he could find them, talk with them, he'd build a stronger case against Montague.

Francis typed in *Robbie Johns*, the boy who had broken his wrist climbing over the back wall. Robbie had been quiet, withdrawn, and the target of some of the other bigger boys. In the photo, his hair had been long, jaw length, and a messy black mop with bangs covering his eyes. Francis guessed his age and added the local area to the search to narrow the results.

Several possible results came up, but a news article caught his eye first.

Robert Johns, age nineteen, had died of a drug overdose.

Francis clicked a few more links and found a photo of Robbie taken after Stanmore. The article explained he'd tried to join the military but had failed selection.

Francis searched another name from his past, and after more digging, discovered he had died by suicide.

He searched another name, finding no results. Then another. Car accident. Drunk driving.

Were they all dead?

They couldn't be. Perhaps, because he was searching the internet, only those who made the headlines showed up, and the others were very much alive and well, living quiet, normal lives, with normal families.

His office door flew open and Montague charged in, his black gown flowing. "Your conduct earlier was entirely unbecoming of a man of your stature. This will go on your performance report."

Francis lifted his gaze over the top of the laptop screen. His heart thumped, instincts kicking in to defend himself. "What about your conduct?"

"What is it you think I did, Francis?" he asked, circling around the desk to stop at Francis's side.

He hadn't *done* anything, and he knew Francis couldn't prove anything. He'd always been *careful.*

Shh, don't make a noise, this will be our secret.

Those words, spoken long ago. The first time he'd been touched.

Montague had said *secret* as though it would be fun, as though what they were doing wasn't wrong, but exciting. And it had been, because in his innocence, Francis had *liked* it.

"Where did you get that photo?" Montague reached out to grab the picture of the Stanmore boys.

Francis snatched it back. "Fond memories?"

Restrained fury pinched Montague's face. "How dare you." A thread of real threat pulled through his words. "Ever since you came back from Venezuela, you've been... different. I didn't like to say, but you appear to be suffering from some kind of post-traumatic stress."

The only thing he was suffering from was the confidence to speak the truth. "How many of these boys did you groom for sex, or was it just me?" Francis's heart fluttered with fear now he'd spoken the secret aloud.

Montague's throat moved as he swallowed. His back

straightened, shoulders rising, like a bear standing his ground. "You are mistaken. You—"

"No, I don't think so. I distinctly recall the weekends at your house, in which you were *very* thorough with your teachings." These words were real, just like the memories, and coming from his lips, spoken aloud for the first time in over a decade. The more he said, the more he lit the fuse, and the more the fire inside burned, building to a rage he'd been keeping stifled for so long that it had become a part of his soul.

Montague glared and breathed hard through his nose. "You little pervert. It was *your* fault. You with your questions, and touching. I wouldn't have—I didn't want to—"

"I was eleven years old."

Montague looked away. "I resisted, but you..."

"I what?" Francis breathed hard too, still sitting in the chair, as though fixed to it. "What do you think a jury will make of you fucking an eleven-year-old boy, whether I encouraged you or not? I was a child, you were in a position of authority. And frankly, the things you did to me were no accident, archbishop. I didn't ask if I could suck your cock." Yes, his words lashed the archbishop like a whip, and it felt *good* to have the sins exposed between them.

Montague clenched his fists at his sides. "You little fuck."

"And there you are, there's the truth. You have everyone fooled, but not me, not anymore. I'm not the same boy you—"

Montague lunged. His thick fingers locked around Francis's neck and shoved him deeper into the chair. He gasped, clawed at the hand, and writhed, but Montague's weight was twice his, just like it had always been. He was back there again, under him, unable to move, confused, wondering if he'd made this happen, if he was broken, if it was all his fault, because he'd encouraged him, told him, in his stupid innocent way, how he'd loved him and wanted to be just like him. Montague had said he'd make that happen, and all Francis had to do was keep their secret.

"You ruined me," Montague growled, his eyes so big and bloodshot with rage, his grip crushing, his smell inside Francis's head all over again. "You tempted me. All of this is your fault!"

Montague's hand landed on Francis's crotch, groping through his cassock.

Francis gasped and bucked, dislodging hm. He kicked out, forcing Montague off, and gulped air.

Montague smirked and clutched the crumpled photograph like a victory flag. He crushed it in his fist. "Stay away from the past, Francis, or you'll end up like the rest of them." He marched from the office, taking the photo with him, and slammed the door.

Francis closed his eyes. His heart galloped, trying to escape. He rubbed his throat and winced at the burn. He should have done more, said more, but when Montague had held him down, he'd been thrust into the past and pinned there, buried under the weight of shame and guilt.

He choked on air and spluttered, or sobbed—it all felt the same. The guilt covered him again, as though he'd rolled in thick oil, the kind that didn't wash off. His skin crawled. He felt filthy, felt exposed, turned inside out. It had been years since Montague had threatened him, touched him, but now it felt like yesterday, as though his past sins were in the room now.

"God, come to my assistance, and Lord make haste to help me." He rummaged around the desk drawer for his personal mobile, grabbed it, and dialed Vitari's number. He still couldn't breathe, but it would be all right, Vitari would answer. Francis *never* called him. He needed him now, needed to hear his voice.

"—I can't talk right now."

A sob lodged in Francis's throat. He shouldn't have called. What had he been thinking? Vitari wouldn't care. He had women in his bed, other people in his life. Whatever they'd had no longer existed.

"What's wrong?"

He breathed, swallowed, rubbed his throat. "I uh... God." He scrunched a fist in his hair and squeezed his eyes closed.

"Let me get somewhere, hold on..."

He heard Vitari moving. Traffic hummed and honked in the background, a door swung shut, and now the traffic was louder. Vitari stood on a street somewhere, a whole different world away.

"Francis, what is it? What's happened?"

He gulped, choked, sobbed. Hated himself, hated how it sounded, and hated how he'd called Vitari, who would think him weak, pathetic. Vitari didn't fall apart when another man grabbed his cock. He'd probably put a bullet in that man's head.

"Francis, talk to me. Shit—are you hurt? Do you need help?"

"I need you..." Francis croaked. "To help me... kill a man."

Vitari inhaled. "Be very careful what you ask for."

Francis buried his face against the desk and willed himself to stop shaking. He wished he was back in Venezuela, back among honest, kind people. Westminster was Hell compared to El Cristo, but even that had ended in disaster. "I can't be here. I can't do this."

"Hey, whatever it is, you'll beat it. You hear?"

He wanted to tell him all of it, but Vitari had suffered too, suffered worse than Francis. He thought Francis had it easy at Stanmore, and he had, compared to Vitari. Vitari had left his initials scrawled on the wall of the dark room. Francis had no right to be such an idiot when Vitari's suffering had been a hundred times worse.

"Hey, do you remember the house in El Cristo?" Vitari asked. "You remember that night? It was a good night. One of the best. I might be a few countries away, but if you remember it then I'm there, with you... if you need me to be." Sirens wailed past Vitari. "Shit, I can't talk for long."

Francis did recall that night; he rarely slept without thinking about how free he'd been with Vitari. Free of guilt, free of shame. Free of everything. But that night had been a dream in a world of never-ending nightmares.

"I uh..." Francis sighed. "I'm sorry." He sniffed. "I don't know why I called. I just... I just did."

"I'm glad you did."

He slumped back into the chair with the phone clutched to his ear. "I wish you were here."

"Yeah?"

"I've stirred up old ghosts, and I'm not sure I can banish them alone."

Vitari breathed in. "Right, so you need my fists, huh?" Another voice mumbled in the background of the call. "I have to go."

"Yes. Of course." Francis dragged a hand down his face. He didn't feel as though he was coming apart any longer so that was good. But he didn't want the call to end. Vitari calmed him, made everything seem possible, made him feel... safer. Which didn't make any sense, as Vitari was the most dangerous man he knew.

"Hey, Padre Blanco, you're the bravest, most bad-ass priest out there. You don't need me to banish your demons." He heard Vitari's smile, and smiled too. "Tell me you're okay? Tell me you've got this."

"I am. Okay, I mean. And I do got this—*have* this."

Vitari hung up, leaving Francis holding the phone to his ear. "But I do need you," he told the dial tone.

It was crazy, clinging to that one night between them as though it meant something.

He shouldn't have called him. But he was glad he had.

Vitari saved him, whenever he was drowning.

He set the phone down and sighed the last of the panic away.

He'd lost the photo of the Stanmore boys to Montague. But he'd also gained new information. Montague had threatened that Francis would end up *like the rest of them.* The boys were all dead, and Montague knew it, had perhaps been behind it? All Francis needed was to find the evidence to condemn the archbishop.

Evidence that had to be in the boxes in his apartment.

He hurried from his office toward the apartment building at the opposite end of the cathedral grounds. The streetlamps blinked to life as dusk approached. Distant London traffic murmured. Francis entered the converted chantry and hurried up the stairs. He'd bring Montague down with facts. It was the only legitimate way. Find something to connect Montague to the abuse, to prove he was complicit in what went on at Stanmore, and he couldn't deny it.

His apartment door hung ajar.

He stalled on the landing. Was somebody in his home? His blue Mercedes stalker? He collected his door key in his fist, jutting its pointed end from between his fingers, and gently pushed open the door. In the gloom, one thing was immediately clear—the Stanmore boxes were gone.

All the papers, the documents, potential evidence. Gone.

He checked the rest of the rooms, but whoever had taken the boxes had left long ago. Probably when he'd been at the fete. He stifled a scream.

If they were so fucking desperate to silence him, why didn't they just kill him? The others were dead. All of the Stanmore boys! Why was Francis still breathing?

The church.

Francis was *protected*.

Was Montague the only one keeping him alive? The archbishop owned him in every other way, so why not that too? What if Francis tested that protection? What if he flew to Rome? How protected was he? Would they come for him there?

He couldn't do that; he wouldn't even know what to do in Rome, or how to find Vitari. Vitari had his life, which included women in his bed and all the things Francis had tried to run from. But what if Francis had been running from the wrong people this whole time?

He'd tried running, but he always seemed to end up back in Hell.

He had to do something. He couldn't stay, knowing they'd been inside his apartment, taken his research, were watching him...

What if he went straight to the top? Crime, politics, religion. Rome.

What if he went to the only true sanctuary he knew? The Vatican.

CHAPTER FIVE

Vitari ambushed Sal in the east wing of the villa, wrestled him by the collar, and slammed his bulk against the wall. Sal grunted, surprised, and threw up his arms. "Woah, fra!"

"You fucker, you gave my phone to Giancarlo."

"I had to." He spluttered. "Nobody says no to your father."

That was true. Vitari glared into his friend's eyes. "Some warning would have been nice."

"You'd still react like this."

Jesus, Vitari couldn't stay mad at him when he'd have done the same thing in his position. He shoved off him and Sal dropped his hands, then righted his suit. "Sorry, Angel," Sal grunted. "We tight?"

Vitari rolled his eyes and offered his hand, then hauled Sal from the wall. "You eating too much of your mamma's puttanesca?"

"Muscle," Sal corrected. "And you could use some. I

could put you on your ass with my eyes closed."

They laughed, and Vitari threw Sal a loose fist. Sal deflected and jabbed back. It was all harmless. When Sal landed a real punch, his target didn't get back up.

They sauntered together through the gardens, basking in sunlight. "Another fucking day in paradise." Sal grinned. "How are *things* with Giancarlo?"

"Yeah. All right. Nice. Suspicious."

"Maybe he's realized he's getting old and you're his best bet for an heir?"

"I dunno, fra. I always thought Little Toni was next in line?"

"Yeah, but my father ain't blood, Angel. You think Giancarlo hates you? He hates everyone. Safer that way."

Maybe, but unlikely. Vitari was expendable. Always had been. Which made the father/son talk by the pool unusual.

They walked on, chatting about Rome, about the business, about life. Sal was the only person Vitari could talk with like this, as though his every word wasn't being weighed and measured. And he needed it. The paranoia wore on him, especially when snitches like Ricky swung from bridges right after talking with Vitari. He hated loose ends.

"So, listen, your priest is in Rome," Sal said.

Vitari's heart swooped. He stopped dead on the garden's gravel path. "What the—" He slammed down the mental barriers, but Sal had heard his shock. Vitari threw his gaze toward the sky and counted down from five. Francis was in Rome? "He's not my priest."

"I'm telling you now so your face doesn't do *all that*—" He waved at Vitari's face. "—when Giancarlo tells you."

"It's not... It's..." What was it exactly? He'd thought

Francis was wrapped up safe and tight in some cloistered cathedral, far away from Vitari's world. But no. He was in Rome, in the Mafia's backyard. With a hit out on his life. Of course he fucking was. He was Francis. If there was trouble, he stumbled into it.

"Whatever, Angel, but I'm telling you this because you need to stay away from him," Sal said. All his smiles and easy-going manner had vanished, replaced by the hard, cold enforcer who would not hesitate to follow orders. "Something is going on, pieces are being moved, and we're not being told why. Even Papá is quiet when it comes to the church. I love your papá, but I don't trust him. Vitari, for your own sake, stay away from the priest."

Everyone was so damn eager to warn him off Francis. Vitari screwed up his nose. "It's fine. Why would I even see him? The whole fucking Venezuela operation was a fiasco because of him."

Sal smiled and flung an arm around Vitari. "Right. Sure. Maybe delete his number off your phone, eh?"

Vitari half laughed. "Right." He pulled his phone from his pocket, showed Sal the name Frank, then hit *delete contact*. "You're going to tell Giancarlo that?"

Sal laughed but the sound was strained, and so was Vitari's smile. They chatted and laughed and walked some more, as though everything were fine.

Vitari didn't need the number in his phone anyway. He'd memorized it long ago.

The Vatican was its own state within Rome, with its own laws, police, and government—and all of it answered to the Catholic Church.

Such a state sounded a lot like the Mafia, but instead of worshipping God, the Battaglia worshipped status, honor. And money.

Vitari hurried over one of the many bridges and threaded through ambling streams of tourists. As he approached the Vatican City limits, a familiar guard waved him through a gated personnel entrance, tucked down a narrow side alley.

Every time he stepped onto the Vatican's holy ground, he expected to combust from sin. That didn't happen today. He strode up the almost empty street. Voices echoed from somewhere nearby. He couldn't stay long. The Vatican had as many eyes as the Battaglia, and his face was likely known. He wouldn't have needed to come at all if Francis had picked up his phone.

He'd tried to call him, to yell at him, tell him to get the fuck out of Rome. But he hadn't answered. Which left Vitari with no choice.

The Vatican—behind St Peter's Basilica—was a sprawling, tangled labyrinth of old walled roads, ancient limestone terraced houses, churches, spires, battlements, manicured gardens, and statues of angels and demons, like a living fantasy novel. He walked briskly into an open courtyard area framed by endless limestone archways and then hung back, trying to get his bearings. Francis wouldn't be anywhere near the tourist hot spot of the main thoroughfare. He'd be tucked away to the east, among the residential buildings, with all his other priestly cohorts.

Vitari pulled up the map on his phone. He was in the right place. He just had to wait and hope nobody grew suspicious.

After pacing for thirty minutes, he kicked at some lose cobbles. This was ridiculous. He shouldn't be anywhere near the Vatican. Or Francis. Giancarlo would have his balls.

Then, by luck or fate or maybe even God, a nearby doorway opened, and all of the concerns and doubts vacated Vitari's head.

Francis walked fast, black gown flowing, eyes ahead, on a mission to save someone or something, in stark contrast to the last time Vitari had seen him, holding a gun on Luca. That brutal, unforgiving side to Francis bared no resemblance to this poised and graceful one, but he was in there. Naive, yet ruthless. Sweet, yet cunning. The contradiction was half his attraction, that and his ability to see good where there wasn't any. If God didn't want his disciple to be fucked, why make him so damn fuckable? Although knowing Catholics, irresistible temptation was the point.

Vitari dashed through the arches to intercept him.

Francis would hate him for this. Vitari *liked* that thought. He lived to get a rise out of Francis, in whatever form that rise took.

He dropped to a knee, took Francis's hand, heard his gasp, and kissed the backs of his fingers. Yes, this was perfect. He looked up and smiled at the shock on Francis's face.

Vitari's heart sprang to life. It had been too long since Venezuela, so long since he'd felt like this, as though he'd been brought to life. The first time they'd met, in a little English church in the middle of nowhere, Vitari had been on his knees then too. So much had changed, but also remained the same.

Francis glanced around frantically. "How did you get in here?"

"I know some people."

"You *can't* be here," he whispered.

Vitari slipped a note into Francis's fingers. "Meet me."

Francis snatched his fingers back and clasped both hands in front of him, hiding the note. His shoulders straightened, as though he were the epitome of discretion. He peered down his nose, while Vitari gazed up at him, imagining all the ways he could ruin that flawless act. He'd shove him against a wall and make him moan for more, lift his hand up under that black robe, seeking all the hardest parts of him, and he'd tell him all the wicked ways he'd make him beg for more.

Francis's soft, hazel eyes widened, as though he knew Vitari's thoughts. "Please—"

Another priest emerged from an arch and glanced over. "Buongiorno."

Vitari rose and dipped his head, as though in prayer or out of respect. As was right, for a man of the cloth.

"Peace be with you," Francis blurted, glancing at his fellow priest.

Vitari took the opportunity to make his escape, but with every step Francis's gaze weighed heavier on his back, right up until Vitari turned around the corner of a building, breaking their connection. Vitari grinned. Inviting Francis out had to be one of the most idiotic, suicidally stupid things he'd done, but Giancarlo wouldn't find out, and having seen Francis in the flesh again, feeling the heat the priest had ignited within him, it would be worth it.

If Francis came, which he would, Vitari planned to seduce him all night long. Venezuela had been frantic and desperate. They'd only just begun to realize how good they were together.

Vitari's smile faltered, and his pace quickened.

Rome would be so much more, but also a goodbye. Because it could never happen again.

CHAPTER SIX

Francis

The little restaurant Vitari had asked him to meet at appeared to be a family-run business tucked away in one of the many winding side streets, far from Rome's tourist hot spots. Francis bluffed his way in using some basic Italian he'd been trying to learn with *Duolingo* between all his other commitments. Whether the owners knew to expect him or not, they were eager to seat him inside, near the back, at a table for two with a single red rose in a small vase.

Francis played with the rose as he waited, unsure what he was doing, waiting for Vitari at a quaint restaurant.

According to the quirky olive-shaped clock on the wall, Vitari was late. There was still time to leave, which was probably the right thing to do. Being kidnapped by Vitari Angelini was one thing. Meeting him at an intimate dinner for two was entirely another. But he didn't want to leave. He *wanted* to be here. Once he'd gotten over the shock of

Vitari appearing in the courtyard, he'd been counting down the minutes to now, to this very dinner.

Vitari felt like the one good thing in his life, the one stable thing, despite him being far from good, or stable.

"Scusa il ritardo." Vitari appeared from the back of the restaurant. He removed his jacket, flicked it over the back of his chair, and sat. Their knees bumped under the table. His watch glinted. So did his dark eyes, and then his smile. His perfect hair made Francis wish he knew how to style his own, and while Vitari wore an expensive suit, Francis had come in his Marks & Spencer slacks and sixteen-euro sweater. Vitari was always so glamorous and well-groomed, and so handsome. Francis blinked away, overwhelmed and embarrassed and all kinds of other *things* he couldn't think too hard on.

"Sorry," Francis said, shuffling, unsure what he was apologizing for.

Vitari's smile grew. "You look good."

His heart fluttered. He hadn't been nervous, until now. The little table, the restaurant, the music. Was this... a date? He'd never been on a date before. "Oh, uh... Thank you. I er... I didn't bring much with me. To Rome, I mean. It was a... uh... spur of the moment decision." Which he did not want to get into now. His heart galloped. Nerves had parched his throat.

"Wine?" Vitari asked, then went ahead and ordered for them. "Best pasta in all of Rome. Trust me."

"I do."

Vitari's smile stalled and his sharp eyes softened. The weight of his gaze warmed Francis's face. He wasn't used to being gazed upon as though Vitari could see beneath his clothes. "How are you?" Vitari asked.

"Better. I had to get out of England... I..." He trailed off, not wanting to bring his emotional baggage to whatever this evening was.

The wine arrived, and the server fussed with that for a few minutes. Francis lost his thoughts in watching Vitari as he spoke. The last time he'd seen him, he'd lain unconscious in a Venezuelan hospital. Francis had been forced by the police presence to leave him there, unsure if he'd survive. None of that ordeal was evident in his sly glances now, or the upward tic of his lips.

The server left, and Vitari picked up his wine. "You were saying... about England?"

"It's not important. Later." Francis raised his glass to celebrate their being together again, but the right words wouldn't come. Venezuela had been a whirlwind, much of it too traumatic to dwell on. He hadn't even been sure he'd ever see Vitari again. Yet here they were, eating dinner together on a warm Rome evening.

Vitari lifted his glass. "To surviving, si?"

"Surviving." Their glasses chinked, Francis's nerves smoothed, and just like that, he was at ease.

As they sipped wine, Francis spoke of his decision to visit the Vatican, but not why. And Vitari told him how the family business was thriving, as usual, but steered away from details. He ordered food for Francis, and when it arrived, it had to be the most colorful plate that Francis had ever seen, with exotic fresh fish and vegetables and pasta drizzled in golden dressing along with fresh bread. They ate, talked about nothing of any real importance—the weather, Rome and its history. Vitari clearly loved the city. He spoke of hidden ancient villas, all underground and off the tourist trail, that so few took the time to visit.

"I'd love to see it with you."

But it had been the wrong thing to say. Vitari set his

wine glass down and skipped his gaze away. Of course, they couldn't be seen together. Even coming here was a risk. "I'm sorry, that was a... That was a silly thing to say." He laughed at his own giddy foolishness. He'd forgotten, for a moment, who and what they were.

Mob boss's son and an archbishop's protégé. Forbidden in so many ways.

They fell quiet as the chatter from the other customers bubbled around them. Vitari glanced toward the restaurant's front door, and his dark eyes narrowed, as though searching for threats.

The thrill of the dinner faded. This meal, this evening, it felt shallow, like a veneer over something rotten. As nice as it was, it was all pretend. It couldn't go anywhere, couldn't *become* anything. Not that Vitari would likely want it to. The joy in Francis's heart snuffed out. This was all a fairy tale.

"Vitari, what are we doing?"

Vitari placed his wine glass down. "Shall we skip dessert?" His mischievous grin ensured only one possible answer.

"Yes."

He asked for the check and chatted animatedly with the servers, complimenting the food. He paid, and an older gentleman arrived, shaking Vitari's hand with vigor. Francis watched it all with a strange kind of bewildered envy. Vitari's life here seemed so free, without all the rules and duties of Francis's world. He supposed that was much of the reason he was drawn to Vitari, to his freedom.

They left the restaurant by the back door and stumbled outside into a steep, cobble-lined street too narrow for cars. Rome hummed all around, but the little side street was empty.

The wine had lightened Francis's head, or maybe it was the company. He glanced over at Vitari and how his eyes glinted in the dark. He had a lopsided grin, too, as though he were always half laughing at the world.

Francis had missed him, missed the relief he felt whenever he was near Vitari. He didn't have to pretend with him. No rules, no religion, no etiquette or hierarchy. With Vitari, he was just Francis.

"So, we can't... You and I, we can't walk around," Vitari said, slurring a little. "There's a little townhouse up ahead. It's mine. Do you want to... join me? There's more wine."

Francis stopped. This was more than a clandestine dinner—a whole lot more. "Are you asking me to stay the night?"

Vitari, two steps ahead, turned and he scratched at his nose. "If you like—"

"I can't do that." Guilt made the wine in his belly churn.

Vitari's smile froze.

"I can't. I'm staying at the Vatican, I can't..." Francis waved a hand. *I can't sleep with you.*

"Is this about your vows?" He laughed. "I think those are beyond repair."

Francis closed the distance between them and as he looked into Vitari's eyes, Vitari's smile faded. Did he think Francis's life—his commitment to God, his vows—were a joke? "Just because something is broken doesn't mean I give up on it."

Vitari shrugged and stepped back. "You think this isn't a risk for me? You have no idea what it means that I'm even here, talking to you."

"Why are we here? What is the point in this?"

"I don't know." Vitari threw up his hands, turned away, hurried on, then turned back again. "I just thought…"

"Thought what? Secret notes, an intimate dinner, a midnight walk? I don't understand what we're doing here." It was more than that. He needed to know what they were doing. Because if it was nothing, then he should leave. But if Vitari wanted *something*… If he wanted more, then perhaps the risk was worth it? But he had to know.

"Jesus, I just wanted to give you something like Venezuela," Vitari snarled. "You sounded like you needed it, the last time we spoke."

So Francis was supposed to go along with it, and then go back to Vitari's house and what, have sex? Was that what all this was for? "Why don't you take one of your women to bed? Wouldn't that be easier than going to all his trouble for me?"

"Fuck, Francis, that wasn't—"

"I know what she said, Vitari. She was in your bed."

"Why are you being like this? I'm trying to do something *nice*."

"No, you're trying to *sleep with me*." That last part came out in a low whisper.

Vitari marched up and met Francis face-to-face. "Tell me you don't want it. Fuckin' tell me, right here, that you haven't thought about it, like we had before." He whispered the words, hissing some of them, but they still seemed loud, as though the whole of Rome might hear them.

"What difference does it make?" Francis asked. "There are a thousand reasons why we can't do this."

"Do you think I don't know that?"

"We can't—"

"Yes, we can. I'm here and so are you. Tomorrow we might not be." Vitari stepped closer. His light, gentle fingers skimmed Francis's cheek, scattering shivers down his spine. "I want you, Francis. I never stopped wanting you. If it was a choice, I'd choose not to. But you're in some part of me I have no control over. This—" He leaned closer still, his mouth a whisper away from Francis's lips, his body a hot, firm siren song. "—could get me killed." He lifted his eyes. "You're right, it would be easier to fuck women, it would be a whole lot fuckin' safer, but I don't want that. I want you."

His every word landed like a hammer blow to Francis's heart. Vitari was right. This wasn't a choice. Francis could choose to walk away, but he'd still crave Vitari. That desire had never left. If anything, it had grown worse since he'd tasted Vitari's body, ravished his hot mouth, moaned under his biting teeth and the stroke of every part of him. Now he knew the pleasure he'd missed, he craved it.

They were so close, close enough to kiss. Francis tilted his head, pinched his lips together, and swallowed. His heart pounded in his throat. Vitari would kiss him, and he'd let him.

Vitari stepped back. "Not here." When he turned, his lingering gaze begged Francis to follow.

Francis fell into step behind him, and when they came to a narrow little house squeezed between its neighbors, Vitari unlocked the door and stepped inside, holding the door open for Francis.

A short entrance vestibule opened into a chic industrial-style living room with exposed brick and tiled floor. He drifted past the couch, aware of Vitari following close behind, like a wolf stalking its prey from the shadows, and when Francis turned, Vitari was right there, waiting to pounce.

Francis knew he shouldn't be here, that this was all wrong, including what was about to happen, but the rising tide of anticipation would drown him if he didn't surrender soon. They both knew this was inevitable.

Vitari started forward, flung his jacket over a chair, and began to unbutton his shirt. The heat in his gaze scorched Francis's thoughts, muddling them, and the wine tripped them over some more. He couldn't think—didn't want to.

His mouth dried. This was happening. Only he could stop it.

Vitari untucked his shirt, finished unbuttoning it, then shrugged it off his shoulders and dropped it in a puddle of silk. His chest was smooth in the soft light filtering through the shutters. The outline of muscle, and how his physique guided his gaze downward, between narrow hips, emptied all reasonable thoughts from Francis's head. He exhaled after forgetting to breathe and stepped back. Retreating. The backs of his legs nudged the couch.

"The only word that's going to stop me from ruining you, Francis, is no."

He had time to say it. Vitari wasn't yet on him; he even looked as though he might be slowing, doubting himself, and this.

There was no escaping it now.

This had been inevitable since the moment Francis had accepted the note, perhaps since he'd landed in Rome.

Francis lunged and crashed into Vitari, the tide of need and desire having broken all his attempts to hold it back. When they were together, it was just them. No church, no rules, no guilt, no shame. Just the feel of him, hot and muscular, firm and powerful. And with Vitari, he was allowed to feel and taste and touch and drown in pleasure.

Vitari grasped Francis under the ass and marched him back. They kissed hard, bruising lips. Francis fucked with his tongue, trying to devour Vitari whole. Vitari laughed, interrupting the rhythm, then pinned Francis against the back of the couch. Vitari grasped his hair, yanked his head back, and sucked on his neck, holding Francis prone, at his mercy. God, Francis rubbed his cock against him, needing more friction, more everything.

"Easy, Padre," Vitari purred. "We've got all night." He freed his fingers from his hair, and with one hand on Francis's lower back, Vitari leaned Francis away and rode his free hand up, under Francis's sweater, skimming his palm up, past his navel, over his chest. The touch, skin on skin, caught Francis's breath and wedged his heart in his throat. "And I'm going to make you beg for every minute of it."

Beautiful eyes undressed Francis, and Francis almost whined with need. He wasn't going to last all night. He wasn't going to last another five minutes if they didn't slow things down. But he didn't want to slow down. He wanted everything, all of him, and he wanted it now.

Vitari jerked him upright, slamming Francis's chest into his, and at the same time dropped his hand to cup Francis's dick through his trousers. "Fuck, you're hard." Vitari bit Francis's lip, and the tiny spark of pain triggered Francis to lunge. He sucked Vitari's lip between his teeth, but then Vitari rubbed him and Francis flung his head back, mouth open, desperate to bury his cock into Vitari's hand.

Vitari rubbed, and Francis flung his arms over Vitari's shoulders and rocked, grinding against him. This was good; as long as they had clothes between them, he could control himself. Hopefully.

But then Vitari tore at Francis's belt and plunged his hand inside, and all at once, he had his fingers wrapped around Francis's naked dick, his thumb stroking up precum, and Francis momentarily lost his mind to the riot of pleasure surging through him.

Vitari hovered his mouth over Francis's, breathing in his gasps. "I'm going to make you come like this. Don't fight it. Just fuck my hand, fucking give yourself to me." Francis's pace quickened. "Yes, fuck me, do it faster." Francis rocked, Vitari pumped, their mouths mingled, hardly touching, bodies rocking. "You want me on my knees, Father? You'll get it, but you've got to fuck my fist like it's the tightest hole you've ever come in. Harder, amore. Fuck me like you hate me."

Oh God. His words were filthy, and Francis was falling, lost to the inferno, burning up. The pressure built, Vitari pumped, his face vicious and victorious, and as he switched to Italian, Francis couldn't hold back. The blinding climax rolled over him, and he came hard, hips juddering, slumped against Vitari, his teeth pinched into Vitari's shoulder to keep from crying out.

"Gah, fuck, Francis—" Vitari clutched Francis close, holding him up as Francis spilled his load over Vitari's hand and chest. And abs. Francis gasped at the sight of his own cum gleaming on Vitari's dark skin. Then Vitari grabbed his chin, looked him in the eyes, and kissed him. "Good," he mumbled against Francis's mouth. "You were going to blow whatever I did. Now we can slow down."

"I'm sorry, I..." Francis swallowed. He'd tried not to indulge in masturbation, but since meeting Vitari, that had become a losing battle. But the Vitari in his head was nothing compared to having the man in his hands, for real. Vitari was right. Whatever they did, he wouldn't have lasted.

Vitari eased off. "Stop apologizing, amore." He scooped up his shirt, wiped his chest clean, then tossed the shirt again and returned to Francis—still propped on the back of the couch, his cock half hard where it lay out of his fly.

Vitari said something smooth and delicious in Italian. *Duolingo* hadn't prepared Francis for this. He had no idea what the words meant, but the way he said them, and how his eyes darkened, it was surely filthy.

"I'm going to ruin you all night." Vitari pushed in between Francis's knees and nudged his mouth open. "This is no place for guilt, Padre. You can do no wrong with me."

He hadn't known how much he'd needed to hear those words, or how he'd needed to be given permission to let go. To be himself.

Relief rolled over him, and to keep from collapsing into an emotional wreck, he kissed Vitari, kissed him softly, kissed him gently, so Vitari could feel what this meant, even if Francis didn't know the words to express it.

Freedom and lust and... maybe this soaring feeling inside might be love?

CHAPTER SEVEN

Vitari

Francis wouldn't have been Francis if he hadn't resisted. He was wired to push back, to fight, but he always surrendered, at least with Vitari.

Vitari flicked open the buttons of his own fly and Francis's gaze dropped, tracking each of Vitari's movements. He still leaned against the back of the couch, cock out, sweater hitched up, looking like spoiled goods. A throb of warm pride rolled through Vitari. He'd been the one to spoil him.

"Sei la cosa più bella che mi sia mai capitata," Vitari said. Francis didn't understand, but his eyes widened, his enjoyment obvious at the sound of the words. It was probably for the best he didn't know Italian. Vitari had already said too much.

Vitari eased his trousers open but kept them clinging to his hips, then closed the distance between them again. "You do it. Take my cock out, Padre."

Francis's hands dropped to Vitari's waist and eased his

trousers down, while he searched his eyes, reading a thousand things Vitari couldn't hide. As Francis's soft hands dove under Vitari's ass and his firm fingers dug in, Vitari stroked his knuckles down Francis's cheekbone. He was the most precious thing in Vitari's life, worth more than all his possessions combined. This man, with his soft brown eyes and painfully innocent face, had killed for Vitari. He'd saved Vitari's life, costing him his soul. Vitari wasn't worth it, he didn't deserve him, but he'd do everything in his power to keep him safe, to protect him. Maybe... love him, even though Father Francis Scott deserved so much more than a broken bastard like Vitari.

Francis shifted his hips, bringing them closer together. Vitari needed to feel more of him.

Francis reached up and plucked the stiff priest's collar free, tossing it aside without a thought. There had been a time when he wouldn't have found it so easy to discard his layers. He pulled his sweater over his head next, fluffing his chestnut hair. Vitari loved to grip his short locks. There was so much of him to explore, he hesitated, not knowing where to begin. His pale chest, pert nipples, his lithe waist that fit so well under Vitari's hands. His ass, that fine fucking ass.

"No going back," Vitari whispered against his cheek, and swept his hand up his bare chest, soaking in his every shuddering breath and rapidly beating heart. "You're mine, all night."

Francis's hand caught his. "Or maybe... you're mine?" he said, then went to his knees and swallowed Vitari's dick. His big eyes peered up, so fucking innocent and pure, even as he sucked head and stroked Vitari's shaft.

Vitari leaned back, giving himself to Francis's hot, tight mouth, giving himself to his priest, the one and only man who truly knew him.

Vitari told him to *take it* in Italian, and as Francis's sucking teases began to unravel Vitari's control, he confessed other things in Italian too: told him he'd keep him safe, told him he wasn't good enough for him, thanked him, over and over. He said he was sorry—sorry for the things he'd done, for the things he'd yet to do. And as he spilled over Francis's tongue, half out of his mind, he told him he wished their lives were different so they might be free to live them.

Francis kissed him on the mouth, tasting salty, tasting like sin. Vitari kissed him back, lost to the feel of him. Seduced, heart, body, and mind.

As he came down from his high, he found Francis studying his face. "What?" Vitari smirked.

"Nothing."

Vitari thrust a hand into Francis's hair, making him gasp. Fuck, he was too damn precious. "Liar."

Francis mumbled something about not lying, like he always did. *Too precious.* He guided him into the bedroom, gasping between kisses, and laid him on the bed. Francis kicked off his shoes, then shuffled his trousers down, and now naked, he lay back, propped up on his arms, gloriously displayed in all his ivory-skinned perfection. He was lean, wiry, with several sharp edges that Vitari planned to kiss away.

"I uh... I'm not used to this." Francis gulped. A blush warmed his face and neck.

"But you're so *good* at it, Padre." Vitari didn't know where to start, so he began at Francis's mouth, making him arch like a flame reaching for fuel. The more Vitari kissed him, the more Francis moved like liquid, no longer rigid and restrained, but smooth like honey under Vitari's hands. He twitched and trembled, gasped and moaned. And Vitari drank it all down, drowning in Francis, and loving every moment.

How could Francis's God claim such passion was unholy when he came alive in its throes?

Vitari sucked and teased all the way down his body until he reached Francis's twitching dick, then sealed his lips over its hardness and molded his mouth to firm cock.

Francis garbled a moan for more, so Vitari spread Francis's thighs and with a slick finger, he stroked from his balls toward his rear, testing how far Francis would allow him to go. When he didn't resist, Vitari stroked over his hole while working Francis's dick over his tongue. There was a flicker of resistance, a stutter to his breath, but it seemed like a good reaction. So Vitari pushed in, widening him, then eased out, stroking. Francis hadn't told him to stop. His breaths had quickened, his chest flushed. Vitari cupped his balls and gently pumped his finger into his ass, while also lavishing attention on his dick.

Then, with Francis writhing, his knees in the air, Vitari eased off his cock to focus on his ass and fucked him there with his finger, wishing it was his dick instead. He needed to see if Francis was receptive, and it seemed he was. At least to a finger up his ass.

Vitari's own dick twitched from the need to bury inside that tight, muscular hole. In his head, he imagined flipping Francis over and fucking him into the bed. But they had time. They had all night.

He didn't know what the time was, didn't care to know. Francis lay spooned against him, and Vitari had him trapped under his leg, his arm thrown over him. Francis's fingers traced the tattoo around Vitari's wrist, his thoughts far away. He'd made Francis come again, and this was the calm before another lustful storm.

Tiredness tried to tug Vitari toward sleep, making his eyes heavy, but there was no way he'd waste these precious moments. Not when he knew it might never happen again. He hadn't told Francis yet, how this was the end. Couldn't tell him.

He stroked Francis's messy hair and watched his mouth tic up in a little smile.

Francis breathed in, filling his lungs, making his chest rise, and rolled onto his back. Vitari propped his head on a hand and stroked lazy circles down Francis's chest, marveling at the tiny goose bumps his touch summoned.

"I've been learning Italian," Francis said. He threw his arms back, laced his fingers behind his head, and lay sprawled, his whole body on display for Vitari's hands to roam. "You said a lot earlier. I only caught some of it."

He *had* said a lot, thinking Francis had no clue what any of it meant. Heat flushed Vitari's cheeks.

"Are you blushing?"

He snorted, then sucked a nipple to distract him. Francis's hand landed in his hair, clutching him close, but then Vitari pulled away with a laugh. They'd fuck again soon, but he was enjoying this quiet moment for now, absorbing every gentle second, committing them to memory.

"How many languages do you speak?" Francis asked.

"English, obviously. Italian, Spanish, French. Some Russian, enough to get by."

"Russian?"

"Я не могу жить без тебя."

"Hm, it sounds... harsh." Francis twisted onto his side, facing Vitari. "What did you say?"

"The weather is nice today."

He frowned. "Really?"

Vitari laughed him off.

"Is that all the languages you know?" Francis asked.

"Those not enough for you, Padre?"

Francis smiled, but his smile faded, and he got that long-distance gaze in his eyes, signaling his wandering thoughts. "You're brilliant, you know? You could do anything you put your mind to."

"Maybe." Perhaps if he was free to choose his future, but he wasn't. His life had been mapped out for him long ago.

"I came to the Vatican to find myself," Francis said, filling the soft quiet.

"Like a spiritual thing?'

He nodded. Shame averted his gaze.

"And you found me, huh?" Vitari almost apologized. Francis had been on a spiritual journey, and he'd swerved him so far off course that he lay naked in a mob boss's son's bed. Not so long ago, Vitari wouldn't have felt bad about corrupting a priest. But that was before he knew Francis. There was no denying, every time Vitari entered Francis's life, Vitari fucked it up.

If he told him how sorry he was, he'd have to admit this meant something, admit this was real. And tomorrow, it was over anyway.

"You remember when I asked in Venezuela if I could stay? Before it all fell apart?" Francis asked, his voice all dreamy and thoughtful.

"Yeah?" Vitari croaked.

"I don't know if it was the place, or the fact I wanted to run away. I don't think I'm meant to have this life. I keep trying to be everything I'm supposed to be, like a square peg in a round hole. I'm not sure I'm even supposed to be a priest."

Vitari propped himself onto an elbow, making sure to level him under his glare. He'd known from the first time they'd met that Francis was all tied up in the restraints of a life he didn't want, but it wasn't God he loathed. "You want to know what I think?"

Francis's grin bloomed, like the sun on a rainy day. "I always want to know what you think."

"You'd walk over razor blades to save a stranger. If that's not the behavior of a good Catholic, I don't know what is."

"I killed a man," Francis whispered. "There is no greater sin."

"A man who would have killed me and dragged you back to someone who either wanted you dead or silenced. You need to be kinder to yourself, save yourself once in a while." Francis would shred his soul to save a man who wasn't worth saving. To save Vitari.

"That's easy for you to say. You don't have a lifetime of Catholicism breathing down your neck, telling you desire is a sin. *You and I* are a sin. What we just did... There's a whole room in Hell *just for that.*"

"Really? Sounds like fuckin' Heaven." Vitari grinned and rolled onto him, pinning Francis under his thighs. "As we're already damned, we should sin some more." He poked Francis in the ribs, startling a laugh out of him, and now he'd found a weakness, Vitari attacked, ruthlessly extracting Francis's laughter until he descended into rocking against him in waves, cocks and bodies rubbing. Vitari loved to hear him laugh; he might never get enough of it.

"Stop!" he begged. "Vitari, stop. I can't... Oh God."

Vitari let him go, chuckling, and waited, listening to

their panting in the quiet. *This* was fucking Heaven. In bed, free to fuck a man he... liked a lot.

Francis pounced, clutched Vitari to his chest, and twisted, rolling him over. Vitari was under him suddenly and so consumed by this new, demanding side of Francis that he didn't realize what Francis had in mind until his hand slipped beneath Vitari's balls, fingers sliding toward his asshole.

Panic fluttered inside Vitari's head, flushing all lust and desire from his body, dumping him in ice.

He gasped and snatched Francis's hand, breathing hard through his nose. Francis jerked his head up, shocked. *Please don't.* Vitari gave his head a small shake. *Don't ask, don't make me explain.*

Francis froze. He thought he'd done something wrong. But it wasn't him. There were few things Vitari wouldn't—couldn't—do. "It's n-not you," Vitari stuttered.

An array of thoughts showed in Francis's eyes. Concern, then understanding.

Vitari freed his wrist. What if he'd ruined this? What if Francis no longer wanted him?

Francis bent forward. His warm, wet mouth swept up Vitari's chest, then his tongue swirled around a nipple, and the heat simmered back to life.

Vitari clutched at Francis's messy hair. "Si, amore."

Then Francis's hand plunged south again, but this time he grasped Vitari's dick and stroked him back to desperate hardness. Yes, this was what he needed: Francis close, so close he was in Vitari's head, chasing the past away. In his heart, making it beat for him. In his veins, setting him ablaze.

Francis straightened, and with his hand still on Vitari's dick, he adjusted his position, rising over him. Francis rode him like a white knight. Well, not quite riding him. Not yet. Then, as though reading Vitari's thoughts on his face, he angled Vitari's cock, sliding it up and under him, until the slick head wedged against his hole. No condom. Fuck.

"Wait—side drawer."

Francis hesitated, poised, confused. Then leaned over and opened the side drawer. He gasped. "Do you want a bottle of something I assume is uh... lubricant, the condoms, or the uhm... gun?"

Vitari laughed. He'd forgotten about the gun in the drawer. Francis stared at it, then flicked his sultry gaze back to Vitari, his eyes full of need.

In Spain, when he'd gotten Francis off with the gun, Francis had *liked* it. In Venezuela too, there had been a moment when Vitari had rubbed a gun over his cock—Oh fuck. He had a kink. "Pick up the gun, Francis."

"I don't know if I should..."

"Sure, you do." Vitari stretched his arms back, over his head. Francis would pick up the gun. Any second now. His dick knew what he wanted. His head just needed to get out of the way.

Francis picked up the gun.

"Hand it over."

He blinked and obeyed, cock hard and straining.

Vitari slid the clip free, checking the rounds, while Francis stared like a man possessed.

"I see we're goin' all in with the sinning, Padre Blanco."

It was supposed to be a joke, but Francis's face fell. "Is it wrong?"

"Fuck, no. I told you, there's no wrong with me. How do you want it?" He rammed the clip home, noted Francis's twitching dick, then made sure to check the safety. Francis watched all of it with widening eyes.

"What kind of gun is it?" he asked, voice rasping.

"Ed Brown. Evo, K-C-Nine. Nine mill." Vitari propped himself up on his left arm and pressed the gun under Francis's chin. Was it the gun he liked, or the feeling of Vitari holding it against his skin?

Francis gasped, teeth clamped shut. Yeah, Vitari knew what he wanted. He dragged the gun's muzzle down his chest, then stroked the slide against his dick. "You like that?"

Francis's glare switched from desperate query to snarling demand. Yeah, he liked it.

A few strokes was all it took for Francis to rock, thrusting his dick against the gun. Maybe Vitari had a gun kink too. Or maybe it was a Francis kink. Because this was some of the hottest shit he'd ever done. Both of them naked, just the gun between them, and Francis on fire.

Francis opened his eyes. "I need you in me, Angel. *Now.*"

Vitari dropped the gun as Francis grabbed the condom from the drawer and tossed him the packet. Vitari used his teeth to tear it open and had barely rolled the condom on before Francis straddled him, wasting no more time. His quick fingers grasped Vitari's dick, and he slowly lowered himself, his own dick twitching at Vitari's eye level. Slick tightness ringed Vitari's cock, taking him all the way in, so fucking deep. Francis had clearly used the lube too.

Vitari gripped his thigh, afraid he might hurt him. But Francis narrowed his eyes, daring him to stop this. And then, with a hungry, unforgiving glare, he began to rock.

Vitari clenched his teeth, breathing through his nose, and clutched Francis's leg, holding on. God, he was beautiful. "Amore mio," he whispered. Francis stole his world in that moment. Stole his heart too. Ecstasy raced up his spine.

Francis rocked his hips, rising and falling, riding Vitari's dick with incredible slow stokes. Then he braced forward, changing the angle, and as Vitari slow-fucked his ass, Francis's rigid dick stroked Vitari's navel.

This could never be wrong, not when Francis was so perfect. But if Francis stayed where he was, peering into Vitari's eyes, their intimacy scorching his soul like an iron brand, Vitari was going to come.

Vitari pushed upright into a sitting position, hugged Francis to him, then cupped his ass, spreading his cheeks around his dick. Francis's flushed face filled Vitari's vision. They shared sawing breaths, shared heartbeats, shared souls, so close the lines between them blurred. Francis rocked some more, stroking his own dick up Vitari's lower abs.

"I need it harder," Francis moaned. "I need you to fuck me, Vitari." He bit his own lip, as though to punish himself.

Vitari locked him tight in his embrace and switched their positions, laying Francis under him. Still buried inside him, Vitari pumped. God, he was going to come, he couldn't last, not like this. It was too much, too perfect, too Francis. Vitari hammered his asshole, balls slapping, fucking him hard, and Francis clutched at his hips, digging blunt nails in. "My God," Francis spluttered.

Vitari hardly heard it; he was far away, yet had never been more present. He fucked him faster, grunting, chasing the high, needing more, so close to coming. Francis flung his head back, and Vitari bowed forward, buried his face in his neck, and came with a ragged shout, stuttering and gasping, losing himself so thoroughly in Francis that he only noticed the slickness between them as the exquisite high faded. Francis had come too.

Vitari could fuck him all day and night, and it would never be enough.

How could he let him go? How could he walk away? He kissed him, hiding the fear that would surely show on his face. "Sono pazzo di te."

Francis's eyes widened. He'd understood that one. *I'm crazy for you.* And he looked afraid too, as though this were something bigger than them, something they had no control over. The forbidden, the unspoken.

This was love.

But it could never be.

CHAPTER EIGHT

Francis

Vitari was chatting about how to craft the perfect espresso with his impressive stainless steel coffee machine, but all Francis cared about was how his smile came so easily, how he gestured at everything, hands always in motion—hands that had summoned magic last night... and this morning.

He didn't even know what day it was. He'd be missed at the Vatican. They might send someone to look for him. But he didn't care. His body felt used and his muscles were sore in the best way.

He wanted to go back to bed, to lose himself in Vitari all over again. But Vitari had insisted they share a morning espresso together, so here they were.

Vitari handed him the tiny espresso cup, then dropped onto the couch beside him. "Try it." He'd thrown on a crumpled shirt, and his trousers weren't buttoned. Vitari took pride in his manicured appearance. To witness this rare messy side to him was a treat. Vitari Angelini, unwrapped, leaving just the man without all his swagger and flashiness. Like this, he was a wonder.

Francis was only half dressed too, wearing just his trousers without socks. He couldn't ever recall a time when he'd casually walked around without a shirt on. It was strange, to be so free, but good. The company *made it good.* Vitari made him comfortable in his own skin.

Francis sipped the coffee. "It's strong."

"That's the point." Vitari threw the shot of coffee back in one. "Italians don't mess around with milk. You've seen the way we drive, there's no time for lattes. It's fresh. Get notes of chocolate?"

Francis snickered and sipped the tiny coffee some more. "Maybe?" He didn't taste chocolate, just strong, thick coffee.

Vitari's right eyebrow arched. "Heathen."

He chuckled. Clearly, one of Vitari's passions was coffee. "So um..." There was one thing he'd wanted to ask, but there hadn't been a chance, and now they were here, relaxed, drinking coffee, it seemed safe.

"So um?" Vitari echoed, teasing.

"Who was the woman... in the background... when you called, that time?"

Vitari smiled, then laughed quickly, like he did when he was trying to brush something off. "She was nothing."

Francis frowned. "She was a person."

"You know that's not what I meant."

That smile. Francis knew it to be a lie he used to hide a multitude of sins. Like right now. "Am I nothing, then?"

His smile grew into a grin. "Are you angry with me, Padre?"

He was. A little bit. If Vitari was so flippant with his lovers, then how was Francis any different?

He laughed and draped his arm across the back of the couch, half fencing Francis in. "Shit, you are. Non rompermi le palle."

"In English?"

"Fuck, you're hot when you're mad." Vitari walked his fingers toward Francis's shoulder.

"I don't think that's what you said." Now he *was* getting mad. He flicked Vitari's wandering hand away. "I'm serious. I want to know who she was. The fact you're laughing me off makes me think I should be mad."

His fake smile faltered. "You're going to make me say it, fine, all right..." He sighed. "I have to pretend, okay?" He shrugged and looked away.

"'Pretend' what?"

"Like I'm straight, to the family, to anyone watching." He leaned forward, hunching over and closing down. "It's stupid. I hate it. But I can't be... I can't be gay around them."

"Oh." And now Francis felt bad for making him admit it. "Sorry."

"I don't do anything with them. I just fool around, make sure I'm seen."

"Okay." Unease squirmed inside. He knew what it felt like, hiding who you were every single day. He should have realized Vitari was trapped in the lie too. "You don't have to say any more."

"Is that honest enough for you?"

Francis needed to do something to relax him again, so he didn't ruin their lovely morning by asking stupid questions. "May I make breakfast? Do you have groceries?"

Some of the mischief returned to his eyes. "You cook?"

"Some. Not much. I'm alone most of the time, and cooking for one always seems... pointless..." He trailed off under Vitari's intense gaze. He probably thought him terribly dull. "Do you?"

"I can. But as you're offering... There's some things in the fridge. Mushrooms, eggs."

Francis would do anything to make this morning last longer, to drag out the inevitable goodbye. Leaving Vitari watching from the couch, he moved to the kitchen and examined the contents of the cupboards. Then gathered the eggs and mushrooms.

"What happened, before you called me last?"

Francis glanced over. Vitari rested his chin on his arm, draped along the back of the couch. Content to watch. Where to begin with the archbishop and the files, and the photograph of the dead boys? Bringing the Stanmore horrors into the room didn't feel right. Worse than that, he feared those truths might change the good thing they had together. Would Vitari hate that Francis had seen his initials on the wall?

"You asked me to help you kill someone," Vitari prompted.

"I was er..." He grimaced at the memory of Montague overwhelming him. It seemed like a distant memory now, one left far away in England. "I was angry. I shouldn't have said that."

"Who pissed you off?"

He turned his back on Vitari, broke the eggs into a pan, added seasoning and some mushrooms, and stirred. There was no telling half the Stanmore story. Once he began, it was all or nothing, and he did not want to end their date with a toxic conversation. "It was nothing."

"You're a better liar than this."

Francis laughed. "I don't lie."

Vitari's warm arms wrapped around Francis's waist—

ambushed from behind—and Vitari nibbled his earlobe, adding a growl, making Francis's legs go weak. They weren't going to get to the omelet if he kept that up. Francis tried to focus on the pan, but Vitari murmured soft Italian into his ear and rocked his hips, grinding against Francis's ass. He blushed, thinking of all the things they'd done. Of how he'd... demanded things in the madness of passion, and how Vitari had answered. They'd been together, in a physical way, a way he'd always been told was wrong, but during those moments, as he'd had Vitari inside him, while holding his gaze... He'd felt nothing like it before, as though they were two halves of a whole. It had been beautiful, not ugly.

But then he'd tried to offer Vitari the same, thinking he might like to have Francis *inside* him too. But he'd frozen, almost... terrified. Francis had never seen him scared, until then. Maybe he just didn't like to be touched there. But the fear in his eyes had suggested it was much more than that.

Francis should have been more understanding. He knew some of what Vitari had endured at Stanmore.

Talking about it might help.

"There was something," Francis began.

Vitari sucked his neck, alternating between sweeping kisses and tiny bites, sending shivers down his back. He could feel himself getting hard, even as he tried to steer his thoughts away. Soon, he wouldn't be able to resist, and they'd be wild with lust. He used a spatula to poke the eggs around the pan, attempting to distract himself.

"I've been investigating Stanmore."

Vitari stilled, then withdrew and turned his back on Francis, to move away. It hurt, to see him hurting. But if they talked about it, discussed it, it would help them both, and perhaps help the investigation.

"I just think—"

"Are these the *old ghosts* you mentioned?" All the warmth had vanished from his voice, leaving it hard.

"Yes, I went back and—"

A bang sounded near the front door. "Angel!" a man yelled. "We just wanna talk!"

Vitari grabbed Francis and shoved him toward the back corridor. "Bedroom. Go."

Francis bolted into the bedroom, still holding the spatula, and froze. A few thumps sounded, then murmured voices. What if this was El Cristo all over again? What if they'd come to kill them?

Vitari's gun lay on the bed, nestled among tousled sheets.

He tossed the spatula and picked up the gun. A flash of a brutal memory kicked his heart into his throat. He'd aimed a gun at Luca, pulled the trigger, killed him. He saw in vivid detail how the blood had spread over his chest, and how Luca had fallen backward. He couldn't do it again. He couldn't hurt another soul.

He didn't want the weapon in his hand. But Vitari might be in trouble—

The bedroom door opened.

Francis swung the gun up—aimed at a stranger.

"Put it down," the man said in guttural English.

"Who are you?" He listened for Vitari. Anything to know he was all right and Francis was overreacting, but there was nothing. What if he was already dead? What if they killed Francis next? "*Who are you!?*" he screeched.

The stranger had a gun too, pointed at the floor. "C'mon, Father. You're not going to use that." The man held out a hand, urging him to surrender the weapon.

Luca had said the same too, told Francis how he wouldn't kill a man. But he had. And he'd do the same now.

Cool clarity smoothed his rattling thoughts. He *would* shoot. Because he was already damned. "Where's Vitari? Is he hurt?" Francis stepped closer, and the man showed his palms, the gun pointed away. "I'll kill you," Francis snarled, meaning it. "Tell me!"

"Fuck…" The stranger's face fell, no longer smiling. "Angel!" he called. "Tell your priest to back the fuck down."

More voices sounded, and then Vitari's throaty voice rumbled, "It's all right. You can come out." But he didn't sound content. He sounded strained.

Vitari didn't have a gun, but Francis did. And he wasn't giving it up. He'd been threatened, beaten, kidnapped. The gun was staying in his hand until he knew Vitari was all right.

Francis inched toward the door, keeping the gun up. "Stay there. Don't move."

The stranger shrugged, hands still up. "Easy."

No, he wouldn't be *easy*. That was the mistake everyone made, thinking he *was* easy. Not anymore. Not since Venezuela.

Francis made it to the door, but now he was close to the stranger, the bed blocking the man's retreat as they side-stepped each other, and Francis needed to look into the corridor to make sure nobody was out there waiting for him—

The stranger lunged and snatched the gun from his fingers lightning fast. He grabbed Francis by the arm and rough-handled him down the corridor, into the lounge, where Vitari sat on the couch, wrists draped over his knees, head bowed. Defeated.

Oh no.

Another man sat opposite him, holding a gun on Vitari. A big man. Older, with cold eyes, wearing a black t-shirt, and dark tattoos painting his arms. This gun was different. It had some kind of attachment on its barrel, making it longer.

Vitari lifted his head and gave Francis a slight nod, probably trying to convey how everything was fine, when everything clearly was not fine. It was two on two, and these intruders were armed.

"Father Scott," the tattooed man said, his accent very different from the other man's. It took Francis a moment to place it as Russian. "You're a difficult man to meet, Batjushka."

Whoever the Russian was, he had gravitas. Dark chestnut hair was styled to sweep back from his square-jawed face. Even dressed casually, his broad shoulders and tall stature meant he'd never blend into a crowd. He had to be over six feet, when standing.

The man who had stolen Francis's gun clamped a hand on his shoulder and shoved him down, making him sit on the couch opposite. He then circled around, keeping Francis's gun loose in his left hand, with his original weapon in his right. "This is nice iron, Angel," the man said, examining Vitari's gun. "A few thousand euros. Must fire pretty rounds too, eh." He thrust out his arm, aiming the gun an inch from Francis's head.

"Fuck!" Vitari barked. "Don't!"

Francis closed his eyes. *Our Father, who art in Heaven, hallowed be thy name, thy kingdom come.* He didn't want to die. Not yet. Not here. Not like this.

"We're not resisting!" Vitari said. "Fucking shoot me, not him."

Thy will be done on Earth as it is in Heaven.

"You going to shoot a fucking priest?"

Give us this day our daily bread, and forgive us our trespasses as we forgive those who trespass against us.

"Sasha, you piece of shit! Hurt him and neither of you will leave this house alive."

And lead us not into temptation, but deliver us from evil. His tasted his heartbeat and breathed hard, knowing the next breath might be his last. Would he even hear the shot that killed him or would it just, instantly, be over?

"Lower the gun," Sasha said, his accent thick.

Francis opened his eyes. The stranger pointed the gun down but smirked at Francis as though he'd enjoyed every second he'd had him in his sights. Francis swallowed his beating heart and swung his gaze to Vitari, who sat panting and pale faced, far from the stoic enforcer he'd been moments ago. If Sasha hadn't already known they were close, he did now.

Sasha appraised Francis. And so Francis assessed him in return.

The DeSica were Russian mob, and this man, Sasha, was important. Had Vitari mentioned the name? He couldn't recall, but if Vitari was scared, then so was Francis. The DeSica had begun all this. They'd killed Adelita and left her body in Francis's graveyard. The two men who had attacked him in St Mary's had been DeSica, two men Vitari had killed. The bogus Spanish cops had been DeSica.

The DeSica had done more to hurt Francis than the Battaglia.

Now, here they were. With a gun on Vitari. Another on Francis.

Sasha leaned back in the chair. "It's good to meet you, Angelo della Morte. I've spent much time and money cleaning up trail of dead behind you."

"Then maybe you shouldn't fuck with the Battaglia."

"Perhaps your father should not fuck with me?" Sasha carelessly waved the gun at Vitari. "A bullet in your head seems like good way to remind him."

Vitari stared at the Russian. "Kill me, and you'll start a war."

Wicked satisfaction gleamed in the man's eyes. "Your father made it clear, we are already at war."

Vitari shifted. His knee jumped. He was wired, scared, and like this, he was dangerous too.

Francis wet his lips and considered their options. The DeSica didn't want them dead, or they would be. Which meant they wanted information. Information they'd always been convinced Francis had.

"You are both well-protected," Sasha went on. "Finding you alone... like this—" The Russian raked his gaze over Francis's naked chest and chuckled. "—it is as though Christmas has come early. For me, anyway. Not so much for you."

"What do you want?" Vitari asked, voice clipped.

"Nothing too difficult, Angel. I want you to bring down your father and the Battaglia."

Vitari smiled his thin, sharklike smile. "You may as well shoot me now."

The Russian shrugged and nodded at his colleague.

The stranger raised his gun again and aimed at Francis. His finger twitched.

Francis's heart lurched. "Wait!"

He fired.

The muffled shot struck the cushion next to Francis's right arm, jolting him. He froze, flushed with cold sweat, and gulped a sob. *Don't pass out, don't pass out.*

Vitari lurched from his seat, as though he intended to throw himself between Francis and the gunman. The gunman swung his weapon up, aiming at Vitari, freezing him half off the couch.

"Sit, Angel," the Russian ordered.

Vitari reluctantly sat. "Let Francis go. He has nothing to do with any of this. Let him go and I'll do what you want."

"That almost sounds like demand. Why do you think you can ask anything of me?"

"He's just a priest."

The Russian's smile grew as he glanced at Francis. "A priest with the power to ruin the Battaglia."

Vitari lifted his gaze and snorted. "Nobody has that much power."

"He hasn't told you?"

Vitari looked over. Francis swallowed. "I don't know anything." He'd told them that a thousand times. Why did nobody believe him?

"Don't you, Father?" the Russian asked. He leaned forward and gestured in a circle with his gun. "All around you, there are many questions. I received information. A priest in rural England can ruin Giancarlo Cinci, and this priest is so dangerous, Giancarlo is sending the assassin the Angel of Death to kill him. And so I must see for myself who this young priest is that has Giancarlo so frightened. But Angel takes you before I get my answers."

"I don't know anything about Giancarlo," Francis admitted. "I'm not whatever you people think I am. I never have been, I'm just a priest."

"This is my thought too," Sasha said. "A mistake. But why, then, does Giancarlo send his loyal son to kill you? Don Giancarlo rarely makes mistakes. So I researched you, Father Scott. You're very young for a priest. Popular. Many news articles on you, and your past, and your patron. Archbishop Charles Montague."

Francis tried not to flinch, but the Russian saw it.

"You are close with the archbishop?" Sasha asked.

Francis clenched his jaw so hard it ached. The Russian couldn't know *how* close. Nobody knew. "He is my patron, as you say."

Sasha smiled, as though sympathetic. "He seems to be a good man. Lots of charity work. Many good causes. I often find those who try too hard to be good have the darkest stains on their souls." Francis closed his eyes, as the words cut deep, but the Russian went on. "Crime and religion. For some crime is religion, and religion is crime."

Francis opened his eyes to find the Russian peering at him.

"The Battaglia and the church are—" He closed his free hand into a fist. "—this close. Some say the Vatican's wealth flows through a Battaglia bank. So, they must be good allies, yes? You know something, Father Scott. You may not even be aware of your power, but if Giancarlo believes you dangerous, that knowledge exists."

Francis hadn't known Vitari had orders to kill him. He'd suspected, but hearing it twisted his insides. He slid his gaze to Vitari, who'd remained uncharacteristically quiet. Vitari raised his eyebrows, questioning Francis. He'd never quite believed Francis was innocent. What if all this were a ruse to use Francis, to find out what he knew? What if last night was a lie? "Is that true? You *were* sent to kill me?"

Vitari averted his eyes. "I didn't know you then."

In all they'd shared, the passion, the moments, Francis had almost forgotten the man Vitari was—a ruthless killer. That night they'd first met, when he'd walked into Francis's church, had he come to murder Francis? "So why didn't you?" he asked.

"Because the whole thing stinks. It did then, it does

now. You don't know anything. A blind man can fucking see it."

"Did you lie to get close to me?"

"No," Vitari said, his unblinking glare locked on Francis.

"Was..." He had to be careful how he worded the next question. "Was Venezuela a lie?"

"No." Vitari's voice quivered. "You know the truth, Francis." And there was much in that sentence. Everything he couldn't say, not with witnesses. He always had seen the truth in Vitari's eyes, and it was there now.

It *was* real; what they had was real, *they* were real. Francis sighed. At least he had that, if little else.

"Angel took you to keep you out of our hands," Sasha said, swinging the topic back around. "But Giancarlo will give the order to kill eventually, Father. You are no fool. You must know this. The only reason he hasn't yet is because someone in the church," Sasha opened his free hand and squeezed his fingers into a fist, "holds his balls in a vise. Someone with control over the Battaglia."

Vitari snorted. "This is all fantasy. Giancarlo controls the Battaglia, not some mystical higher-up."

Everything the Russian had said so far was true. Somebody had pointed him toward Francis as a weak link in Giancarlo's armor, and there was only one force in Francis's life powerful enough to unsettle the Mafia. The church. Giancarlo had sent a killer, the DeSica had wanted answers... Someone out there was convinced Francis held a loaded gun either against Giancarlo or against the church.

The only thing in his past he knew people had died for was Stanmore.

The boys in the picture Montague had stolen were all gone. The place itself was nothing but cobwebs and rubble.

Even the documents were gone. But Francis remained. And so did Vitari.

"What can Francis know? He's spent his whole life closeted. He has no Mafia ties. Nothing to link him back to organized crime. Believe me, I've looked. He really is as naïve and fuckin' innocent as he looks."

Francis wasn't sure he was innocent. Not anymore.

"Well, Father Scott?" the Russian asked. "What do you know?"

Francis swallowed. These men would kill to get answers. Was the horror of the past worth Vitari's life? "Stanmore."

Vitari swung his gaze to Francis.

The Russian noted his reaction. "What is this... Stanmore?"

"It's nothing," Vitari said.

"Just like this priest is nothing, hm?" The Russian shifted in his chair, angling toward Francis, giving him his full attention. "*You* tell me what Stanmore is?"

"A boys' home, where I grew up. A charity, sponsored by the Catholic Church. I had uh... I had been about to bring some things to light—" He stroked the creases from his trousers. "—that the church would consider a scandal. But I didn't pursue it after I was kidnapped."

"And when you did not pursue it, the church made it clear, through the Battaglia, that *you* were protected."

Francis blinked. He hadn't considered the two things connected, but he should have. He hadn't sued, he hadn't revealed the secrets, and now he was safe.

"What are these *things* you were going to reveal?" the Russian asked.

"What does Stanmore have to do with Giancarlo?" Vitari asked, rushing on.

"That is the question, isn't it. Perhaps you should let the priest speak?"

Vitari glared. "We're done here. You're grasping at straws and making connections where there are none. Francis doesn't know anything. You need to go."

The Russian's smile grew. "I was just beginning to get comfortable."

Vitari sneered, "Stanmore is in the past. Let it die there. Get out of my home."

"You seem very passionate about *not* discussing Stanmore. Perhaps there's a reason for that? Did Giancarlo order you to silence the priest because he was about to expose Stanmore? It sounds likely, doesn't it? You must agree there, Angel."

"We're done. Shoot me, or get out."

There was a reason Vitari had shut down, but it wasn't what the Russian thought. Vitari didn't have orders to not speak of it, he *feared* Stanmore and everything it had done to him.

The Russian sighed. "You, Angel, are going to get me proof of Giancarlo's ties to the Stanmore scandal. Proof that I can use to expose him and the church. You will do this or your priest dies."

"Francis doesn't fucking know anything," Vitari snapped. "He's not part of any of this. Let him go, and you and me will talk this through? I'll tell you all you want to know about Stanmore."

Sasha hesitated, considering it. "No, I need proof. Not your word. Get me proof or the priest will swing from a Vatican bridge."

"You touch Francis, and I'll—"

The Russian's silenced gun kicked, and Vitari jolted, gasping. He clutched at his side and fell back in the couch.

No, no, no... Francis flew to his side and reached toward the swelling patch of blood on his shirt. "Vitari?" He couldn't be shot, he couldn't be.

Blood squeezed between Vitari's fingers. So much blood.

"Your phone—where's your phone?" Francis asked. "An ambulance, I'll call an ambulance."

Vitari shook his head and squeezed his next words through gritted teeth. "No ambulance. Are they gone?"

Francis glanced behind him, having forgotten about Sasha. "Yes, they're gone." He faced Vitari again and was sure he'd paled in those few seconds. "Does it hurt?"

"Yes, it fucking hurts!" He slumped, breathing hard. "I'll be fine. You need to go."

"What? No. I'm not leaving." Francis grabbed a clean cloth from the kitchen and hurried back. "Hold this tight against it." Vitari took the cloth and with bloody fingers pressed it to his side. "Where's your phone?"

"Francis, you have to go, you can't be here."

Francis took a step back. "I'm not leaving. I left you in Venezuela, I'm not leaving you now."

Vitari smiled. Why was he smiling? He was *bleeding*! There was nothing to smile about.

"I'm going to be fine" he said. "It's just a warning. But you have to go. If my father's people find you here, it will be worse for both of us. Do you understand? This bullet is nothing, but if... if we're discovered together?" His eyes said what his words could not. "Just go."

"I can't." Francis paced. *Walk away, with him bleeding on the floor?* "I can't do that."

Vitari hissed. "Fuck, Francis. Listen for once. Save me by leaving."

Francis hated this. Hated that he couldn't be here to see

Vitari safe. It wasn't right. He sat bleeding on that couch, hurting, and every part of Francis told him to stay, to be with him, to comfort him. "You're going to call someone?"

"Yes."

"You'll get help?"

"Yeah. Go. I'm okay. We'll talk later. Go back to the Vatican and don't do anything, not a fucking thing. Carry on like you normally would. None of this happened. Understand?"

Francis lunged and kissed him hard and fast on the mouth, then stared into his eyes. There was too much to say, too many questions and no time. Vitari's glare fixed on him, willing him to go, but also begging him to stay. He felt the same. "Go," Vitari whispered.

Francis straightened, and Vitari pulled his phone from his trouser pocket. He dialed a number with bloody fingers and raised the phone to his ear. "Go, amore mio."

Francis stood, nodded, and headed for the door.

"Clothes!" Vitari laughed, then gave a cough. "Put a shirt and shoes on, Padre."

Right, clothes. He hurried back to the bedroom and flung on his shoes and shirt, then after casting Vitari one final glance to capture his smile, he walked out into bright sunlight and buzzing city noise as though stepping into a different world. Blood stained his trembling hands. He wiped them on his trousers and walked. Just walked, not even sure if he were heading the right way.

Go back to the Vatican.

Do nothing.

But with every step his heartbeat drummed for him to turn around, to make sure Vitari was safe. But Vitari was right. He couldn't be found with Francis, for many, many reasons.

Do nothing, Vitari had said. But how could he *do nothing?* The Russian wanted to know about Stanmore, and so did Francis. It all went back to Stanmore. Vitari being sent to kill Francis had not been a coincidence. Giancarlo could have sent anyone. But he'd sent his son, a son who had also spent years at Stanmore.

Francis walked Rome's streets, hardly seeing the people he passed.

The Russian implied the church was embroiled in organized crime. And Francis had been about to sue an archbishop for child abuse. What if Giancarlo hadn't wanted Francis gone at all, but the church had, so they'd leaned on Giancarlo, making him send his assassin?

He stopped on a street corner, having passed over a bridge. Traffic churned. The wind tore down the curve of the River Tiber and rustled the leaves on the riverside trees. Somewhere not too far away, police sirens wailed.

No, his church would never sanction murder, not even to cover up a scandal like the one Francis had been about to expose. Would they? They'd survived proven cases of historical child abuse before, and many more had been paid off, never seeing a courtroom. Unfortunately, claims like his weren't unique.

Which meant something about Stanmore was different.

Perhaps it wasn't about Francis at all.

He looked around him, at the passing cars and ambling people, a slice of normal life, while blood dried on his trousers and under his nails.

What if this was about Vitari?

Francis's abuse had been mild compared to locking boys in a dark room for years on end, to making them available for the sexual pleasure of adults. Vitari had only briefly mentioned the things done to him. He'd thrown the facts at

Francis like knives. But the things he *had* revealed were devastating.

Nausea moistened Francis's mouth. He pressed the back of his hand to his lips and staggered back against a tree trunk, needing something to hold him up. His head was a whirl. Tiredness and fear tugged him apart.

If this was about Vitari, and the boys in Stanmore's back room, then it could damage the recovering Roman Catholic Church's reputation beyond repair. And if those boys had been killed... *murdered*... then Vitari might be capable of ruining the entire church.

What if the explosion on the superyacht had been meant for Vitari?

What if Luca's insane raid on El Cristo, butchering half a town, had been sanctioned by Giancarlo? Kill two Stanmore boys with one stone. Francis and Vitari. The last survivors.

If the Russian got hold of the evidence, it would absolutely bring down the church *and* Giancarlo.

But that evidence could also be the leverage Francis needed to keep them alive.

Francis could not *do nothing*.

He needed to get to work.

CHAPTER NINE

Sal glared while the doctor stitched Vitari's side in the living room. The bullet had grazed him just enough to deliver Sasha's warning: get the evidence to bring down Giancarlo, or the priest dies.

"Take these for the pain," the doctor said, dumping several blue pills into his palm. "Change the dressing morning and night."

Vitari thanked him and waited until he'd left before facing Sal's judgmental gaze.

"What happened?" Sal asked, arms crossed, unimpressed with having his day ruined.

With his side throbbing, Vitari levered himself off the couch and limped into the kitchen area. He filled a glass with water and washed the tablets down. "Sasha was here."

"Sasha?" Sal's stance went from pissed off to alert in a blink. "Fuck! Here?! Call Giancarlo now—"

"Slow down." Vitari waved a hand and slumped

against the kitchen counter. He had no idea how he was going to explain any of this. Sasha turned up, threatened him, wanted details of an Essex children's home from Vitari's past life, or the priest would get hung from a bridge. None of it would make any sense to Sal. But it would to Giancarlo. Too much sense. Vitari was so fucked.

He couldn't give Sasha anything that could implicate Giancarlo. It would help if he knew Giancarlo's involvement in Stanmore, and the church. So he could somehow protect his father, and Francis. He was going to have to ask some painful questions and did not relish that conversation with Giancarlo.

This was not how his *One Night in Rome* date with Francis was supposed to go. It had been great, the best fucking night of his life and the perfect goodbye, until Sasha had shown up.

"The DeSica boss was here and you're still breathing?" Sal was still waving his arms around. "What did he want?"

"I don't even know, fra. I need to meet with Giancarlo."

Sal sighed and glared, with an expression on his face that said he knew Vitari was in trouble, but it was above his pay grade. "Yes, you do. I'll drive."

"I'm good. I don't need an escort."

Sal breathed in, filling his chest, making himself bigger, and charged toward the kitchen like a bull. "What if he tries again, huh? There's no way I'm letting you walk outside alone."

"He didn't *try* to kill me." A flare of heat surged up his side, stealing his breath. "This is a message," he wheezed.

"Why are you so fucking calm?" Sal flung his hands out. "Sasha was *in your home!* We should be out there, putting a fucking bullet in the fucker's head. We need to round up his known men and cut their fucking balls off, then send them to him, send our own fucking message—"

Vitari let him rage and pace. "We will be," he said. "After I've spoken with my father. It's all good, Sal. Relax, fratello. He'll get what's coming to him."

With his rage burned out, Sal huffed through his nose, dragged a hand down his face, and glanced around him, muttering about cutting off balls and disrespect.

Vitari needed to think, which was proving hard with Sal losing his shit and a deadening ache in his side. At least Francis was safe. There had been a moment during the altercation when Vitari had been sure they were going to execute Francis and Vitari had gotten a glimpse of true fear.

"Were you alone?" Sal asked.

"Huh?" Vitari looked up.

"Here. Were you alone?"

His mind raced. "Yes, I was alone."

"So you decided to make two espressos?" Sal nodded toward the countertop. "One for each hand?"

Vitari glanced down at the incriminating evidence of Francis's untouched espresso and his own empty cup. Since when the fuck was Sal so damn observant?

"Please tell me it wasn't the priest," Sal groaned.

"Why would it be the priest?" His pounding heart choked him. This day just kept on getting worse, after beginning so damn fine. He should never have gotten out of bed. He should have stayed with Francis, tangled together, kissing him where he knew it made him gasp. Fuck his life. Fuck the world.

Sal held his gaze, then sighed as though he was as tired of this shit as Vitari. "I'm just gonna put this out there. How did Sasha know you were here? Who told him, huh?"

Was Sal throwing shade on Francis, implying he'd told

the Russian mob boss where Vitari was? For what purpose...
to get Vitari killed?

Vitari laughed. If Sal had met Francis, he'd know
that kind of bullshit wasn't on Francis's radar. He
didn't do betrayal. He'd probably have to pray for a
week if he accidentally watched a non-Catholic video
on TikTok.

"You know what, Angel? I don't want to know. Let's
just go. I'll put someone on the house, just in case the fucker
tries to hit you again."

Vitari gingerly shrugged on his jacket and followed Sal
out of the door. At least he'd had the One Perfect Night, the
date he'd wanted, with Francis. They were unlikely to get
another anytime soon.

Vitari should cut him off. End it now. Deal with Sasha,
and keep Francis far away from Giancarlo, the DeSica,
Sasha, Battaglia, all of it. But he couldn't, not even to save
him. Francis was his drug. And like an addict, he'd do
anything to get his next fix.

Perhaps even betray his father.

The villa was abuzz with activity. Glossy, expensive cars
crowded the sweeping drive, and the driver of the catering
truck was swearing at the housekeepers. Vitari rubbed at his
forehead as Sal pulled his car to a stop among the chaos.
He'd forgotten Giancarlo's birthday celebration was tonight.
He'd have to put on the smiles and would be expected to
play the perfect son, while everyone sneered behind his
back.

Giancarlo wouldn't be here yet either. He hated the set
up and preferred to arrive like the guest of honor.

"Shit, I forgot. He probably won't be here," Sal was saying, coming to the same conclusion.

"I'll wait." Vitari closed the car door and sauntered across the undulating, sweeping lawn. Two caterers carried an enormous multitiered cake across the driveway. Vitari snorted. He was lucky if he got a card for his birthday. The last few years, he hadn't even gotten that.

He headed into the house, passing staff filing back and forth with table arrangements and chair covers. A few of his father's inner circle nodded a greeting. They'd be making sure the caterers didn't wander into places they shouldn't.

He needed to get out of the bloody shirt and cleaned up before anyone asked why he looked like shit. He entered his bedroom and shrugged off the clothes. He couldn't shower with the new dressing, but wiped himself down, shaved, and dressed for the evening. He then fixed his hair—it was crazy thanks to Francis's grabbing fingers. Once he let go of his inhibitions, he fucked like a man trying to make up for all those years of celibacy.

Before Sasha had barged in, things had been good.

And the night—fuck, the night had been amazing. Francis was a god-damned diamond, outshining all the bad shit in Vitari's life. All that passion and fight wrapped up in his tight, agreeable body. Vitari chuckled at the memories and clipped his cuff links in place. He didn't deserve him. This life, Vitari's world... He'd get Francis fucking killed.

But that wasn't going to happen.

Vitari would get Sasha his evidence, if that was what it took. Whatever it was, it couldn't be as bad as Sasha hoped. Giancarlo would survive it, he always did, and nobody had to know Vitari had been the source. It was a shame Luca wasn't around, or Vitari could have pinned a leak on him.

He left his room, headed through the villa, and

approached Giancarlo's study. Vitari knocked, and when no reply came, he checked he was alone in the corridor, opened the door, and stepped inside.

A slow fan whirred above, stirring stuffy cigar-tainted air. Giancarlo kept his desk drawers locked, but Vitari knew from his early teens, after the many hours of being locked in this room as punishment for acting out, that the tall display cabinet contained multiple historic documents and a bunch of old flash drives.

He opened the cupboard, removed some of the box files, and pocketed the flash drives. The chances of there being anything incriminating on them was slim, but without access to the locked drawers, it was as good a place to start as any. He skimmed some of the printed documents, but nothing stood out as a smoking gun. Giancarlo wasn't likely to leave sensitive information where anyone could stumble onto it.

Vitari returned to his room, opened his laptop, and plugged in the first flash drive.

The party didn't kick off for a few hours. He had time to flick through a few of the drives. The first one contained old accounting files for several overseas land holdings. A good accountant could probably follow the breadcrumbs to something incriminating, but nothing jumped out as damning. The next just held two files of random photographs. The third was corrupted and wouldn't load. He hadn't expected to find a smoking gun on old files stuffed in a cupboard, but something suspicious would have been useful...

He plugged in the fourth drive and opened the first file.

Pictures of him filled the folder. In the first, he was maybe fourteen, sitting on a lounger by the villa pool, smiling. Another photo showed him with Giancarlo, leaning over the hood of an old sports car. He remembered that day.

It was one of the few when his time with Giancarlo hadn't felt as though he'd been squeezed into his father's endless schedule. He'd been fifteen years old.

All of the photos were of him in various places, not posed, just natural. And most had been taken by Giancarlo.

Vitari sat back. There were no photos of him on display anywhere in any of his father's houses. Giancarlo displayed images of his cars, his dogs, his other houses, some of his lovers—he'd never married. But none of Vitari. Because Giancarlo was ashamed of the whore's son, ashamed of Vitari. The open secret.

So, why keep the photos at all?

Vitari skimmed the other folders, but came up with just more of the same. Hundreds of relaxed, content pictures of himself.

The next drive was useless—again full of accounting documents.

But on opening the sixth, and seeing a woman and a child in the photos, he leaned forward. A double click displayed the images in a larger gallery. The woman was young, perhaps late teens, with tumbling dark hair and a broad, kind smile. She held a swaddled baby in her arms and looked at that child as though they were the most precious thing in all the world.

Vitari's heart stuttered. He scrolled through more pictures. The woman on a lawn, her arms out, beckoning a toddler toward her. Another with a boy attempting to ride a bike. Then pictures of her alone, posing for the camera, beautiful, graceful. Pictures of her on a familiar Rome bridge, posing with the grand domes and arches of the Vatican behind her. Pictures of her in a Vatican park, outside a Vatican house, in the Vatican gardens.

He scrolled back through the pictures, returning to the

one with the woman holding her arms outstretched. He knew that lawn. He'd walked across it just a few hours earlier.

He scrolled forward again, quicker, needing to see more. Needing to know...

And there, one of the final images, was of the boy, no more than four years old, sitting on a pony with his mother's hands around his waist, supporting him. He wore a silly straw hat and a faded Voltron T-shirt. He didn't seem that happy to be on the horse, and his dark eyes had narrowed, suspicious and fearful of the four-legged creature he rode.

He was that boy.

He didn't remember that day, but he recognized his own scowling face.

Vitari wasn't a fucking mistake. He wasn't a dirty secret. These pictures were proof he'd been loved, proof his mother hadn't been some cheap whore.

He jerked from the desk and paced. The graze in his side throbbed anew. Everything hurt, but the worst of the pain came from inside.

Why had Giancarlo hidden everything about his mother? Why had he let him believe she'd been nothing?

And how had Vitari gone from that silly, pink-cheeked boy in a straw hat to the ruined boy in a windowless room in Stanmore Boys' Home?

Giancarlo had kept all this from him—kept the fact he was the product of love, the fact he was wholly Italian, and how he had been cherished. Giancarlo had kept the identity of his own mother from him!

He sat back down, made copies of all the files and photographs, and numbly plugged in the final drive.

This one was numbered, with no file names, and the pictures were too blurry to make out at thumbnail. He clicked, and as the dark, gloomy images cascaded onto the screen, the images took shape. His brain translated the flashes of white as glimpses of pale skin against dark brick walls. A young boy, with his hands raised, his head down. Naked.

Vitari's guts swooped, then churned.

He couldn't look, but couldn't look away. He scrolled, seeing but not seeing, as though he were far away from everything, wrapped in numbness. The boy was thin, his Mediterranean skin wheat-pale, as he sat on the end of a metal-framed bed. His big eyes were so like his mother's it was a wonder Giancarlo could look at him today and not see her.

The pictures ranged from Vitari as a six-year-old, to almost nine or ten. It was hard to tell. He seemed so young, so thin and vulnerable.

He'd made it so that weak, pathetic boy didn't exist.

But there he was, staring back with Vitari's own eyes.

Vitari yanked out the drive and held it over the trash can. If he threw the photos away, they never had to exist, which meant that time didn't exist, like that boy did not exist.

But the images were also proof of how he'd been sold like a piece of meat.

Proof his father had known.

He set the drive down on the table beside the laptop, stared at it, daring it to hurt him some more, and then he plugged it back in and scrolled through every gut-wrenching, disgusting image, making himself *see*, even though each one burned like a fresh cut to the veins. There were others in the pictures. Older men. Prominent politicians, celebrities. The pictures would be worth millions in blackmail, which was likely the whole reason they existed.

Money from Vitari's shame.

The door to his room opened and Sal entered.

Vitari yanked the drive clear of the laptop and closed the file window.

"Giancarlo is here."

His heart pounded in his ears.

"You all right?" Sal asked.

"Uh huh. Fine." He closed the laptop, stood, but as the room spun, he grabbed the chair to hold him up.

"You sure?"

"I said I'm fucking fine, Sal, Jesus!"

Sal backed off, hands up. "You want to get a drink? You look like you need it."

He wanted to get so fucking wasted that when his veins sloshed with alcohol, he'd set himself on fire, scorching all the images from his head. He couldn't burn the memories away though, they went soul deep. "Yeah..."

He shoved the other flash drives into a drawer, but dropped the worst one into his pocket. Nobody could ever, *ever* see those photographs. Nobody could know how worthless he'd once been.

He'd take that evidence to his grave.

Sal had abandoned him. He couldn't blame him. Vitari hadn't been in the party spirit. Neo had tried to get a smile out of him by sharing a story about how he'd once almost shot his toe off. There was plenty of ammunition there for Vitari to use for further jokes at Neo's expense, but he couldn't bring himself to care. The numbness that had set in since viewing the photos clung on, suffocating him even as it shielded him.

He didn't want to be here, among the shiny, shallow people, all laughing and smiling as though they weren't all terrified *not* to come. He didn't want to be Vitari Angelini anymore. It was too much. He was trapped, just like Francis had said months ago. Vitari had denied it, told him he had no idea what he was talking about, but Francis had *known*.

Stumbling from the main room, where most of the guests were gathered, Vitari pulled his phone from his pocket and staggered outside, through the parked cars, to the sprawling front lawn where he'd once, apparently, lived a happy, normal life.

He flopped onto the grass and called "Frank." Francis probably wouldn't pick up. Since he'd been in Rome, he hadn't answered any of Vitari's calls. Maybe priests weren't allowed their phones in holy places.

It rang and rang, and Vitari's heart thumped harder and harder.

He shouldn't be calling him.

But he needed to hear his voice, needed to feel close to someone who made him feel like he was worth something.

"Are you all right?" Francis asked.

"I love you." The confession fell out of him. He hadn't planned on saying it, but there it was.

Francis's intake of breath had Vitari's insides fluttering. Had he just ruined it all?

"You were shot," Francis said. "Are you okay?"

So, he was just going to ignore Vitari's words, then. Fair enough. Vitari could ignore them too. "Ish...fine."

"Are you drunk?"

"What? Nah. Maybe." He flopped back on the grass and stared at the twinkling stars.

"I can hear it in your voice." He sighed, making Vitari

feel like a scolded teen. "Are you really all right... from earlier?"

"Yeah." He closed his eyes and listened to Francis's breathing. "You should hate me."

He waited a beat. "Sometimes I do."

"I hate my life."

"Did something happen? Something... more than this morning?"

"Yeah." He couldn't say it. Already the emotions were welling up, choking him. He'd never get the words out, and then he'd break down here on the lawn, at Giancarlo's party, crying like a fool to a priest. "I want to see you."

Francis sighed. "I can't right now. It's evening mass, and we... can't keep doing this."

"Run away with me?"

Francis's little laugh thawed some of the numbness. "We tried that."

"I'm not who I thought I was," Vitari mumbled, plucking at the grass beside him, removing each blade, one by one.

"Angel, are you going to be all right?"

"Uh huh."

"I can maybe... get out later... the gates are locked at midnight, but I can meet you before then."

Nobody would know or care if Vitari wasn't at the party. "I'd like that."

"Outside the restaurant you took me to? I can meet you there, at eleven? But it has to be quick. I need to be back by twelve."

God, he loved the sound of Francis's voice, so reasonable and smooth and calm. Vitari checked his watch, blinking a few times to clear the blur. "I can do that."

"Are you going to be able to get there safely?"

"I'm not as drunk as you think," he slurred. "It's the drugs."

"That doesn't ease my concerns, Angel," he said, all stern and chiding.

"Not *those* drugs... Pain medication drugs."

He chuckled. "All right. Good. Then... I'll see you soon. Goodbye?"

"Ciao."

Francis ended the call first, but Vitari still held the phone to his ear, listening to the call-ended tone. He'd told Francis he loved him, and it had felt right, even if Francis had ignored it.

"There you are." Sal stomped over. "What the fuck are you doing out here?"

"Nothing." He tried to stand and fell onto his knees with a snort.

"Jesus, you need to get your shit together." Sal grabbed his arm and hauled him upright. "Giancarlo wants to see you." He patted Vitari's face, just lightly, trying to wake him up. "C'mon, this isn't you."

"What is me, huh?" Vitari stumbled into Sal and slumped in his arms. This was... good. Sal was good. Sturdy. Dependable.

His big hands tried to peel Vitari off him. "I can't take you to the boss like this. Go back to your room and sober up. I'll tell him I couldn't find you."

Vitari grinned at his friend and patted his cheek. "Love you, Sal."

"Right," he drawled, then flung an arm around Vitari and together they stumbled around the side of the villa, and in through a back entrance. "Take a cold shower, get focused, and I'll come get you in ten—"

Sal swung Vitari's door open. The light from the

corridor illuminated Giancarlo standing by the desk where Vitari had earlier viewed the worst of his nightmares.

"Leave us," Giancarlo snapped. He loomed large in the dark, his silhouette broad.

"Yes, boss." Sal was gone, leaving Vitari swaying on his feet, alone. He righted his clothes and faced his father. He could do this. He could stand up to him.

"What has gotten into you this evening?"

"Nothing." He sniffed and dragged a hand down his face, trying to clear away some of the drunkenness. "It's fine. I'm fine. Everything is fucking fine." He drifted toward the window. His father's glare weighed down every step.

"This behavior is intolerable, Vitari."

Vitari smiled at his reflection in the dark window. "Yeah, I am intol-able." The Battaglia's open secret, Giancarlo's attack dog, the whore's son. L' Angelo della Morte. He just had to get through this, then after Giancarlo returned to his party, Vitari would hire a taxi and go find Francis. The only place—the only person who made any damn sense in his life.

"Happy birthday, Father," Vitari drawled, and somewhere buried far at the back of his mind he knew he was making it worse, that he should grovel and beg his father's forgiveness, but he didn't feel much like getting on his knees since seeing those vile photographs, since realizing Giancarlo had known everything he'd lived through.

"Do not leave this room for the rest of the night."

Vitari snorted. What was his father going to do, lock him in as though he was fifteen again?

"What was my mother's name?" He remembered her smiling face from the photographs—always smiling. She was beautiful. And happy. So happy.

"We're not discussing her. That whore has no place on this night, on my birthday—"

Vitari turned and leaned against the windowsill. "She wasn't a whore though, was she? You call her that because you hate her?"

His father's face twitched. "You are a drunk disgrace to the family, to the Battaglia! You behave like this, you dishonor me in my home—"

Vitari laughed at the ineffective insults. He'd heard them all before. "Did *you* put me in that boys' home? Whose idea was it? What happened, and where is she now? Did she grow tired of your bullshit?" Vitari pushed from the window and marched toward his father. "Did she try and get away? Did you kill her?"

The slap struck him so hard he fell to the floor on his knees. Bitter, coppery blood filled his mouth. He swallowed and wiped his lips on the back of his hand. And here he was, on his knees, right where he'd always been.

The hand Giancarlo had used to strike him with trembled as he lowered it to his side. "Stay here until you are sober, and never speak of your mother again. Her name will never touch your lips." He turned on his heel and hurried toward the door.

No, Vitari wasn't going to be dismissed like filth. He'd seen the evidence. He knew he'd been lied to. He sprang off his back foot and flew out of the door, after Giancarlo.

"Hold him," Giancarlo ordered. Two guards lunged in, grabbing Vitari like cargo nets, hands all over him, forcing him back. "Make sure he stays in that room," Giancarlo ordered. "If he gets out, you're fired."

"Fuck, get off me!" Vitari bucked, tried to writhe free, but the two men—men he knew, men he'd respected—muscled him back into the room and flung him at the bed.

"Stay down, Angel," one of them warned.

Angel had lost. He was a mess. He knew it. They all knew it. But worse, he wasn't meeting with Francis...

That was probably a good thing. Wasted like he was, he was a liability. A stain on the Battaglia. An embarrassment. Shame made his skin crawl.

But he'd make his father hurt, he'd fucking ruin him, like he'd ruined the little boy in the straw hat and Voltron T-shirt. The boy Vitari should have been, not the monster he was today.

CHAPTER TEN

Francis

He waited until the last possible minute, but Vitari wasn't coming. Considering the drunken state he'd been in during the call, he'd likely passed out somewhere, or forgotten. Francis hurried back to the Vatican.

Texting Vitari was out of the question. Texts could be saved and used as evidence against them. It would be better to wait until Vitari had sobered up. He'd probably call in the morning.

Putting Vitari's absence to the back of his mind, he returned to the apartment building he'd been allowed to stay in—a stunning, if intimidating, high-ceilinged ancient piece of history in its own right. The building had a private chapel, used only by Vatican staff. The chapel felt small and safe and less overwhelming than the grandeur of St Peter's. With only three pews, he knelt in the middle one and prayed.

Vitari was hurting. Something had happened, something to make him call Francis in that state, to make him reach out, to make him say those words: I love you. Of course, it didn't mean anything. They were just drunken words. Vitari would never say that and mean it, even if Francis wished for it to be real. The times in the past, when he'd been so drunk he'd slurred his words, those times Vitari's soul had suffered.

Francis prayed for guidance, and for strength. For them both.

He prayed that he'd make the right decision, because something had to give.

Francis had fallen down the same misguided path, unable to prevent himself. It wasn't wrong, being intimate with a man—he firmly believed that—but it was in conflict with his life and role as a priest.

He had a choice to make.

The church or Vitari. He could not have both in his life. Yet... he couldn't imagine leaving either.

Francis clutched his hands tighter together, bowed his head, and prayed *harder*. He wasn't here to be redeemed. He could never cleanse himself of the sins he'd committed. But he could help others cleanse theirs, as he'd always wanted to.

He prayed that God might forgive him, and forgive Vitari.

"Oh, I'm sorry, I thought the chapel was empty."

Francis jerked awake and blinked at the smiling, blond-haired older man leaning over the end of the pew.

"Were you sleeping?"

"I uh..." Francis glanced around. He was still in the

chapel, slumped in the pew. Sunlight poured through the high stained glass window. He'd been there all night. "I think perhaps I was."

"Don't worry. I won't tell if you won't." The priest—American, by the accent—offered his hand, and Francis shook automatically, his thoughts slow to catch up.

"Father Davis," he said, shaking Francis's hand with gusto. "You're Francis, right? Not the Pope Francis." He winked and let go. "But arguably just as famous. I saw you on the news. Seeing you in the flesh, like this, it's like meeting a rockstar."

"Oh, well, I don't know about that." Francis rubbed his face, trying to sweep away the remains of sleep and embarrassment. He needed to get back to his apartment, take a shower, and see if he could make it to the morning service.

He shuffled from the pew and thanked Father Davis as he stepped aside. "I'll leave you to your prayers, Father. And I'm sorry, for... well, for what you saw."

"Call me Riley. There are too many fathers around here, eh." He chuckled. "And don't worry, I've seen worse things than a man asleep during prayer."

He seemed nice. "Riley." Francis smiled politely. "I should be going."

"Sure thing."

Francis turned away and was certain Father Davis's gaze stayed on him until he left the chapel.

Returning to his apartment, he showered, dressed in his robes, and fell into the comfortable routine of fulfilling his daily duties. The day passed in a rush of tasks, and while mobile phones weren't allowed sin the working areas of the Vatican, Francis snuck his in on silent and checked it during the day. No calls.

He couldn't call Vitari, could he?

He knew he *shouldn't* call him, but last night's conversation had been strange. Vitari was likely fine; he would have slept off the alcohol by now and would be going about his day, just like Francis, although with less prayer and more whatever he did as the Mafia don's son.

It was best not to think on that.

So... Perhaps, a quick call? Francis groaned at his own idiocy.

"Ah, Father Scott, two times in one day. It must be fate, no? Or it's more likely we're all rattling around the same buildings."

"Father Davis." Francis straightened, caught leaning against the wall and staring at his phone. He glanced at the Swiss guard—the only other person in the same stretch of corridor. He'd become so accustomed to the guards' blue and orange livery, they were like elaborate pieces of furniture dotted about the Vatican. "I'm sorry, every time you see me, I appear to be slouching or asleep."

Davis laughed, and the sound filled the arched ceiling. Davis's blue eyes sparkled with a kind of vibrant mischief, making Francis doubt his initial "old" assumption. He couldn't be more than early forties.

"No need to apologize to me, only God." He laughed. "Did you want to grab a coffee? Seems we could both use the caffeine."

It would take Francis's mind off Vitari, and he had some time before his next duties. He could also do with socializing more. Since arriving, he'd felt a little like the outsider, with everyone being so busy.

"Thank you. I'd like that."

They left the Vatican grounds, walking in bright sunlight among tourists, down the main promenade of Via della Conciliazione, and found a small pizzeria down one of the side streets. Father Davis suggested they eat, so Francis sat at the window, with good company and good food, feeling more normal with every passing minute. Davis talked about his Midwest church, his parishioners, and how he missed the simpleness since he'd been *drafted* in as an American representative for the Vatican's world-renowned Easter events.

Francis recognized his own struggles in the priest's life, and although he didn't say it explicitly, it appeared as though Davis battled much of the same demons as Francis. Perhaps they all found their lives difficult, and Francis wasn't alone in his strife.

"Waiting for a call?" Father Davis asked, noting Francis's less than subtle glances at his screen.

"Something like that." He almost told him who, then shut himself down. Of course he couldn't mention Vitari Angelini by name. His kidnapper, the Mafia boss's son, his... lover. Sometimes, he felt as though the volume of secrets was drowning him. "A friend of mine had a rough few days. The last time we spoke, he was... He didn't sound like himself," Francis explained. "I was hoping I might have heard from him by now, so I know he's all right."

"Oh, I'm sure he will." Father Davis beamed and finished off his pizza with a messy bite. He licked his fingers clean. "How bad can it be, right, if he has you as a friend?"

"That's kind of you to say."

"You seem like a good guy, Francis."

Davis wouldn't say that if he knew all the things Francis had done.

"I try to be." He may not have been trying as hard as he should have.

"Ain't *that* the truth." Davis smiled, with a little too

much weight behind his words, as though he bore the weight of his own sins and knew how heavy they could be.

Francis's phone rang. His heart leaped into his throat. "I have to just... I must take this." He left the table, then glanced at the screen, where Father Hawker's name was displayed. Not Vitari. His heart sank. But it wasn't all bad. He hadn't heard from Father Hawker since moving to Westminster.

"Father Hawker, hello?"

"Oh, hello Francis."

They chatted briefly, the usual small talk, but then Father Hawker's tone turned serious. "I uh, well I... I wanted to call and ask if you're all right, Francis? I'm afraid I was rather remiss in my duties and then you were gone, so... we didn't really have a chance to discuss everything you went through."

"I'm fine, thank you." It was a bit late, but welcome nonetheless. He had wondered if Father Hawker had been glad to see the back of him.

"Oh good, good..." He trailed off, waiting, or thinking.

"Was there something else?" Francis prompted.

"You're in the right place, Francis. You'll be fine."

Strange. Was something wrong with Father Hawker? "Are *you* all right?" In the months he'd spent with Father Hawker, he hadn't once asked him how he was. He'd always been the pillar of priestly life, content, with his church and the parish in order. Everything Francis had aspired to be.

"Yes, I just..."

"Is something wrong?"

Silence.

"Father, what's going on?" Francis moved farther from the busy eating area, away from listening ears.

"Forgive me for saying this. I think perhaps, some things

you shared with me in the past, well, I wasn't as aware of the implications as I should have been."

This was about Francis's confessions. But which part? His being gay? He had told Father Hawker of his desire for men before he'd begun his post in St Mary's, but it hadn't bothered him then. So, was this something else? He tried to recall all the things he'd revealed, but he'd been careful. He hadn't spoken much at all of Venezuela. But the Mafia wouldn't know that. And Father Hawker was a soft, easy target. "It's all right, tell me what's wrong."

"I read the letter... from your solicitor. I know I had no right to, but we were all so worried about you..."

Then he knew about Archbishop Montague's abuse. But more than that, he knew about the boys' home. Francis's solicitor, in that letter, had asked for more witnesses, more *victims*. At least he now knew who had opened the letter. "Did anyone else see it?"

"No, I... I hid it from the church, when they came to investigate."

"It was nothing. A mistake." If Father Hawker began to dig into Montague and the boys' home, he'd find himself tangled up in this horrible mess alongside Francis, and he did not deserve that. "I didn't go through with it."

"Francis," Father Hawker said, in his stern voice. "He took you to Westminster. I thought to protect you, but it wasn't that at all, was it—"

This man was too kind. He couldn't bring him into this world too. "It's all in the past, it doesn't matter. Please, just forget it."

"I can't do that."

"Father, please... I'm... I'm dealing with it. You don't need to do anything."

"I'm sorry." Father Hawker's voice trembled. "I'm so

sorry, Francis. I feel shame, for what was done to you. He is *not* the church. We are better than that. Just know... you can talk to me. I will always be here for you. I will always listen. God will always listen."

He'd needed to hear those words, to know all was not lost. The world wasn't as corrupt as it seemed. He just happened to be in the middle of a pocket of darkness. "Thank you. But Father, please do not mention any of this to anyone."

"Is it... is it over? I mean, does he... Is it still happening, Francis?"

Francis sighed and leaned against the wall. Was it over with the Archbishop? Sexually, it was. The man wouldn't dare touch him like he'd used to. But was it over, in general? No. The boys' home, the archbishop, the dead with no voices to tell their truths, and now the DeSica. It was all so tightly twined, like a web of abuse and lies and corruption, that a pluck of one string reverberated through the others. "I'm dealing with it," he repeated, and made sure Father Hawker heard the severity in his words.

"Does it have anything to do with your kidnapping?"

He glanced behind him at Father Davis gazing out of the window at the passing tourists. "I can't talk anymore about this now. Thank you for calling, it means a lot."

"I'm here for you."

"I appreciate that."

They said their goodbyes, and Francis ended the call. Strange, how the sunlight seemed to have dulled. Father Davis sipped his coffee, still staring out of the window. At least he didn't have anything to do with it all.

Nice, normal people who didn't want to extort, threaten, or bribe did exist. And Father Davis was one of those.

Francis returned to the table and thanked him for joining him for lunch. Father Davis offered to pay for his food and Francis's mind had gotten so bogged down in the quagmire of his past, he didn't have the energy to insist. Even outside, walking back to the Vatican in blazing sunlight, he couldn't shake a growing chill. He apologized to Father Davis—who again insisted he call him Riley—for souring the mood and offered to make it up by inviting him for lunch the next day.

Riley agreed and left Francis alone in one of St Peter's many closed-to-the-public rooms, swamped by high ceilings and four hundred years of Catholic history. He pulled his phone from his pocket and hovered his thumb over Vitari's number. If he didn't answer, what did that mean? And if he did answer, what was Francis going to say? Thank you for the date, it was amazing, but we can never do it again?

Francis dropped his phone back into his pocket.

Sasha seemed to believe the boys' home and Giancarlo were linked enough to ruin the mob boss. And the boys' home had been linked to Montague, since he was its patron, and Francis had met him there. Which likely meant all three were tangled together. And as an archbishop, there would be records of Montague's rise through the ranks in the Vatican archives.

Archives that were just a few rooms away from where he stood.

After Francis surrendered his phone to the archivist guard and signed the security log, he stepped through the vacuum-sealed door into the Vatican vaults. Rack upon rack of red box files ran the length of the enormous archives, stretching far under St Peter's grounds. There were records and documents here Francis would never be allowed to see, and some only the most stalwart lifelong servants of the Catholic Church would ever lay eyes upon. As fascinating as it all was, Francis wasn't here for any of the older records, or those kept locked away inside metal cages. He needed more recent records pertaining to personal files of the ordained.

Within a few meters, the files on the shelves switched from red to blue, and ahead, the infamous metal cages came into sight. The documents behind those metal doors were the most treasured, or controversial. But opposite those, shelves of newer box files waited.

He stopped in front of them. These files were probably all computerized somewhere, but knowing the church, he'd have to jump through hoop after hoop to get access. Whereas, he was already here. Although, the task did seem daunting. Even alphabetized, he was staring at several hours of work ahead.

An hour later, he found the personnel files.

"May I help you?" A nun appeared at Francis's left shoulder, startling him. She laughed a little at his surprise. "I did not mean to sneak up on you, Father," she said in English.

"No, it's my fault, I was lost to reading. You may be able to help." He asked after the recent files on European ordinations, explaining he was writing a piece on declining priest numbers—a small white lie he'd atone for later—and was met with several files of names and placements. The nun left him to his browsing, and after a little while, he found Archbishop Charles Montague's file.

A quick skim of the information revealed Francis's own name and a number beside it, referring to another file. He found it and a table, and spreading out the documents, he scanned for anything that might link Montague with the boys' home. And there it was, along with his own name again, as a person of special interest to the archbishop. Francis's own brief time as a priest had been slotted in on a clean, white, crisp piece of paper, with a mention of how he'd been ordained at twenty-four years old, with the archbishop's consent. *Consent* sat uneasily with him, but he pushed those feelings aside. While swallowing the bitter taste in his mouth, his gaze caught a familiar name:

Stefania Angelini.

There were likely many Angelini's in Italy, but to find one among Montague's files seemed significant, although the name only appeared once: under *dependents*.

Francis stared at the innocuous little words. His heart pounded in his ears. It could be a coincidence, or it could be exactly what it appeared to be. Montague was linked with Vitari Angelini by way of this Stefania. Who was she? Cousin, sister, aunt?

Returning to the racks, he searched for a file on just Angelini, but there didn't appear to be anything related to that name. He asked the nun, Sister Lucia, who helped him search. "Stefania Angelini lived here," Sister Lucia said a little while later, kind brown eyes peering out from the hooded shadow of her habit. "Part of the Angelini family, living in the Vatican grounds."

"People live at the Vatican?"

"Oh yes, but not many. Less than a thousand. In some cases, generations of the same family live and work at the Vatican."

"Are the Angelinis still here?" Did Vitari have living relatives inside the Vatican? Did he know?

"No," she explained, shaking her head. "The Angelinis ended at Stefania. Oh, I remember this, I'd just joined the library staff. The poor girl disappeared over fifteen years ago, after stepping outside her house."

"Did she have a brother? Or a... son?"

"Oh, no. No child, and her aging father died not long after. Her mother had died long before them. So sad. She wasn't ever found, although there were rumors and theories of her whereabouts, of course."

"Rumors, such as?"

"Oh, I don't like to pass on gossip. But I'm sure you can find all the theories online, if you want to Google it later. Much of it is nonsense though."

Stefania Angelini. Vitari thought he was nobody, thought he *had* no one. Whatever it meant, he'd want to know about Stefania. "May I take a copy of these files?"

"I'm sorry, we do not allow that."

"All right, thank you."

She glided away, and Francis went back to studying the files. Stefania Angelini—a dependent of Archbishop Montague. How was Stefania Angelini connected to Montague as a dependent if she'd disappeared, likely died, over fifteen years ago? She'd had a life, a family in the Vatican. Where was the connection with Montague? And it couldn't be a coincidence how Vitari shared her last name.

With nothing else of use among the records, he left the archives and retrieved his phone Stepping into the Vatican gardens in the waning day, he Googled *Stefania Angelini Vatican.*

Missing Vatican Girl Sparks Probe into Catholic Church.

Stefania Angelini – the Angel Who Never Returned.

Pictures of a young, smiling Italian woman populated the search results. Francis sat on a bench in the fading sun and scrolled through the results as several gardeners wandered by and pigeons picked at grit on the pathway.

Pope John Paul Issues Public Apology for Vatican Failings.

Father Orders Exhumation of Vatican Grave. No Body Found.

Father of Missing Girl Dies Without Knowing Daughter's Fate.

Article after article, most dated from many years ago. Stefania Angelini had vanished early evening outside her Vatican home. The Vatican City police wrote off her disappearance as a young woman acting out. The case was never investigated.

She'd walked out her door and disappeared.

Theories ranged from running away, to aliens, to Vatican conspiracies and plots against the church. A true crime podcast had even tried to resurrect the story a few years ago but found nothing.

Francis screenshotted a few photos of the young woman and the articles. He needed to show them to Vitari. If nothing else, her link to Montague as a "dependent" and subsequent disappearance were too significant to ignore.

With the sun warming his dark robes, but his thoughts mired in shadows, he leaned back on the bench and dialed Vitari's number.

"Father Francis Scott," a deep, gravelly male voice answered.

Francis froze. This man was not Vitari.

"Listen well, Father Scott. Do not call this number again," the man said. "Do not reach out to my son. Live a long, content life among your church. Hai capito?"

"Don Giancarlo," Francis whispered. Vitari's father.

Where was Vitari? Was he safe? Had something happened to him, was that why his father had his phone?

"If you see my son again, photographs of you breaking your vows will reach your superiors."

He'd wondered when Luca's photographs of him and Vitari engaged in intimacies would make an appearance. If Giancarlo had seen them, then Vitari was in trouble. "I see."

"Then we have an understanding?"

"Is he all right?"

"He is not your concern, Father Scott," Giancarlo grumbled, losing his patience.

"I... understand." He had to say it, there was no other answer. Giancarlo had the photographs, which meant he knew his son was gay, and Vitari had been very clear he lived a life that did not allow for such things. What if he was hurt somewhere? "Just... Please..." He might be making it worse, he knew that, but he had to know. "Is he safe?"

"He is my son."

What did that mean? That he was fine or damned? Giancarlo wasn't going to tell him anything, that much was clear. But this call might be the only time Francis ever got to speak with Vitari's father, the one chance he had to ask him anything.

"Who is Stefania Angelini?" he blurted.

The line clicked, and the dial tone hummed in his ear.

Francis slumped forward, shivering in his robes despite the day's heat.

There was no way of reaching Vitari. There was nothing he could do but trust Vitari would reach out to him when he could.

He would be all right.

Vitari was always all right.

The Russian still needed proof, and Francis still needed answers.

Whatever all this was, it was big. Bigger than them, just as Luca had said, all those months ago. And Francis wasn't letting it go. A girl had vanished, boys had died, the abuse would not go unpunished, and all of it could be traced back to Archbishop Montague.

Francis needed to go back to London, back to Montague, and demand answers. But to do that, he needed a smoking gun. He needed evidence. Or Montague would deny it all. Francis's gut, his intuition, perhaps even God, told him Stefania Angelini was the answer to it all.

CHAPTER ELEVEN

Vitari

Giancarlo had taken Vitari's phone as though he were a child. Probably because he'd acted like one. He'd fucked up. He'd been drunk and angry and stupid. That wasn't him. He'd worked too damn hard to throw it away on the past. So what if he'd once had a caring mother, someone who had loved him. It didn't change a damn thing.

Tonight, he was L' Angelo della Morte, and he was at a commercial dock, waiting for a supplier of product who'd been skimming profits. Tonight, he was doing what he always did, before a priest had turned his world upside down. Vitari was about to remind a thieving idiot not to fuck with the Battaglia.

Thieves lost fingers. And other things.

He was more powerful as L' Angelo della Morte than as the family's dirty secret hidden away in England.

As for Francis, just so long as he stayed in the Vatican and didn't make waves, he'd be fine. There was still that little problem of someone taking out a contract on Francis, but Francis was still known as being protected. Only Ricky had been stupid enough to go asking about the hit and had gotten himself a trip off the side of a bridge. The hit wasn't going anywhere.

A refrigerated box truck clattered along the dockside. Vitari checked his watch. Two a.m. Right on time. He pushed off his car and sauntered toward the slowing truck. Two nearby cameras had been turned off by the dockside staff, paid to look the other way. Nobody was watching.

The driver rolled down his window. "Who are you? Where's Ginelli?"

The lone driver was just some middle-aged mule, hardly worth Vitari's time. "Get out of the truck."

"What the fuck, man—"

Vitari produced a gun and gestured with it for him to open the door. "Get out of the fucking truck."

The man's face fell. "You don't want to do this." He opened his door and stumbled out, then raised his hands. "This is Battaglia product. They will come for you. Don't be stupid. They'll get you."

Vitari grabbed his arm, kicked his legs out, and dropped him to his knees. "I *am* the Battaglia."

"Oh shit, shit, shit, what is it?" he whined, his voice pitching higher. "I did what you said, I always do it!"

"This is just business, man. Relax."

"Fuck. They're here, in the back, what did I do wrong? I haven't done anything wrong. I just maybe used a few, you know? Like, to see if they were good."

"'They'?" Vitari asked, glancing at the truck. The old branding had been stripped off its sides. What was its cargo?

The man on his knees side-eyed him. "The people," he said, as though Vitari was a dumbass for not knowing.

People.

In the truck.

"Stay there. Don't fuckin' move." Vitari moved to the rear of the truck, unlatched the doors, and swung them open. A dozen, maybe more, young faces peered out of the gloom. Boys, girls. Young. A lot younger than Vitari. "Where are you from?" he asked. They stared blankly. "¿De dónde eres?" Nobody replied, although he feared he already knew the answer.

He'd been told the truck was brimming with product, not fucking *people*.

"Where are these people going?" Vitari asked, returning to the driver, who was still on his knees.

"London."

Vitari's mind churned scenarios and outcomes. He knew this shit went on, but he'd never seen it with his own eyes. It had always been someone else's problem. Until Venezuela, and the dead girl in Francis's graveyard. A girl who had gone to Francis for help, whose sister had asked Vitari for help, and who both were now dead.

God damn it, why couldn't it have been drugs?

"You do this run a lot?" Vitari asked.

"Every s-six months."

Vitari filled his lungs and winced into the dull dock lights. His side ached some too, a throbbing reminder of Sasha's warning. This night had just gotten a whole lot more complicated for everyone involved. "You said you 'used' them? How does that work, huh?"

The man blinked, and now Vitari studied him. He'd been a tool before, but now he was a man who routinely trafficked people and *used* them while doing it. His name was Marco something. Vitari usually didn't care to know the names of every mule the Battaglia employed, but this one had made himself special. Marco had been skimming the profits *and* sampling the product.

"I mean, yeah, right." He frowned. "Some of them get loud, so you have to show them what happens if they don't behave." He snorted a laugh, sensing a friend in Vitari, now they were talking. "It's just business, right? You know what it's like."

Vitari crouched to eye level with Marco and gave him his quick grin. "Use them how, huh?"

Marco's gaze skipped over Vitari's face. He half smiled, man to man. "You know, beat 'em an' shit. Some of them are asking for it."

"You ever touch them? Sexually?"

Marco swallowed. His gaze slid away. "No, man."

Vitari pressed his gun to the man's head. "You lyin'?"

Sweat beaded Marco's face. "It's all they're going to do when they get where they're going anyway, so what if I fuck a few. Nobody cares—"

Vitari tugged on the trigger; the silenced gun fired, kicked, blood sprayed the side of the truck, and Marco jerked, collapsing like a card castle at Vitari's feet. Silence rushed back in. Vitari sighed. This was not how the night was supposed to go.

He stood, grabbed Marco's limp arm, and dragged the body to the edge of the dock. There wasn't anything around to weigh him down. Hopefully, the ocean current would carry him out, away from the docks. Vitari kicked Marco over the side and his bloody body landed with a splash.

Returning to the rear of the truck, Vitari huffed a sigh at the blank faces peering out at him.

"Fuck."

Punish the thief, that had been the job. Now he had a truck full of people to deal with. This was *not* the plan.

"Goddammit. Just..." He had no idea what to say or what to do. "You'll be fine. Siento que estarás bien." He shut the door, latched it closed, and climbed behind the wheel.

What the fuck was he supposed to do with a truck full of smuggled people?

CHAPTER TWELVE

Francis

Church bells tolled at five a.m. Francis showered, dressed, and checked his phone. Fifteen missed calls from an unknown number had stacked on the screen. He'd flicked it to silent during evening prayers and forgotten to turn it back on. As he gawked at it, the phone vibrated.

"Hello—"

"Fuck, why don't you answer your phone? I've been trying to reach you all night."

"Angel." Dizzy relief washed over him. "You're all right—"

"You like helping people, Padre?"

"I uh... Yes?" Why did the question feel like a trap?

"I have a situation which I am fast running out of time to deal with. Meet me?"

"Today?"

"Si, now. Immediately."

"I uh, I have a whole day of scheduled duties and

appointments. I'm supposed to be with the nuns handing out food parcels to the homeless—"

"Food parcels? Jesus-fucking-Christ, this is more important than that. Trust me."

"What is it?"

"I can't... It'll take too long to explain. Meet me at the south end of Via del Commercio, Ostiense. Take a taxi. Make sure you're not followed."

"What? I didn't catch the address—Followed? Why would I—"

The line died.

Francis blinked at the wall. Whatever the reason Vitari needed him, it was clearly important. He'd sounded... concerned, harried even.

He stripped out of his cassock and into civilian clothes, took the coward's way out and texted the deacon with an excuse of sickness, then ordered a taxi on an app and ventured from the apartment building. Another blazing Rome day had begun to scorch St Peter's. Francis glanced over his shoulder a few times, checking for any tails, although he wasn't sure how he'd spot them among the crowds.

The taxi arrived, he fumbled the address, hoping it was right, and settled in the back seat to watch Rome's ancient buildings sweep past the window. The old gave way to new, more modern buildings, then the taxi trundled into a tired, graffiti-strewn industrial area.

Maybe Francis had gotten the address wrong?

The taxi pulled up outside a storage yard ringed by rusted nine-foot-high fencing, trash lining the sidewalks, and overgrown grass sprouting everywhere. Whatever had been processed in the warehouses here, they'd long ago closed down. This couldn't be the correct place. If he got out of the taxi here, he'd be mugged in ten minutes. "Oh uh... I'm not sure if I..."

The driver's door on a box truck opened several meters up the road, and the unmistakable impeccably attired Vitari climbed down from behind the wheel.

"Oh."

"Correct, si?" the taxi driver asked.

"Erm, yes." Francis paid him and waited until he'd turned the car around before approaching Vitari.

He looked good, but then he always looked good. Francis mustered a smile and shielded his eyes from the glaring sun. "What's in the truck?" he asked, half smiling. It probably wasn't drugs. Was it drugs? Oh God, what if it *was* drugs? That would be ridiculous. Vitari wouldn't be driving around Rome in a truck loaded with cocaine in broad daylight.

"People."

"What?" Francis lost his smile.

"We need to get them somewhere safe. Get in."

We? This was one of those times where his head told him to leave and wash his hands of everything Vitari Angelini. But his heart knew he wouldn't have asked Francis here if it hadn't been important.

He climbed into the truck's cab, acutely aware being here made him complicit in whatever crime Vitari was in the midst of committing. "I was going to say it's good to see you're all right, but now I'm wondering if I'm about to regret this."

"No regrets, Padre." Vitari turned the truck away from the old industrial yards and smiled his flashy don't-look-too-hard-at-this smile. "It's good, you're doing a good thing. *We're* doing good. I think."

"Did you say there are—" He swallowed. "—people in the back of this truck?"

"Yeah."

Francis swallowed the weird, squirming unease churning his insides. "Is this illegal?"

"Technically, it's the opposite."

"Then it's legal?"

"Hm." Vitari scratched his cheek. "Yeah... no."

"God help us."

They rode in silence a while, until Vitari mentioned the truck was refrigerated so the people in the back wouldn't be boiling in what was effectively a tin can in thirty-five degree heat. Francis was not comforted by that information. What was he was supposed to make of all this? Why had Vitari asked him to come along? He'd gone from thinking Giancarlo might have killed him to riding shotgun with him in some kind of criminal activity.

Vitari glanced over a few times. "You're doing that thing you do when you want to say something I won't like, so you brood on it a while."

"I... No. I don't... Well..." He did a thing? There was a lot to say, and ask. But one question seemed more pressing than all the others. "Why do you have a truck full of people?"

"They're product. And I know, before you get your cassock in a twist, I don't have anything to do with this side of the business, but this time I did, and when I saw it was people, I couldn't let it go. So I took them."

He *took* them. Then his father didn't know he had them? "Where are we taking them, exactly?"

"There's a farm a few hours north of Rome. It's isolated and antiquated. Barely any mobile signal. We use it for—" He glanced over. "—disappearing things. We'll take them there, you'll look over them, make sure they're okay, and then I figure…" He winced some, but Francis couldn't tell if it was from feelings or the sun's glare shining through the windshield. "We own the polizia. But the Spanish cop—Catalina Diaz, remember her?"

"How can I forget?"

"I think she'll want to handle this."

Francis twisted in his seat and fixed his glare on Vitari. "You're going to hand them over to the police?"

He laughed. "What else am I supposed to do? Set them free in the Italian countryside?"

"I'm surprised, that's all."

"Surprised I'm letting people go?"

"Yes, I suppose."

He arched an eyebrow. "You think so little of me, Padre?"

"That's not what I meant."

"No, that's fine. It's not as though I've done anything to earn your respect, right? I must be bad to the bone, because I don't grovel to God?"

He had witnessed Vitari kill four people. Saving a few didn't make up for murder, but Francis wasn't here to argue over past sins. "Don't do this." Francis sighed and faced the front again. Heat haze rippled up from the road the truck rumbled down. "You know I don't think like that."

"No, you're right." He sighed. "Scusa, it's been a long night. I'm tired. And… you look good, by the way. The way we left things was… not ideal."

"With you bleeding on the floor? No, that wasn't ideal."

"The gunshot was just a scratch… But I meant the call I made to you. I uh… I was drunk. You're angry, I understand—"

"Angry? I'm relieved! I thought… " Francis sighed hard.

"When you didn't meet me, I called your phone, and your father answered."

"Fuuuuck, Francis!" The truck hit a hole in the road and swerved. Vitari clutched the wheel, swore again, then wrestled the vehicle under control.

Francis clutched his seat and said a quick prayer. "I had no idea he would answer, obviously."

"I don't want to know what he said," Vitari said with a groan. "Don't tell me. Did he know it was you?"

"Yes."

"Fuck."

"I'm sorry."

"What did he say?"

"You just said not to tell you—" Vitari glowered. "Okay. He told me never to call you again and implied if I did, he'd kill me."

"Figlio di puttana." Vitari narrowed his eyes. "I am in so much shit. When was this?"

"A few days ago."

"He didn't tell me. He probably thinks his warning will stick." Vitari growled a few more creative-sounding Italian words and glanced over. "You okay?"

A thin laugh fell out of Francis. "I'm here, in a stolen truck, transporting illegally trafficked people into the Italian countryside, defying a mob boss's threat, stealing *his* people, with his son, after he ordered me not to talk to you again—and I'm doing all that because you called me and said 'Hey, let's meet up.'" Francis managed a smile. "Oh, I'm doing just fine."

"I also executed the driver."

"Vitari!"

"He deserved it."

"Dear God. Please don't tell me anymore." He

harrumphed. Leaning his elbow against the door, he rubbed an ache from his forehead. The truck rumbled on.

"For what it's worth, I'm glad you're here," Vitari said after a few soft moments of silence.

Francis pulled his gaze back inside the cab and studied the complicated man behind the wheel. The man he couldn't say no to. Even now, he was clearly exhausted, his clothes were creased, but he still had a mischievous charisma Francis couldn't resist. "Tell me *why* I'm here, Vitari? Why have you dragged me into this?"

"Because the people in the back of this truck are terrified, and you're good with people. They'll trust you."

"You didn't need me for this. You could have handled it on your own."

"But I do... need you." He stared ahead, determinedly not looking over. His hands flexed on the wheel. "About what I said... on the call... I didn't... I was drunk, and... I'd had a really bad night."

His idea of a bad night was likely a blood-soaked nightmare. And Francis couldn't stay mad at him. "I know. It's fine."

"Are you mad? I can maybe drop you off somewhere—"

Strangely, he wasn't mad at all. If anything, he was glad Vitari had reached out to him. It meant Vitari trusted him, and it meant neither of them were alone. "Let's just get these people you stole somewhere safe."

An hour later, Vitari pulled the truck down a dusty track toward a collection of single-story thrown-together buildings that didn't appear to be more than cowsheds, but at least it was private, with no other buildings around, just a lot of arid land, olive trees, and distant mountains. Whatever the place had once farmed had long since died in the heat.

"All right, you ready?"

The way Vitari asked, he was certain he *wasn't* ready. They jumped from the cab, walked around the back of the truck, and Vitari opened the back doors. Fifteen people huddled together in the back. Francis had definitely not been ready. His heart broke for their sad, terrified faces. Taken from their lives, their family, and everything they knew, into a strange, brutal world.

"Right." He said a quick prayer and nodded. He was ready. "Let's get them looked after. Can you translate for me?"

"Let's do this, Padre Blanco."

Vitari rolled up his sleeves and spoke Spanish in soft, gentle tones, comforting them while also introducing Francis.

Whatever he told them seemed to work, as one by one they emerged from the back of the truck, big eyed, weak, and filthy. Francis got them inside the dusty farmhouse and asked Vitari for water. He disappeared a while, returning later dripping with sweat and carrying buckets of clean, cool water. And together, they set to work helping the people feel safe.

Most of the fifteen were teenagers taken off Venezuelan city streets, either kidnapped or sold lies about how they'd be taken to a safe place in Europe for a better life. Clearly, some were already traumatized by their ordeal. Francis helped clean them up, get them hydrated, and prayed with them, while Vitari translated their needs, helping in any way he could. Occasionally through the night, Francis glanced over and found Vitari was speaking with each of them, comforting them, making them feel safe. So kind and gentle, with his sleeves rolled up, his shirt untucked—like a different man to the vicious Angelo della Morte he knew him to be.

He really hadn't needed Francis to do this.

Vitari laughed with one of the young girls and it struck right at Francis's heart. He'd seen his swagger, his attempts to show the world how untouchable and powerful he was, but here, in a little rural farm, he was just someone who wanted to help.

The farm wasn't equipped to sleep seventeen, but they set up beds with blankets and cushions on the floor. And once they were all settled and comfortable, Vitari went to the well to draw more water, while Francis prayed over them.

Later, as the Venezuelans slept, Francis ventured outside into the cool night air and spotted Vitari leaning against the old stone well, illuminated only by moonlight. Vitari hadn't yet seen him, as he stared off at the mountain, sleeves rolled up, hair sticking out at odd angles.

Vitari didn't think of himself as a real angel, but for the people sleeping in the farmhouse he was. By God would this man ever cease to amaze him? Francis cleared his throat and approached with a cup of water. "Here."

"Thanks." Vitari took it and downed the contents in a few gulps.

"You did a good thing here, Vitari."

His teeth flashed in a moonlit smile. "*We* did a good thing, Padre Blanco. I knew you'd be perfect for this."

Francis propped his ass against the well beside him. "It's nice here."

"Yeah... just watch for snakes."

"What?" He lifted a foot and searched for anything moving in the crisp, baked grass.

"Don't worry, they're rare." Vitari chuckled. "God will keep you safe, right?"

"You'd think so, but I've wondered lately."

"You mean your faith is wavering?"

"Not wavering, maybe... sliding sideways."

Vitari reached out and took Francis's hand, as though it were the most natural thing in the world to do. He held it tight and sent his gaze far off into the mountains again, just... holding hands. Francis squeezed gently and swallowed the small lump in his throat trying to choke him.

"Your God's a fuckin' idiot if he doesn't see the good in you."

"Erm... thank you? I think."

Vitari laughed at that too, but then his laugh fell away, and his face turned serious. So serious that it skipped Francis's heart.

A twitch of pain crossed Vitari's expression, and his eyes turned sad, and that tiny trip of fear in Francis's heart turned into a chasm of emotion, swelling out of nowhere. Francis leaned in and pressed his lips to Vitari's. A soft, delicate touch. Vitari opened his mouth so carefully, it was almost as though this were their first kiss, as though this was the first time they truly knew each other.

As though this was the first time Francis knew love.

This wasn't about sex, or even physical pleasure, it was just Francis telling Vitari he was loved, and together, they could make good things happen. The kiss faded, and Vitari's dark eyes glistened in the moonlight, full of too much emotion.

"Are you all right?" Francis asked.

"Yeah..." he croaked, then laughed. "I... It's been a long

day. It's just... a lot." He swiped at his face, hiding tears before Francis could see them. How was it this man could be so brutal, so vicious, but also so gentle, so caring, and so deserving of love?

"You should get some sleep," Francis said.

"What about you?"

"I will, but I like it out here. I'm going to sit for a while, just drink in the stars."

Vitari looked down at their entwined hands and gave Francis's fingers a squeeze. But when he lifted his gaze, the emotion had become raw, turning to sadness. "There's no tomorrow for us, is there? Our lives won't allow it."

He wanted to tell him he was wrong, that there was always hope and always a tomorrow. But it would have been a lie.

"Good night, Francis." Vitari smiled sadly, pulled free, and made his way back toward the farmhouse.

"Good night, Vitari," he whispered after him.

He wanted to hope, but how could he? The Catholic Church would never recognize their love. And Giancarlo had made it clear, what they had could never be allowed.

Neither of them were free to be who they were.

Leaning back, he lifted his face to the heavens and prayed for God to watch over everyone in the farmhouse, including Vitari.

He knew why Vitari had helped these people, and why he'd killed the driver. In every one of those boys' eyes, Vitari had seen himself. He'd always fight for the innocent.

Francis admired that, admired him.

And he loved him. He knew it to be true, and real, and not as terrifying as he'd once thought.

Something rustled behind him in the gloom. A snake? He straightened and turned. More rustling. Something large was out there, in the gloom. Did Italy have bears? No, Vitari would have mentioned those.

His heart galloped. He backed toward the farmhouse, one careful step at a time. If he could just make it close enough to bolt—a figure! "Vit—" A gloved hand slammed over his mouth from behind and a firm arm locked around his waist.

CHAPTER THIRTEEN

Vitari

He drifted between sleep and wakefulness while slumped on the floor against the kitchen units. Exhaustion rode him hard, but it was the good kind of weariness. The kind that warmed the soul. He hadn't minded today... Working with Francis, helping people, nothing else on his mind, nobody riding his damn back or wanting more than he could give.

Today had been a good day.

Gravel crunched outside, jolting him awake.

Vitari drew his gun, got to his feet, and listened. Just the sound of gentle snoring filled the farmhouse. But as the cool breeze drifted in through the open windows, stirring the drapes, it brought with it a thick silence. A *disturbed* silence. No crickets, nothing. Someone was out there, someone who wasn't Francis and was trying very hard to be quiet.

"Angelini, ¡manos arriba!"

Spanish. "Fuck."

Guns rattled, boots thumped the ground. It wasn't just one person outside, but several, and they knew who he was.

A few of the kids lifted their heads. He waved at them to stay down. "I'm coming out," he said in Spanish. Tucking the gun into the back of his trousers, safety on, he raised his hands and walked out into the glare of multiple flashlights. "Easy..." He couldn't see their faces, just knew there were many. "I'm cooperating."

Two rushed him, dropped him to his knees, stole the gun, yanked his hands behind his back and cuffed him. They rattled off instructions to go with them—not that he had a choice. Flashlight beams danced. There had to be eight men, at least.

Where the fuck was Francis? He didn't see him among them. Had he gotten away? Good. He didn't need to be a part of it any more than he already was.

Orders barked inside the farm.

"There are innocent people in there!"

The man holding him hauled him to his feet by his bound wrists.

Three 4x4s rolled down the track, high beams piercing the night. *Shit.* This was bad. Alone, without a gun, he'd never make it if he broke free and tried to run.

A car with all-black windows pulled to a stop. Vitari was manhandled into the back seat, the door thunked closed, and the car sped off, wheels spinning in dirt, bumping down the track. "Hey, where are you taking me?"

The driver glanced in the mirror, then slid his gaze away. At the end of the farm track, they pulled onto the road and sped up, racing along, until reaching a left turn. Slowing, he turned off, onto another dirt track, and rolled to a stop. They hadn't traveled more than a few miles from the farm.

A short distance ahead, another car waited, headlights pointed at them, high beams on. Vitari's driver climbed from behind the wheel and opened the door. "Out," he grunted in English.

The only time you drove someone out into the middle of fucking nowhere was to trade illegal shit or put a bullet in someone's head and their body in a shallow grave. Although, if they'd wanted him dead, they could have shot him back at the farmhouse. Vitari licked dry lips and climbed out.

"L' Angelo della Morte," a Spanish woman said, breaking the silence.

He knew that voice.

Catalina Diaz emerged into the glare of headlights, black hair pulled tight in an unforgiving plait. The white letters on her black ballistic vest read *POLICIA*.

"Fuck, Diaz. This is... *What* is this?"

"*Inspector* Diaz to you. And this is precautions," she said, stopping in front of him. They'd never met before. She looked him over, head to toe. "Thought you'd be taller."

He snorted. "You're early."

"Early is good. Early keeps bad people on their toes, si?" At least she was smiling. But she hadn't removed the cuffs yet. There was a strong chance she wouldn't. He'd known that when he'd called her.

"Where's Francis? The priest? You have him, right?" He squinted into the high beams. If they'd picked up Francis, he would not be pleased.

Catalina nodded at someone in her car. A door clunked, and a wide-eyed Francis stumbled into the light. What had she said to him while he'd been in the car with her? Horrible things about Vitari, probably. Would he have told her anything? Not knowingly, but people like Catalina Diaz were clever and observant. She was a wolf, like Vitari, and Francis the lamb.

Francis came forward. "You all right?"

"Yeah, you?"

"Yeah, they grabbed me by the well," he muttered. "I thought... I thought it was El Cristo all over again."

Fucking police. Vitari instinctively stepped forward, guarding Francis behind him. "You didn't have to go in heavy-handed like this," he told Diaz. "I explained what I had for you."

She narrowed her eyes. "Day I trust a Battaglia is the day I eat a bullet." She circled around him and unlocked the cuffs. "Why are you doing this, Angelini? What do you get?"

"I told you why." The cuffs fell away. He rubbed his wrists. "They're innocent people. They're not supposed to be here."

Catalina's hard glare slid back to Francis and softened. Vitari knew that smile. He'd worn it himself a time or two. She had a soft spot for Father Scott. Sucker. Although, he couldn't judge her, when Francis had inexplicably, by some miracle, wormed his way into Vitari's cold heart too.

"Is this your doing?" she asked Francis.

"No, Vitari did this. I just... I just followed along."

"I'm trying to understand how you end up *following along* with a known criminal, Padre," Diaz said.

He sighed, like he did a lot around Vitari. "I struggle with that same question every day, Inspector."

"This..." She nodded. "This is something quite... unbelievable, no? A priest and an angel?" Her radio blipped. She raised it to her ear, then returned an acknowledgement. "It seems we have the people, just as you say, Angelini."

"Good." Then this little meet-cute was over. "Can we go?"

She nodded. "My men will take you back to the farmhouse."

"You're not going to arrest us?" Francis asked, his voice pitching higher.

"Not today, Padre." She jerked her chin at Vitari. "You could do much more than this. Maybe not be angel of death, si? Maybe turn around, and be good?"

"The day I turn on the Battaglia is the day both of us eats bullets."

"Think on it." She held his gaze. "You and the priest can make a big difference. Do good." As she headed back to her car, she said, "This could be the beginning of something."

"This is one-time only," he called, then nodded at Francis to hurry and get in the car.

Francis stared out of the window during the short ride back to the farmhouse. They arrived in time to see the Venezuelans they'd saved climbing into multiple cars, beginning the next leg of their journey. They were going to be all right. Vitari trusted Diaz in that. And now they were no longer Vitari's problem.

Francis stood by the farmhouse door, watching the cars leave again, and then it was just the two of them in the middle of nowhere. No people, no neighbors, just the stars.

"We shouldn't stay long," Vitari said, when the quiet got too thick. "I don't trust her not to turn around and arrest me."

"If you have an agreement, then she won't," Francis said, so confident.

"You two friends now, huh?"

"No, but it's obvious she wants you as an informant. She won't break your trust now if she can rely on you later." As the taillights from the cars vanished in the dark, Francis looked over. "We don't have to go yet, do we?"

Vitari smiled, and after sauntering back inside the house, he flopped onto the old couch with its frayed cushions. Torn blankets lay about, evidence of their good deed. It wouldn't be enough to keep Vitari out of Hell, but it had felt good to make a difference to those lives.

Resting his head back, he eyed Francis loitering in the living area, stewing over all that had happened. At least he wasn't yelling at Vitari, or throwing things, but he was clearly troubled. Getting jumped by armed police would have scared him, like Venezuela had.

"She wasn't supposed to be here until tomorrow. I would have told you, but I wasn't sure she'd show..." Francis didn't reply, and still paced. "Are you all right?"

"What are you going to tell Giancarlo... about this?"

Vitari shrugged. "If they didn't show up in England, that's not my fault. I saw them leave the dock. Hopefully, he buys it."

He stopped pacing and stared. "They were going to England?"

"Yeah, they probably thought they were being sold as domestic slaves, at worst. We both know that's not where they were heading." Vitari dropped his head back and let his eyes close so he could push all the bad thoughts from his head. He needed to sleep, to let his mind drift and his body rest.

"If you know about this, why don't you do more to stop it?"

And here it came. In Francis's world, there was always room to blame Vitari for something.

The couch dipped as Francis sat. Vitari kept his eyes closed and mumbled, "I don't deal with that shit."

"So you... look the other way?"

There was that tone again, the judgmental one. "Yes, I look the other way." He wasn't discussing this, not now, not ever. "You can't tell me you agree with everything the Catholic Church does. What about all those payoffs in the nineties when it emerged a whole lot of priests couldn't keep it in their pants?"

"That is *not* the same, Vitari." As angry as Francis was, Vitari still smiled to hear it. He was so fucking easy to rile. So many buttons to push. And he loved to poke at them. "The Battaglia traffic vulnerable people," Francis said. "You could do something to stop it, but you won't."

"What am I going to do?" he asked, keeping his eyes closed because he liked listening to Francis's voice without distractions.

"You did *this*."

"This is a one-off. I can lie my way around this once, but any more, and it gets a lot harder to explain why the product doesn't get to where it's going on my watch. You want me dead in a ditch?"

"You looked in their eyes, Vitari. You saw them. Now tell me you're going to let that carry on. Young kids, like them, bought and sold into the sex trade. You're going to let it happen, with your past, with our—"

Enough. "Stop."

"Catalina Diaz is right. You could be a real angel to a lot of people."

He opened his eyes and stared at Francis's defiant, indignant expression. It was so easy in his perfect world to do good. It didn't work like that in Vitari's world. "Saving a few people changes nothing. But it will get me dumped in a shallow grave. One man can't fight the Battaglia. I'm not discussing this."

Francis huffed and sat back in the couch cushions. Vitari waited for more words to fly, but instead, Francis shuffled against Vitari's arm. His warmth and comforting weight calmed Vitari's wired mind and soothed the rattle left from his words.

He tucked him close. They both smelled like stale sweat and hot dust, but it didn't matter.

Just for a little while, he was going to hold Francis and pretend that, in the morning, everything was going to be fucking fine.

Vitari woke alone with a blanket draped over him. The early morning sun was up and blazing through the windows. He tossed off the blanket, stretched, and peered from the back window. And there was Francis, filling buckets of water from the well. *Shirtless.* His pale skin gleamed in the low sunlight. He dunked his shirt and wrung it out. Then knelt, plunged his face into a bucket, and brought it out, spraying an arch of water all over.

How was this man still a part of Vitari's life, when Francis was meant for better, greater things? It was probably out of some misguided attempt to save Vitari, but he'd take that excuse if he got to see him like this.

Torn between watching him or getting in on the washing action, the reek of his own body odor won out, and he approached Francis while he hauled up more fresh water from the well. Vitari shrugged off his own shirt and balled it up. Francis did a double take, then tried to pretend seeing Vitari's bare chest hadn't stopped his thoughts by staring at the bucket in front of him.

Francis's chestnut hair, now wet, had darkened to a light brown. He'd slicked it back, making his face lean and unforgiving, even with a few damp curls. Only his little smile softened the severe appearance. That little smile twitched on seeing Vitari as he thought of something amusing.

Vitari opened his mouth to ask for the bucket.

A blast of cool water smacked him the face. He gasped, shocked breathless, reeled, then shook the water off with a laugh.

Francis grinned. "You needed it."

"Some warning next time?" Vitari scooped up one of the full buckets, pretending to reach for it to dunk his shirt, then swung it up, from his low angle. The contents sloshed under Francis's chin, knocking him backwards—toward the well.

Fuck!

Vitari lunged, caught him in his arms, and laughed. Francis spluttered, eyed the gaping well beside them, and laughed. "Saved your life, Padre."

Hm, this was good—despite almost killing him. Francis was in his arms, wet and warm and chuckling. Vitari kissed his neck, unable to resist, tasting salt and dirt and not caring, especially when Francis hummed an agreeable sound as encouragement. They rocked, as though dancing to silent music, and Francis's light laughs faded, turning to heavier gasps.

Vitari bumped him against the well and listened to his rapid breathing, kissed his chest where his heart raced. Francis's fingers clutched at his hair. Vitari would never get enough of him, not if they spent days like this, weeks, years. It wouldn't be enough.

Francis clutched at his hips, as though afraid to let go, as though at any moment this—whatever it was—might be ripped from them.

Vitari dropped his hand, molded his fingers to Francis's hard dick through his trousers, and freed a growl. Fuck, every time Francis got hard, Vitari lost his mind to an animal need to own him.

"We can't," Francis moaned breathlessly. "I'm filthy."

"I love filthy," Vitari growled in his ear as he worked on Francis's fly, jerking it open. He spat into his hand and plunged it inside Francis's briefs, sliding down Francis's cock. "I'd prefer to have you on your back, fucking you hard, Padre, but right here, you fucking my hand, is just as good. And you're going to fuck it, aren't you? You're going to fuck it like it's my mouth, like my lips are on your cock, like your dick is down my throat."

Francis's eyes fluttered closed and his peachy mouth opened, so inviting. Vitari sucked his bottom lip between his teeth and pinched, and at Francis's stuttered breaths, he swept his thumb over his cock's head, gathering slick pre-cum, then went back to stroking him so he could devour every one of his hitched breaths and tiny, sinful moans.

Like everything in his life, this wouldn't last. They had to go back to Rome; they'd be separated and their lives would pull them apart over and over again. But for now, Francis was Vitari's in every way—mind, body, soul. The need to sink into him made his whole body burn. If he'd had lube at hand, he'd clutch Francis's hips and ram himself home, balls deep, over and over, faster and faster. He could almost feel it, hear the slap of his thighs on Francis's ass. "Touch me," Vitari demanded, voice raw.

Francis grabbed his crotch, then fumbled with Vitari's fly, trying to get inside.

Vitari helped him—undid the zip—and grabbed Francis's hand, holding it on his dick. Francis's thin fingers wrapped around him, too dry, but it didn't matter. Vitari returned to lavishing strokes on Francis's erection. Then Francis spat into his own hand, his pretty, innocent eyes looking at Vitari as though asking for forgiveness, and then he grabbed Vitari and ruthlessly pumped. They rutted wildly, clutching, breathing hard, fucking each other's fists with a feverish madness.

"I want to spread your fuckin' ass under me, Padre. Want to ruin you until you scream my fuckin' name. My dick inside you, milking you. Until you come so fuckin' hard you lose your mind."

"Oh God. Stop."

"Stop?"

"No!"

"Yes?" Vitari pumped faster, trying to resist falling into the temptation of his own rising climax at the mercy of Francis's faltering rhythm. "You'd feel my dick fucking into you, touching your soul, and I'd come inside you, so goddamned deep you can taste me."

Francis bit his lip. Heat flushed his face. His hips juddered. God, he was going to come and Vitari would spill right there with him.

"Like I'm going to come right now, all over your hand, Francis. Ugh, fuck—"

Francis let out a cry. Cum spurted from his cock, so much it dribbled down Vitari's fingers. Then Vitari was lost, swept up in a blinding orgasm, still fucking Francis's hand, as though he could wring every last goddamn drop from his balls. He clutched Francis's shoulder, his dick, riding the receding waves, then, as the waves faded, he met Francis's sex-drunk eyes.

He wanted to kiss him, like they'd kissed here last night,

as though a kiss could say the words they couldn't speak. Words about a foolish, impossible love of a priest who had turned his world on its head. A priest who had shown Vitari there was sunshine after darkness, if you waited long enough. God, he fucking loved this man. And knew, this love would probably be his end. But it was already worth it.

"We need another bath." Francis croaked a shy laugh.

Vitari laughed too, but it came out raw and strained, tight with emotion he dared not reveal. "A good thing we have you to draw buckets. Have at it, Padre. I'll help when my legs work again."

Francis's eyes widened. He was so fucking innocent, even now, after all the bad shit he'd done for Vitari. Vitari kissed him quickly on the lips, banishing that shocked expression. "Think of me when you're next on your knees in St Peter's. Think of my cock in your hand and my dick filling you."

A lick of fiery lust sharpened his eyes. "You're outrageous."

Vitari grinned. "Exactly the way you like me." He freed Francis, stepping back, and plunged his messy hand into a bucket of water, then swept wet fingers through his hair, perhaps adding a little flare for Francis's benefit.

Francis tracked every move like a priest at a strip show. He slumped against the well, cock out, still hard, shirt missing, in the perfectly-wrecked version of himself. "I love how fucked you look right now, Padre."

He blushed and cleared his throat. "Vitari, I—" The words caught in his throat.

"You what?" Vitari's heart thumped. Whatever he'd been about to say seemed serious. Serious enough to wipe away all evidence of his smile.

Francis breathed in, gathering courage. Straightening

from the well while tucking his cock away, he said, "Before we go back to Rome, I have to show you some things... on my phone."

"All right."

Francis quickly washed up, and whatever was on his mind, and in his phone, had soured the mood. "It's getting hot. Let's go inside."

Vitari trailed after him, carrying fresh buckets they could boil for tea, or coffee, if there was any left.

Whatever was on Francis's phone, he'd left it until now to tell him. Which probably meant he wasn't going to like it.

CHAPTER FOURTEEN

Francis

Vitari snatched the phone from his hand. "Where did you get these?"

"You know her?"

"How did you get these pictures, Francis?" he asked again, staring at the screen.

"Google." Francis folded his arms and leaned against the old wooden kitchen countertop. "Her name is Stefania Angelini."

Vitari looked him dead in the eyes. "Her name is Stefania?"

"Stefania Angelini," he repeated, softer, sensing this was as significant as he'd feared.

Vitari set the phone down on the kitchen countertop, backed up, ran his hands through his drying hair, then returned to the phone but didn't pick it up, almost as though afraid to. He paced some more, back and forth, restless and wired.

If Francis went to him, Vitari would push him away. He needed space, so Francis let the minutes tick by, giving him time to process. "Are you all right?"

A short, sharp laugh escaped him. A smile too. Both were too fleeting to have any real meaning.

"I didn't mean to upset you."

"No, it's not you." He stopped in the middle of the kitchen, hands on his hips, breathing slow. "I never knew her name. I was told my whole life after I was taken to Italy that she was a whore, a nobody. She wasn't Italian. Angelini was a fake name."

"She's your mother?" Not sister, not cousin. His mother.

Vitari lifted dark eyes and nodded. "A few days ago, I found some pictures. A woman, my mother, and me, when I was small. It's her. It's the same woman. Stefania."

"You were lied to."

"No shit." He snorted. "Is she alive?"

"She went missing over fifteen years ago, so I don't believe so."

He nodded. "I knew that, I think. She wouldn't have—I wouldn't have ended up in *that place* if she were." He picked up Francis's phone again, then put it down just as fast. "I can't look—Jesus. What do you know? Why were you Googling her?"

He told him about the Vatican archives, and searching for more information on Montague to link him with Giancarlo in the hope any information might protect them from further threats. And in the documents, he'd found mention of Stefania Angelini, with her name listed as a dependent of Montague's. Vitari listened, and with every passing minute, all the warmth and happiness Francis had seen in him during the last twenty-four hours vanished, leaving the cold, hard, Battaglia don's son.

"A few years ago I searched for Angelinis but there are thousands in Italy," Vitari said. "I even saw that article about the missing woman and dismissed it. A good, honest Vatican woman like her has nothing to do with a piece of shit like me."

"Don't say that." Francis felt Vitari's pain like a blade to his own heart. Nobody should have been treated the way he had been, and by his own family. It wasn't right.

"That's what it felt like." He pushed from the counter again and paced, dusty shoes striking the floorboards. "What I've always felt like. The entire family treated me like an outcast, like I didn't belong. The bastard pet Giancarlo rescued, like my father's the fuckin' hero in all this."

Francis watched him pace, almost wishing he hadn't told him. But he had a right to know.

"Giancarlo did this. Him and that archbishop. That fuckin'—" He glanced at Francis, cutting himself off. "I wasn't ever going to tell you this, but... I saw you and the archbishop on the news, when you were rescued from Spain. I uh... I recognized him." Vitari swallowed hard, and when he next spoke, his voice cracked. "From Stanmore."

He'd known Montague was involved in what went on there, but the way Vitari spoke suggested Montague was more than just a silent partner. He spoke as though Montague had been one of those men who had touched him. *Hurt* him.

"Montague was involved... in that?" he asked, keeping his tone level. Sickness burned the back of Francis's throat. He'd seen the back room, knew what Vitari had been subjected to had been terrible, evil. Montague had sexually abused Vitari. He'd *raped* him?

Vitari folded his arms and nodded. "I should have said, but he's your superior and that place—I don't talk about it.

Ever. Or acknowledge it fuckin' happened. I can't—" he choked. "I just can't."

Francis kept his head down, his eyes glued to the worn tiles of the kitchen floor. He felt wrong inside, as though he'd hurt Vitari, as though it was his fault. "I'm so sorry."

"Fuck, you don't need to apologize."

A swell of guilt and shame clogged his throat, and a sudden rush of emotion made his vision swim.

"Francis?" Vitari was suddenly close, peering into his eyes. "Fuck, hey... It's not you—It was nothing to do with you."

"You don't... I know, I just... You were there, and so was I, but..." He pulled from Vitari's grip and moved away, needing to tell him about the past but feeling ashamed too. Because it hadn't been as bad for him. He had no right to complain. "He groomed me, I suppose. I didn't know what was happening was wrong, I just... It was a thing we did. He'd take me back to his house for the weekends, schooling me for priesthood. He'd teach me about the Bible, we'd have dinner, and after, he'd... do things. When I was older, I started to understand how wrong it was, but by then, I was too tangled in it to stop it. I thought—" He paused to breathe and rubbed his forehead. "—like an idiot, I thought what we did was love and I was *lucky*... to have him. When I tried to end it, he blamed me, said it was my fault for wanting it. And I did want it, so he was right. But it wasn't anything like... what they did with you. Dear God." He braced his hands on his hips and blinked up at the cracked ceiling to clear the tears before they fell.

Shame came rolling back like a sea of oil washing over him, coating him through his clothes, under his skin.

"Does he still... do it?" Vitari asked.

Francis turned. Vitari stood motionless, staring straight ahead, through the wall.

"No, but do you remember that call I made to you, asking for help in killing a man?" Vitari lifted his gaze. "I called him out, said things I hadn't ever said to him. He reacted. Violently."

"Did he fucking touch you?" Vitari growled and clenched his hands into fists.

"I fought him off and right after I... That's when I called you."

"I will kill the fucker, cut his fuckin' balls off and make him choke on them." Vitari marched forward and filled Francis's vision. A wildness flared in his eyes. "If anyone ever touches you against your will, tell me and I will burn them down to ash. I will scorch the fuckin' earth they walk on. Do you hear me?"

Francis swallowed, tasting the threat on his tongue like a sweet, holy wine, soothing the burn of shame and past mistakes. Rightness told him violence was not the answer, but a much larger part of him, a deeper more visceral part, wanted Montague to suffer. "I was trying to find some evidence of his involvement at the boys' home but the records I took were stolen from me, and I just... I couldn't be there anymore, in an apartment right next to his, working *with* him. That's the *real* reason I came to Rome. I had to get away... from him."

Vitari yanked him into his arms. He froze, his body reacting to the sudden contact, but this was Vitari, and there was no other place on God's Earth where Francis would rather be. "They killed the boys from the home, to cover it all up," Francis whispered against his shoulder, struggling to fight the tears again. "Do you know what happened to the others in Stanmore's... back room?"

Vitari shook his head. "I've never looked."

"Then I suspect it's just you and me left. They likely don't know about you being raised there too. It's why I was being targeted. It's why Giancarlo initially wanted me killed, and then for you to bring me in. He knows you and I have that connection. Someone paid him to get to me, or it's personal. He's working with them or for them. I don't know... I wish I did... I wish it had never happened, Vitari. I wish I was better. I wish I didn't want the things I want. I thought being a priest would fix me. But I'm still an abomination. I wish I could wash away the stain of my sin, and what was done to you—"

Vitari's cool hands bracketed Francis's face. He couldn't stop the tears now. There were too many, and it hurt too much, like he'd cut himself open and exposed his rotten insides.

"Jesus, this isn't your fault." Vitari sighed. "It's all right, I've got you. I'm going to make it right. All of it."

Francis nodded, dislodging more tears. Anything he might say had all stuck in his throat. He couldn't stand it and buried his face against Vitari's damp shirt, clinging to him as though he were a life raft in the cold, isolated ocean his life had become. He was so fucking lonely, and alone, and lost. Except when he was with Vitari.

Earlier, he'd almost told him he loved him. He wanted to tell him now. But he'd just told Vitari how he'd loved a pedophile, so what did he know of love, really?

He listened to his strong heartbeat and absorbed his warmth. It felt good, to be held.

The tears dried, and Vitari's embrace eventually eased. He leaned against the countertop beside Francis. "It seems as though the universe is telling me to ruin my father."

"Maybe you should listen?"

"Maybe."

"I don't think it's over." Francis sniffed and glanced out of the open door at the haze-rippling track leading away from the farm. "I think Stanmore was a beginning, not an end."

"It's still happening?"

Francis nodded. "I don't have any proof, but... I feel it. Like it's still out there."

"And Giancarlo knows," Vitari said. He sighed. "Then someone should stop it."

Francis looked over at Vitari, with his sleeves rolled up and his hair a mess. Prepared to bloody his knuckles and wrestle in the dirt for those he loved, for the innocents who couldn't fight. Francis did not envy anyone on the receiving end of L' Angelo della Morte's wrath.

Whatever happened, whatever came next, it was time to get justice for the children who had suffered, for those who had no voice. For those who had died.

It was time to fight back.

Vitari dropped Francis off in the city suburbs, and from there, Francis hired a taxi to return to the Vatican. He hurried back to his apartment and showered off a surprising amount of dust. Cleaned up and back on duty, he explained he'd been sick and hadn't left his apartment for the last forty-eight hours. Nobody doubted his word. Why would they?

He and Vitari had agreed on the ride back to let the dust settle from their human trafficking adventure before diving into a plot to expose Stanmore. Vitari had also said he'd deal with the Russian. That was Vitari's world. Francis had little choice but to trust he would handle it.

The archbishop and the church, however, were Francis's world.

The next few weeks passed without incident. The entire Vatican was buzzing with Easter preparations—from an army of gardeners pruning olive branches to the cleaners using a cherry picker to dust the highest angel statues. Francis allowed himself to be swept up in the frantic preparations too. As the big day approached, the Vatican accommodated prominent church officials from all over the world. It was rather like a fantastic theatrical performance, with chorists, bishops, musicians, and nuns, not to mention the hundreds of maintenance workers and security that bulked out the population.

He hadn't heard from Vitari, but it felt like a good silence. They were back in their lives, in their roles, and they had a plan. Vitari would reach out if Francis was needed.

As Easter weekend arrived, a sea of people flowed onto Vatican grounds and spilled into St Peter's. Early that morning, Pope Francis had spoken privately and prayed with all the deacons, priests, bishops, and cardinals who had arrived to join the renowned ceremonies. Francis drifted through it all, overwhelmed and awed by the love of the people—his family he'd become a part of, all of them united in their love of God. It was beautiful, and breathtaking, and a reminder that although his reasons for becoming a priest had been dubious, he couldn't imagine being anything else.

"Francis?! My, you're glowing."

He must have imagined that voice, because Montague *couldn't* be here. Francis stopped and turned, interrupting the flow of people bustling down the corridor, and there was

Archbishop Montague in his black cassock highlighted by scarlet trim. Montague spread his arms, as though inviting Francis to embrace him.

His heart thumped so loudly it drowned out the burbling of the people. No, he couldn't do this, he wasn't doing this. He turned away again. Montague couldn't be here. Francis had come to the Vatican to *escape* him.

"Francis!" Montague barked.

Others turned to stare.

Francis's heart fell, and instincts to obey took over. Years of conditioning, years of kneeling to those who were above him in all things. He applied his soft smile and crossed a chasm of just several feet to Montague. Gathering his hands, Francis brought the ring to his lips. "What a... *delight*... to see you... here."

This man had raped Vitari.

This man—whose hands Francis held, whose ring Francis kissed—had forced himself on a boy. Hatred and disgust churned inside him.

"Walk with me."

"Perhaps later." Francis straightened and began to pull away. He had to get out, he had to get away. "I'm busy, the day is—"

Montague snatched Francis's wrist, jolting him to a stop. The bustle of the corridor, the distant choir song, and the chiming bells all faded behind the rush of blood in Francis's ears. Heat scorched his cheeks, and rage burned his gut. He yanked his arm free, pinned the archbishop beneath his glare, and left in a swirl of black. If Montague called him back, God help him, he would rage in this very corridor, witnesses and all. But Montague did not call him back, and when Francis glanced behind him, he'd gone.

The rush of blood and emotions, and now its retreat, left him giddy.

He refused to let Montague's sudden appearance ruin the day. Of course he'd be here. Every Catholic priest worth their collar would be here. It didn't mean anything. The Vatican was large enough that he could be avoided.

Francis swept through the corridors and outside, onto the steps above the crowds brimming St Peter's Square. He hadn't meant to end up center stage, but as he gazed at the sea of people spread before him behind a temporary barrier, their colossal number stole his breath. Shielding his eyes, he stood a while and *absorbed* the atmosphere.

Warmth filled his chest. There was love in the world. He could feel it, all around them.

It was going to be all right.

He heard the shot, heard it crack across the square and echo in the vast, open space, as though coming back around again. Someone grabbed his shoulder, yanking him around.

No, wait...

He rocked, flushed cold under blazing sunlight.

Something was wrong. He blinked, tried to clear the blur in his eye.

Someone grabbed him now. A nun, he saw. She asked if he was all right, but her voice was so far away. Were there sirens? Why were there sirens?

"Father...?"

He touched his head, over his right eye, where it burned. Blood glistened on his fingertips. Scarlet blood, like the color of Montague's vestments.

His head pounded, his heart too, drumming into him, pushing him down.

He'd been... shot?

CHAPTER FIFTEEN

Vitari

From the curbside where he leaned against his car, he watched the restaurant staff scurry around, preparing for the lunch rush. Sal was inside, reminding the owner he had a VIP dining here this evening and it would be best not to fuck up in front of Giancarlo. There could be no room for mistakes.

Vitari wasn't expecting any trouble, not on these Battaglia-owned streets. Still, it didn't hurt to rattle a few cages and remind everyone the boss was in town.

He plucked at his damp shirt and squinted through his shades at the brilliant blue sky. The sun was relentless today.

His phone pinged. Whatever it was could wait. He had rounds to make, hands to shake, men to keep in line, one face to break. His day was rammed. His phone trilled from his pocket. He huffed, pulled it out. *Giancarlo* showed on-screen.

It had to be important if he was calling. Giancarlo rarely spoke on the phone. Vitari winced and raised the phone to his ear. "Yes?"

"This was not us," his father said, cryptically.

Vitari waited a beat, unsure if he'd missed half a conversation somewhere. "What wasn't us?"

"The priest," Giancarlo hissed, as though hating the word.

Vitari's heart tripped over a beat and when he next spoke, he tried to maintain a disinterested, mildly bored tone. "What about the priest?"

The call ended.

Just like that.

No explanation.

Vitari scowled at the phone's screen. He couldn't call him back without revealing how he needed to know if this was about Francis. Since returning from saving the smuggled Venezuelans, Giancarlo hadn't mentioned a single word about his call with Francis. Not a fucking mention of the threat to kill him.

So what the fuck was this about now? *It wasn't us.*

Sal swaggered his way between tiny bistro tables, his face grim.

Vitari pushed from the car. "Hey, I just had the strangest call—"

"Angel." He raised his phone. Live news footage showed St Peter's Square, where a huge crowd was scattering like a flock of sheep. *"Reports coming in of a shooting in St Peter's Square..."* the news anchor was saying.

No. No. No... it can't fucking be... He looked up at Sal. His father's call, the simple words. *This was not us.* "Francis?"

Sal sighed through his nose. "Looks like a sniper took him out."

"'Took him out'?" Shock deafened the rest of Sal's words behind a high-pitched whistle. Weakness flushed cold water though Vitari's veins. He reached for the car. "Is he dead?" he croaked. *No, please no.*

"Unclear."

He had to get to Francis. It didn't matter if the whole fucking world saw him—he had to be there. Like Francis had been there for Vitari in Venezuela.

Vitari opened the car door and dropped behind the wheel.

Sal grabbed the door, preventing it from closing. "Where are you going?"

"You fucking know where."

"I can't cover for you, Angel. Not in this. Not this time. He'll know."

"He already fucking knows, Sal." That was why he'd called, to rub it in, to make it hurt. He could have just said *your priest is dead, we didn't do it, but we'll thank who did.*

Vitari tugged on the door, but Sal held it firm.

"Don't," Sal warned.

Sal didn't understand—*nobody* understood. "I have to."

"Giancarlo will punish you for this."

"I know, Sal." Vitari held his glare and said again, "I know." He'd take the hits, whatever they were. Nothing was going to stop him from seeing Francis.

"You really care for him that much?"

I love him. He almost said it, but didn't need to. Sal saw it on his face and stepped back, letting go of the door.

Vitari gunned the engine and sped away from the curb, plunging into Rome traffic.

What if Francis was dying somewhere, what if he

couldn't get to him? Fuck. It couldn't be the end of them. It just couldn't.

He pulled the car to a screeching stop near the main Vatican thoroughfare. People streamed out. Some cried. Most talked on their phones. Police tried to funnel them away from the scene.

Vitari abandoned the car and fought against them, pushed inside, and broke into a run. He didn't even know where to go, or how to find him. But there were ways into the private grounds, past much of the security and the panicked tourists. He ducked into one of the older buildings lining the main street leading to the heart of the Vatican and hit the buzzer on the wall. A glass security door blocked the way into an ancient stairwell.

"Hello?" a reedy female voice said from the intercom.

"Yeah, hi, I'm uh... I'm a friend of the priest who was shot today. Do you know where he is? Can I visit him?"

"We aren't allowing visitors at the moment—"

"Is he alive?"

"I'm sorry, sir. I don't have that information. You should wait for official—"

He shouldn't have come. Of course they weren't going to let him in. "Do you know what hospital he's in? Can you tell me that?"

"Wait, I'll ask."

The buzzing line died and Vitari rattled around the stairwell. Nerves sizzled through him. Francis wasn't dead. He wasn't. His God wouldn't do that. But Vitari knew his fucking God looked the other way too, and bad shit happened to good people all the time.

"Sir?"

"Yes?"

"Try the San Carol—"

He knew it and bolted from the stairwell, back down the street to his abandoned car.

Francis was going to be all right.

Vitari would get there, and Francis would be sitting up in a bed, smiling his stupid smile.

An excruciatingly slow fifteen minutes later, he left the car outside the hospital in the pickup zone and followed the general stream of people through the front door. Most of the wounded from St Peter's had broken wrists and sprained ankles, sustained in the rush to flee. He followed them and rode in an elevator alongside a nun. She frowned at him. He scowled at her and bit back the urge to scare her with sinful language. He didn't have time for her superficial judgment.

The elevator deposited them both on the same floor, and while Vitari queued at the desk, restless and anxious, the nun sauntered toward the wards. Minutes ticked by. People coughed, murmured. Some looked over, glared through him as though they knew his sort and didn't much care for him. Vitari checked his watch. If somebody didn't see him soon he was going to take this fucking place apart.

The man in front stepped aside, and Vitari met the receptionist's gaze.

"Sir, can I help you?"

"Father Francis Scott, is he here?"

She judged him too, drinking in his button-down shirt and expensive watch—or the tattoo, he could never tell what things caught everyone's gaze the most. She had to be able to see he was worried out of his mind.

"Are you family?"

"What? No, I'm a... friend."

"I'm sorry, we aren't allowing visitors."

"Just tell me if he's all right." Did he sound desperate? He *felt* fucking desperate. His heart was in his head, and a great hole had opened up in his chest where it used to be, threatening to swallow him.

"I can't answer that."

Vitari slammed a hand down, rattling the desk and drawing the ire of everyone nearby. "You can tell me if he's alive or not. You can tell me that!"

"Sir, please calm down."

He was scaring her. And himself. "Fuck." He stepped back and thrust his fingers into his hair. This was agony, not knowing. What if Francis was dying just a few doors away? What if he was alone? Vitari had told him everything was going to be fine, but it hadn't been. He hadn't been there for him when he'd needed him the most. A fucking sniper... Goddammit.

He shoved the next man waiting in line out of the way.

"Hey!"

"You need to get someone out here right now who can answer a simple fuckin' question—"

"What seems to be the problem?" a stranger to his right said, in plain, perfect English.

The greying-haired man smiled at him. He wore black, with a thin scarf-like strip of bright red, and a priest's collar. Cold grey eyes blinked, and Vitari knew those eyes. He'd seen them in the dark, seen them in his dreams. Horror filled the hole in Vitari's chest. Memories rushed him. Dark, damp walls. Cold, gritty floor under his bare feet. And this man's hands on his skin.

"Son, do you need help?"

A scream bubbled up his throat, one of pure, vicious rage. He tried to swallow it, but choked instead. Montague couldn't be here. With Vitari. With Francis...

The sick fuck was here with Francis?

Vitari bared his teeth in a snarl and swung a quick right

hook. His knuckles smacked the archbishop's cheek, knocking him against the receptionist's desk. A pot of pens flew. Shouts rose. But Vitari wasn't done. He wasn't thinking either. He just needed to hit him until the horrible slithering sensation inside went away.

He grabbed the thick fabric of the archbishop's robes, yanked him upright, and hit him again. And again. Blood slickened his knuckles. Someone screamed. He hit him again. His knuckles burned. Again.

"Angel!"

Hands locked around him. Heavy, strong hands. He swung at Montague again, but missed when the hands holding him pulled him off.

"Angel, stop!" Sal yelled in his ear, trying to haul him away.

"Get off me!" He bucked and writhed, and broke free. "I'm going to kill that fucker!"

More screams. Montague clung to the desk, bleeding from his mouth. Vitari got his fingers around the bastard's neck and saw the whites of his eyes—real fear. But not the kind of fear Vitari had felt when he'd been taken into the dark room, not that kind of bowel-loosening terror that clung on for life. The rage inside was brilliant and sharp and white-hot.

Sal's big arms hauled Vitari off again, and this time when his fingers slipped from the archbishop, Sal spun Vitari around and landed a punch across Vitari's cheek. He fell against the waiting room chairs, scattering half of them. "Stay the fuck down!" Sal boomed.

Fuck. Vitari, on his hands and knees, spat blood. It didn't matter, he was going to kill Montague here and now. If Sal didn't move, he'd make him.

"Stay down, you stupid fuck," Sal warned, looming like a bear.

Three security guards arrived and picked Vitari up off the floor. He struggled, but surrounded by fearful faces and under Sal's warning growl, he knew he'd lost.

Montague was on his knees. Blood had splashed the desk, the floor.

"You piece of shit!" Vitari yelled, but the guards had him and dragged him away.

They took him down in the elevator, then threw him out of the front door, telling him to fuck off back to Calabria—so they knew who he was.

He slumped on a bench and spat blood into the grass, then dabbed at his sore cheek. Sal's punch had split his cheek on the inside. He hadn't been holding back. Vitari was lucky to be conscious.

He waited, deflated, wretched, kind of feverish, nauseous. And he still didn't know if Francis was all right.

"Fra." Sal blocked the sunlight. "What was that?"

"Nothing."

"You just assaulted a fucking bishop." Sal glared. "That wasn't nothing. If I hadn't stopped you, he'd be dead. Right there. In a hospital waiting room. What the fuck has gotten into you?"

Vitari bent forward. Resting his arms on his thighs, he bowed his head. He couldn't tell Sal why he'd lost his mind back there. "I just wanted to know if Francis is alive," he mumbled around his swollen face.

"He is," Sal said. "The shooter missed, the round skimmed his temple. He's fine, and damn lucky."

Vitari almost wept. A sob lodged in his throat. He swallowed it. "I need to see him."

"No, you don't."

"The fucking DeSica did this!" Francis wasn't lucky. The shooter had meant to miss. It was a warning. Sasha was done waiting. Fuck them, and fuck Sasha. The whole fucking world was going to know not to touch Father Scott, that he was protected by L' Angelo della Morte.

Vitari stood and marched back toward his car.

"Where are you going?" Sal called.

Vitari spun, walking backwards. "To my car. Then to my house. Then to a bottle so I can drink this nightmare away. You want to come and hold my fuckin' hand, Sal?"

"Someone has to." Sal followed. "You'd better hope the bishop doesn't charge you for assault."

"He won't." In those final few seconds, when Vitari had his hands around the archbishop's neck, he'd remembered him then. Just a little flicker of recognition, but it had been there, among the fear. He knew Vitari, and he was afraid. As he should be.

Archbishop Montague was a marked man. He'd die with Vitari's name on his lips.

That day would come.

But not yet.

Vitari climbed into the car and accelerated away, leaving Sal frowning after him.

He'd lied. He wasn't going home.

He was going to find Sasha Zhukov.

CHAPTER SIXTEEN

Vitari

It didn't take long to pick up a tail in DeSica territory. The black German sedan followed two cars back, obvious but not threatening. The DeSica's spotters would have seen Vitari, recognized him, and gotten word to whoever managed the area for Sasha. Vitari recalled a name for Sasha's underboss—Jacobi something. He'd have been Ricky's handler. And probably the reason Ricky had ended up hanging from a bridge.

They knew he was here. But they didn't know why.

Vitari pulled into a quiet, narrow side street lined with four-story terraced houses. The sedan followed, then hung back. Vitari stopped his car. As he climbed out, another Mercedes pulled in from the other end of the street, blocking the exit.

If he'd found a high-ranking member of the DeSica lurking around Battaglia streets, he'd make sure the idiot knew his place too.

This meeting was likely about to get bloody. But they wouldn't kill him. They weren't that stupid.

A heavyset, well-dressed man climbed from the passenger seat of the new arrival. This was Jacobi, and the DeSica underboss did not get his hands dirty for just anyone.

"L' Angelo della Morte," Jacobi drawled in German-accented English.

Two more men climbed from Jacobi's car.

Behind Vitari, the original car that had followed him here sat with its engine idling, its occupants remaining inside.

"What are you doing, Angel?" Jacobi asked, stopping several strides away.

"Just out for a drive." He didn't want these low-ranking idiots knowing he had any connection with Sasha. At this level, loyalty could be sold. The Battaglia, and Giancarlo, could never know he was here to speak with Sasha.

Jacobi snorted, then nodded for his men to close in.

Vitari raised his hands, not that it mattered. They all knew how this was going down. Hands grabbed him, drove him to his knees, and fisted in his hair, jerking his head back. The cold kiss of steel touched his neck. Fuck, these guys went straight for the jugular.

"Hey, hey... wait."

Jacobi crouched to eye level with Vitari. "You want to explain why I shouldn't kill you?"

"Sasha is going to want to hear what I say."

"That so? And what are you going to say?"

"That's between him and me."

"Oh? You're friends now? You couldn't call him? If you're friends."

"Not friends—"

The punch doubled him over. He wheezed, but the fist in his hair yanked him upright again, and the blade returned to his neck. He couldn't see those beating on him, just Jacobi's calm, controlled expression as he studied Vitari, trying to figure out his real reason for stepping into DeSica territory when they both knew it was a provocation.

"Why are you here, little bitch?" Jacobi asked.

Vitari clamped his mouth closed and breathed hard through his nose. This was necessary, for Francis. To keep him safe from further hits, safe from Sasha. And to stop him being used as a pawn in some higher game.

Jacobi sighed, stood, and headed back toward his car.

He clicked his fingers, and his men moved in.

"Wait!"

They descended on him, and there was nothing he could do but drop and absorb the kicks. The blows rained. He curled up and took it. Pain was temporary, always temporary. Even the worst of it would fade.

A pause allowed him to breathe. "When does... the beating start?" he wheezed, smiling.

Hands scooped him up under the arms, a hood fell over his head, and he was marched, limping, into a car. He flopped back in the seat, blinded, ears pounding, and fought his body's urge to throw up. Someone said something in German, then Russian.

They were finally taking him to Sasha.

CHAPTER SEVENTEEN

Francis

He wasn't allowed to leave the hospital. Archbishop Montague had advised against it, until the police had swept St Peter's Square. Montague hadn't visited yet. That nightmare was to come.

A TV, high on the wall opposite his bed, showed footage of the chaos after the shooting. Journalists had been quick to scour the footage from phones on social media and decipher Francis as the victim, and since he'd been in the news several months ago, they dusted off the kidnapping case and were having a field day spinning theories as to why a young, unimportant priest from England was being targeted.

Every time his picture popped up on-screen, he flinched.

He would be questioned after this. How much bad luck could one man have before it became obvious it wasn't bad luck at all, but some rather suspect life choices?

He poked at the large bandage on his forehead and winced at the responding throb of pain.

Someone had tried to kill him.

It hadn't been the first time, but this had felt different. More... professional.

"You look as though you could do with a friend." Father Davis grinned as he parted the curtain and stepped inside the cubicle.

Francis smiled. He'd feared Montague had been lurking somewhere, waiting to ambush him, and he didn't have the energy to deal with him on top of everything else. Seeing Father Davis, however, was a relief. "It's good to see you."

"I brought you a change of clothes." He dumped a bag on the bed and nodded at Francis's dusty cassock. "Something more incognito than that, which will get you mobbed as soon as you attempt to leave."

"Is it bad outside? Are there lots of press?"

He smiled sympathetically and sat on the edge of the bed. "Handsome young priest embroiled in mystery and danger. They're lapping it up."

"I'm really not all that interesting."

"Just bad luck?"

"I fear so." He found the seam of his cassock interesting for a few moments and hoped Father Davis didn't stare too hard, but when Francis looked up, Father Davis was watching him with an understanding expression on his face. "Thank you. For the clothes. And for coming. I... I wasn't sure if Archbishop Montague was here—"

"Oh, he was." Father Davis shrugged. "But he left after somebody attacked him."

Francis blinked. "Oh? He's gone? That's good..."

Father Davis arched an eyebrow.

"I mean… Somebody attacked him?" Francis tried to appear shocked but didn't feel much of anything.

"He's fine. But he left right after, so I offered to come by and help you." He propped himself on the edge of the bed. "Thought you'd want to see a friendly face after such a horrible thing."

"Well, thank you. You're very kind, Father Davis. I could use a hand, honestly."

"Riley, please. Father is so formal between friends." He smiled, and that smile reached his kind blue eyes.

"Riley." Francis hadn't had a *friend* since he'd studied at the seminary. Priesthood hadn't allowed for it. What a relief it was to have somebody normal in his life.

Riley stood. "I'll let you change. I'll just be right outside here."

"Now? Can I go?"

"Yes, you have the all clear." Father Davis left and drew the curtain behind him.

Francis eyed the bag of clothes, then again glimpsed his own picture on the TV. Would Vitari have seen the news? He must have. But he wouldn't have come to see Francis. He'd be doing more important things. If he'd come, it would have caused all kinds of problems for him—not least his father's wrath. No, Vitari wouldn't risk coming. Even if his was the only face Francis *wanted* to see.

Perhaps Vitari would call later?

Francis touched the bandage again.

He dressed, still a little wobbly. Somebody *had* shot at him. Of all the thousands of people in the square, somebody had singled *him* out and pulled a trigger. If they hadn't missed, he might have died, right there on the Basilica steps. His heart fluttered. It had to be the DeSica, didn't it? Sasha making good on his threat for information to bring down

Giancarlo? Or perhaps it had been Giancarlo, since Francis had ignored his threat to not contact Vitari, and they had in fact freed those trafficked people.

Did Giancarlo know? Was Vitari in trouble too?

He said a quick prayer, dressed, folded his cassock away in the bag, and met Riley outside the ward. He really did need to get in touch with Vitari, but it would have to wait.

"There you are. Good. I have a car waiting. Let's take you out the back door. It might be an idea not to leave the Vatican for a while too. Until the next big story comes along and everyone stops staring at you, eh?"

Francis agreed. Keeping his head down felt like a good next move. He followed Riley through the hospital's back corridors to the waiting car outside. Once inside, the air-conditioning hummed, drowning out Rome's chaotic background noises. The car was nice. All leather, very luxurious, and the comfort swallowed him, luring him into feeling safe. Or perhaps that was the painkillers they had him on. Strange, how he hadn't seen a doctor to discharge him.

"Do you have any idea why you were shot, Francis?" Riley asked from the back seat beside him.

"No. I've no idea. I'd only just stepped outside after seeing Archbishop Montague."

Montague. He wouldn't have had anything to do with the shooting, would he? Francis wondered. No, the idea was absurd. Just bad timing.

"I see you're thinking hard." Riley smiled. He was quite a handsome man, with his California-blond hair and tan. "Don't think too hard, eh." He chuckled. "Don't want to further hurt that bruised head."

"Oh, I... I'm just trying to understand it all."

"Did the archbishop say anything to you?" Riley asked. "When you saw him?"

Francis stilled. The way Riley had asked... It didn't sound much like small talk anymore. "No, we didn't have time to speak." Why was Riley asking about Montague?

"He's an interesting man, the archbishop. Are you two close?"

"No." Why did this feel like an interrogation? Francis peered out of the window, hiding his face from Riley so it didn't give his sudden rush of nerves away. Rome's streets blurred by. How long had they been in the car? Shouldn't they have reached the Vatican by now?

He recognized the vast pillars and spectacular frontage of the enormous Vittoriano—but seeing those meant they were heading in the opposite direction of the Vatican.

"Where are we going?" he asked. Unease churned his gut. He'd been in such a hurry to get away from the hospital, away from being found by Montague, he hadn't hesitated to get in the car. Why would he, when Riley was such a good friend?

Riley's broad smile vanished, and the man's easygoing, lighthearted nature went with it. "For what's about to happen next, it's best you do as you're told. You'll be fine."

Francis stared at his *friend*, hearing the words but not fully understanding them. What did he mean? "Where are you taking me?"

The car rumbled over the uneven road surfaces and sped down unfamiliar streets, heading toward a wide sprawl of grand villas and huge palm trees, somewhere on the city outskirts.

"Don't worry, everything is fine."

No. Everything was *not* fine. If he said everything was going to be fine one more time, Francis might scream. "Stop this car." The driver ignored him. "Everything is not fine!" he snapped. "Driver, stop this car!"

It was happening again.

He was being taken... against his will. Again! Why? He just wanted to go home, just wanted all of this to be over.

Riley offered a hand. "Calm down—"

"'Calm down'? Are we friends, or did you just get close to me for this? For whoever you work for? Is it Battaglia or DeSica? Which is it?"

"There's a lot of accusation in your voice that I don't care for, Francis."

"And I don't care for being taken!" His head throbbed. He needed to get out of this car. He groped for the door handle, but it clicked uselessly. This was... too much. What had he done to deserve this? Was this punishment, yet again, for his wayward slide toward sin?

"I am having a *very bad* day. I suggest you let me go, *Father Davis,* or on my return to the Vatican I will report your behavior and your connection to whoever is ordering you to take me."

"And what of your connection, Francis?" Father Davis asked, as cool and calm as though nothing about any of this was criminal. "While I certainly do not claim to be a pillar of priesthood, I did not spend months living with my male lover, a murdering criminal, in Venezuela."

Francis closed his mouth. The word *lover* had landed like a slap to the face. But Father Davis was wrong. They hadn't been lovers, not then, not... yet. "I was *taken,*" he stressed.

Father Davis slow-blinked. "You're a smooth liar, for a priest."

"It's not lies!" Who was this man? How did he know things? Was it an assumption, or did he *know* Francis had been living with Vitari by choice, at least by the end of it.

"The moral high ground will not work with me. I think it's best if you sit there and do as you're told."

"You're Battaglia?"

"I'm trying to help."

Then was he taking him to Giancarlo? It seemed likely. The houses outside the car windows had gotten larger, with more space between their lots. If he was going to Giancarlo, then would Vitari be there? What did this mean? He didn't think he would be escorted to Giancarlo's to be killed, when they could have easily gotten to him in the hospital and even made it look as though he'd succumbed to the head wound.

So what was this? Another warning, or something more sinister?

He sat back and swallowed all the urges to rant at Father Davis. The depth of the man's lies and deception hurt more than anything else and made him feel like a fool for daring to think he'd find a friend.

The car pulled up a sweeping driveway encircling a fountain in front of a grand limestone house surrounded by huge maintained grounds matched only by the Vatican's gardens. Francis waited for the driver to open his door and emerged into bright sunlight.

A couple of armed men approached from the house's arched entranceway and asked him to follow. Father Davis did not join them. What did that mean? He glanced behind him at Riley shielding his eyes and watching on.

Maybe they *had* brought him here to kill him?

He reached into his pocket and checked his phone. He had signal. He could dial the police and leave his phone on in his pocket... But what if this was just a courtesy meeting, and he brought the Italian police force down on Giancarlo for no reason? He couldn't risk further hurting Vitari.

They entered a cool entrance hall with a grand piano tucked away in one corner and a large fan circling above. He followed the two men into an enormous lounge room, then out onto a patio beside a huge pool.

The bronze-skinned, well-muscled older man sitting shirtless by the water, smoking a cigar, had to be Giancarlo. He didn't look over, didn't acknowledge them at all.

The two guards left Francis at the poolside and returned to the shade of the verandah. Francis loitered near a towering palm. What was he supposed to do? Introduce himself? Kneel?

The Battaglia don sighed and turned his head. His glare plunged through Francis, raking his soul. Francis knew one thing immediately,—Vitari was *nothing* like his father.

"You have caused a great deal of trouble, Father Scott," he said in Italian-thick English.

What was Francis supposed to say? Sorry didn't quite cover it. Not to mention the fact this man may or may not have tried to kill him, but had definitely sent his son, L' Angelo della Morte, to do *something* to Francis in England. Kill him, kidnap him... ruin him.

Francis swallowed hard. He was here—wherever here was—on the outskirts of Rome with one of the most wanted organized crime bosses in all of Europe. A man who routinely did terrible things to people. A man who could make Francis disappear with a flick of his fingers.

The armed guards withdrew back inside the house, leaving him alone with Giancarlo.

Was Vitari inside too? Would he be joining them? It seemed unlikely.

He wiped his sweaty palms on the borrowed clothes.

"I'm not sure what I'm expected to say," Francis began. "Just that the Battaglia weren't a part of my life until you sent your son to England, and that I... Well, I didn't want any of this."

Giancarlo's right eyebrow arched. "You blame my son?"

"No, that's not—that's not what I meant." Oh dear.

"Words have power, Father. Be careful with yours." He jabbed the cigar at the air, indicating the chair on the opposite side of the table to his. "Sit, Father. Let us talk."

Francis lowered himself to the edge of the chair. Giancarlo wouldn't have him killed in his own back yard, would he? No, they'd take Francis somewhere, like they did in the movies. Drive him out to the Italian countryside...

Giancarlo twisted, getting a look at him. "How is your head?"

Francis touched the bandage. "Uh... sore."

"That wasn't us." He waved the cigar again. "Although I have suspicions of who it may be. We do not want you dead, Father Scott, just... compliant."

Was he supposed to be relieved? "Compliant?"

"On the phone, why did you ask about Stefania Angelini?"

Francis couldn't backtrack now. He'd blurted the name to shake something free, and here he was, face-to-face with Giancarlo. Something had definitely shaken free. "She's Vitari's mother?"

"You should worry less about my son and more about your own situation, Father. It has come to light you have sensitive information on some powerful men. I'm sure you know what this information is."

Stanmore... This all began with his threat to expose the atrocities at Stanmore.

Giancarlo sat back and took a long draw on the cigar, then puffed out smoke. "I am not your enemy. This is business, and the information you have is bad for business."

"Did you put Vitari in Stanmore as a boy, after his mother's death?"

Giancarlo didn't seem to react, but by *not* reacting, he'd revealed his own concern. He licked his lips, and picked a spec from his tongue. "I am beginning to see why you are such a problem. You're not afraid to ask questions. Not afraid of me."

"I uh... I am. It's just that, I'm here, and we're talking, which seems like a good thing."

Giancarlo nodded thoughtfully. "You are a good man, Father Scott."

"I try to be."

"You know, there is no room for good men in Hell."

"All men are equal in the eyes of God."

Giancarlo squinted into the sun. "Five million."

"Five million...?" Francis waited a moment to see if he might elaborate.

"For your silence."

"Five million *euros*?" A laugh fell from Francis's lips. Giancarlo's unkind glare shot to him. "I uh... I'm not sure what you're asking?"

"Hand over everything you have and never speak of Stanmore. Ever. Take it to your grave. You will get five million euros. Is that clear enough? Spend it, donate it to charity, burn it, do what you like with it. I will see it finds its way to you through legal channels."

Francis held the older man's glare. "I'm not interested in money."

A muscle twitched in Giancarlo's cheek. "Then what do you want, Father?"

"The truth."

He leaned an arm on the table. "The truth of it will get you killed. Is the past worth your future?"

Francis couldn't be bought, not with five hundred million. Not with a billion. His heart didn't beat for money, like Giancarlo's did. He'd expose everything that went on at Stanmore and all the people implicit in the abuse if it was the last act he ever performed. "You know boys died there. And you know the people involved, don't you? Were you complicit? Did you partake—"

"One of those *involved* people is very adamant you are not to be harmed."

Archbishop Montague. Even after all this time, Montague's touch clung to Francis in the guise of protection, but it felt like ownership. "If you know the truth, you can help expose it."

Giancarlo smiled for the first time since Francis had arrived, but it wasn't a pleasant smile. More of a shark grinning at a minnow. "And why would I do that?"

Francis held the don's gaze. Exposing Stanmore would expose Giancarlo. Just as Sasha had hoped.

Giancarlo took another big puff of his cigar and sighed. "I see we are at an impasse. Yes, I understand now. Of course, there is one thing you want. One thing I control. One thing I can take away from you."

Francis's heart stopped. Vitari.

Giancarlo wouldn't hurt his own son... But he had left him at Stanmore, knowing what went on there. Perhaps *because* of what happened there.

Giancarlo's smile grew—he knew he'd found a weakness. "You will cease all investigations into Stanmore. You will destroy all evidence you have already gathered and you will never again speak of Stefania Angelini. I may not be able to silence you, Father Scott, but I can take away the one thing you love more than the truth."

Francis measured every breath. His heart raced and his

blood boiled. The message was clear. If Francis didn't behave, Giancarlo would kill Vitari. This man would use his own son's life to protect himself and the Battaglia.

"Vitari means nothing to me," he lied, voice trembling.

Giancarlo laughed. "You forget who you are speaking with. I know everything. You shot a man stone-dead for my son. No priest takes a life for a man who means *nothing*, even when that priest is on his way to Hell." Giancarlo clicked his fingers. Francis jolted in the chair and spotted the guards moving in. "Get out of my sight, and let us both pray we do not meet again."

The guards grabbed him and manhandled him out of the chair. This might be the one time Francis could speak directly to Giancarlo. He had to make it count. "If you hurt Vitari, God as my witness, I will destroy you with the information I have!"

Giancarlo lifted a hand. "Wait."

Francis hung on the arms of the men holding him, breathing hard, and watched Giancarlo rise from the chair. He wouldn't kill him. He couldn't. Montague protected Francis. Francis glared as the don approached. He was taller, wider, heavier in all ways.

Giancarlo grabbed Francis's right hand, making him tense. Fear galloped through his veins.

Their gazes locked, and in that moment, Francis saw the monster looking back.

The cigar came down—its glowing end pressed against his palm. He didn't feel the burn, at first. Just watched in shock as his flesh contracted and sizzled. The smell of hot meat filled his nostrils. Then the pain hit, flashing like lightning up his arm. He tried to jerk away, to fight, but the men held him, and Giancarlo clutched his hand tighter. The cigar burned and burned and burned, and Francis screamed and writhed, desperate to get away. And then it was gone, torn away, ripping skin with it.

Breathless, sick with pain, Francis sagged.

Giancarlo patted his shoulder. "Something to remember our arrangement by. Every time you pray, you'll think of me, and of how you will never cross the Battaglia. Take him away."

They bundled him into the car, and as he was driven back through Rome's streets, he cradled his scorched and trembling hand and shivered in the heat.

He couldn't lose Vitari. Not even for the truth.

He loved him.

But Vitari's father would absolutely kill him.

The truth wasn't worth Vitari's life.

Francis stared out at what felt like a different Rome. The city had changed around him, or he had changed within it.

He didn't want to concede, he didn't want to surrender. But he knew, in his heart, it was over.

CHAPTER EIGHTEEN

Vitari

The hard plastic chair under him did nothing to ease the throbbing heat from growing bruises. Someone yanked off the hood, and he blinked into a gloomy storage room. Stacks of crates had been moved to the walls to make way for this meet-cute. No windows. An almost-perfect murder basement.

He swirled his tongue around his mouth and spat blood. "You there?"

Sasha's bulk emerged from the thick shadows outside of the reach of the bare bulb. He gave him the obligatory once-over. "These bruises... Good for you. None will suspect you come to me voluntarily."

It was fair—Giancarlo might have had someone on his tail since he'd punched the archbishop. Assaulting a bishop did not reflect well on the family. Neither did Vitari's out of control spiral. But as far as anyone watching knew, he'd been jumped by Sasha's men.

"Now you are here," Sasha said. "You have information, yes?" He was a big guy, and the way he caressed his tattooed knuckles had Vitari wondering if he might swing those fists later.

"I have… information and can get more. But you need to leave Francis—Father Scott—out of it. No more shit like today. Agree to back off, leave him alone, and I'll help you —" The words almost choked him. He swallowed. "—I'll help you ruin my father."

Sasha's dark eyes turned shrewd. "You are very passionate about this priest, why?"

Vitari's heart stuttered. "He's not involved in this. He never was."

"You are wrong. He is at the heart of it…" The big Russian sighed. "What do you have?"

"Valuable proof of… substantial crimes."

"What crime? Is it this… Stanmore?" Sasha smiled. "I cannot take your word, Angel. I need physical evidence. Get me that and I will not touch the priest. But I need to see what you have. Your word is unreliable."

He had proof. And he'd get more. "My father is involved in a sex trafficking operation that stretches back over fifteen years and includes high profile businessmen, men of the church, and celebrities. It began at Stanmore, in England."

"Ah, there it is. This *Stanmore*. Now you want to talk about Stanmore. So you know all this how?"

"I was there." A feverish chill washed over him. He hated this, hated talking about it, making it real again, reopening old scars.

"You were organizer?"

"No." He almost laughed. "I was a victim."

"*You*, victim?" Sasha narrowed his eyes. "You have proof?"

He had the USB in his pocket, but the pictures it contained cut Vitari to the bone. If he gave those images to Sasha, then the DeSica boss would have to believe him. But there was no coming back from that, and those photos only proved he'd been marketed like meat, and that he'd been used by a string of untouchable men. But handing over the images would prove his commitment to Sasha. "Some. I'll get more. And the missing woman, the Vatican woman. Giancarlo killed her. You can add that to his crimes."

"What Vatican woman?"

She'd been forgotten too, like Vitari's past life. Burned up and swept away by Giancarlo. "Stefania Angelini. Google her. You'll find it."

A strange glint of knowing shone in Sasha's eyes, as though this was a game to him. "She is who? Your mother?"

"Yeah. She was."

Sasha breathed in, filling his broad chest. "This is good. Progress. I see you hate your father. This benefits me. We might have a place among us for your talents, Angelo della Morte."

Vitari laughed. Ruining his father was one thing, but working with the DeSica was a whole other shitshow he didn't want to be part of. Besides, after he'd handed over the evidence to bring down Giancarlo and Sasha made his move, there would be nowhere Vitari could run. He'd be dead in twenty-four hours. "Promise me, your word. Francis will be safe."

"You have my word, Angel."

Vitari reached into his pocket. His fingers skimmed the USB drive. Once he handed it over, the horrors of his past would be out there. There would be no returning from this.

He lifted it out and offered it to Sasha. "For your eyes, nobody else's, until it's over."

Sasha looked at the innocuous drive, then at Vitari's face. He took it and nodded. "I'll have my men return you to your car."

The hood slammed down over Vitari's head again, stinking of stale sweat and dust. But none of this scared him as much as the pictures on that drive.

"Angel," Sasha said. "You should know, we did not try to kill the priest."

"What?" His heart dropped through the floor. That hit had been the reason he was here, the driving force behind committing to do this. And Sasha hadn't been responsible? Vitari pulled from the men's grip and tore the hood off. "If you didn't, who the fuck did?!"

The men grabbed him again, but the hood stayed off.

Sasha considered his answer. "I'd look closer to family..."

Had he done all this for nothing?

"You son of a bitch, you let me believe it was you!"

"Not all is bad. I have proof, and I will honor our agreement. The priest is safe from us. I will find out who ordered the hit," Sasha said. "In spirit of our new arrangement."

The hood slammed down again, and Vitari was tugged along, buffeted between the men like a barrel about to go over Niagara Falls.

His heart thumped in his throat. What if he'd made a terrible mistake? But it was too late now.

He'd just made a deal with the devil. Because he loved a priest.

CHAPTER NINETEEN

The call came a few days after his return from Giancarlo's villa. "Francis..." Vitari said, and as though he had a direct link to Francis's heart, his voice warmed him through. It had been weeks since they'd seen each other, weeks since the farmhouse in the Italian countryside, but so much had happened. So much *needed* to be said. He had no idea how to begin.

"Francis?"

"Yes, I'm here... I..." He had to tell Vitari it was over. But how?

His bandaged hand throbbed, his heart ached.

"It's good to hear your voice. Meet me. Behind the Basilica."

This would be better done face-to-face. Francis wet his lips and tipped his face toward the sky. "When?"

"I'm already here."

Francis's heart pounded. "All right, yes."

Vitari ended the call.

He was safe, and that was all that mattered. His father hadn't hurt him. But how long would that safety last?

Francis lowered the phone and gazed over the peaceful early morning Vatican gardens. It wasn't yet six a.m. Only a few gardeners populated the grounds. St Peter's Basilica and the square would be quiet. Tourists weren't allowed in until seven. Although, Vitari clearly had his own ways of getting inside.

Francis clenched the fingers of his bandaged hand, making the burn throb anew.

This had to be done to keep Vitari safe from his father.

Francis walked from the gardens, passing through the enormous Basilica interior with its breathtaking splendor, and back outside via a service door. The road behind was always quiet and mostly used for deliveries.

Vitari waited ahead, leaning on the rail separating the road from the blinding white Basilica walls. He wore shades, black trousers, and a fine striped shirt with the sleeves rolled up, exposing bronze forearms and his glinting watch. He looked like a work of art, especially against Rome's dramatic backdrop.

His smile bloomed as Francis approached, and Francis's heart sank.

He couldn't do this. But he had to.

He loved Vitari, and because of that, it had to end.

"Ciao." Vitari straightened from the rail, his grin now in full bloom. "I would have reached out sooner, but I had some things going on. I heard you were okay, though... after the shooting. How's your head?" He came forward, reaching up.

"Fine."

Vitari flicked Francis's bangs back. They were close, too

close, close enough to kiss, and nobody was around…
Francis snatched Vitari's hand before it could wander and
do something wonderful, like stroke down his face, his neck.
And then Vitari would lean in and say something wicked,
something that would make Francis go weak.

A bruise darkened Vitari's chin. Francis had thought it
was the beginnings of a beard, but the more he looked, the
more bruises he saw, stretching down Vitari's neck. Somebody had hurt him? His father? Dear God, this had to end,
before the truth of Stanmore got Vitari killed.

Vitari's smile wavered. "What happened to your hand?"

Letting go, Francis stepped away and folded his hands
behind his back. "We need to talk."

"Isn't that what we're doing?" His smile cracked, and
another piece fell away. "What's going on? Nobody is here.
Nobody can see us." He looked around, as if to check. "You
okay?"

Francis sighed through his nose and sent his gaze down
the road. They truly were alone, with just the Basilica and
its marble angels looming over them. This *was* right. It had
to be done now. There was no use in dragging it out.

"Okay, fine… Not here. I get it." Vitari thrust his hands
into his pockets, as though holding himself back. "Listen—"

"I need to—"

"I'm going to be away for a while, looking into this trafficking thing."

The trafficking thing? Francis's mind worked. *Oh, the
Venezuelan people smuggling.* "Good. Some distance will
make this easier."

"Make what easier?"

"We…" He cleared the creak in his voice and tried
again. "We can't do this. I should have stopped it long ago. I
allowed it to go on, which is my fault—"

"Stopped what? What are you talking about?" He started forward again.

Francis stepped back, retreating, and Vitari's hand fell to his own side. His smile vanished too, then his mask slammed down, turning him back into the stranger Francis had met in St Mary's so long ago it had surely been a different life.

This was right, this had to happen, but by God, it hurt as though he were cutting out his own heart. "We can't do this," he blurted.

Fine lines pinched Vitari's forehead. "You've said that many times before, Padre."

"I mean it. This time. It's... over, Vitari."

Vitari half laughed, dismissing him. "If this is about the assassination attempt, I have someone working on that. It wasn't my people, and it wasn't the DeSica. You're protected—"

"Stop!" Francis barked. The shout echoed around them. Vitari tensed. Francis hadn't meant to lash out, but that word: *protected*. "Just... stop. It's over. We're done. I don't want to see you again. Please..." Francis fluttered a hand to his forehead. "Just go."

Vitari's smile returned, but it was the sideways, sly version, all swagger and bravado—another mask painting over his hurt. Francis ached to hold him, tell him he was sorry and take all the horrible words back. He loved him. Loved him so much that this moment might have been the worst moment of his entire life, but his hand burned as a reminder of the world Vitari lived in and how his father would kill Vitari to keep his secrets.

"So you're just going to walk away, after everything?" Vitari asked. That sharp smile cut Francis like a knife.

"It's because of everything that I have to."

Vitari smirked, then spat a short laugh and backed away. He raised his hands. "Okay, fine. Go back to your church." He flung a gesture at the Basilica's walls. "I don't need you anyway. You were *nothing*." His lips curled in disgust. "A good fuck."

Francis had wounded him, but hearing him say such things still crushed his heart. Three words would fix this. Three words that, once spoken, would condemn them both. *I love you.* He couldn't say it, so he watched Vitari build his barriers all over again and would have to watch him walk away.

Vitari laughed. "Don't worry, I won't drag you down in the filth with me, *Father*. Have your perfect fucking life." He turned and with the click of his shoes, he marched off. "Good luck confessing it all away."

Francis took a step toward him, then another. He almost called out. But as much as the agony twisted inside, this did have to end, for both of them. He watched him until he vanished out of sight around the Basilica.

And Vitari was gone, with just the burn of his words remaining.

Francis stood alone in glaring sunlight, cradling his sore hand, and he prayed to God for guidance and strength.

This *was* right.

No more Stanmore. No more investigations.

He wiped the useless tears from his face.

No more truth. To save Vitari.

CHAPTER TWENTY

VITARI

It hurt.

It hurt more than Vitari dared admit.

He wasn't sure when Francis had gotten inside his heart —maybe Venezuela, maybe before that, with his doe eyes and floppy brown hair. The way he was both innocent and fucking ruthless when he needed to be. Like earlier, when he'd slammed the door on Vitari.

Vitari had never been so fucking vulnerable with someone like he had with Francis. He'd thought they had something, something good, something pretty fucking special. He wasn't stupid enough to believe they'd get a happy ever after, but since his father knew he'd been in contact with Francis and hadn't punished him, he'd wondered about a happy for now.

Then Francis had ripped his heart out.

"I need to see my father," he told the men who tried to block him from entering the Buona Sera club. The doorman muttered into his earpiece, while the public stood in line, running jealous gazes over him. He ignored them, but with every passing second, his impatience grew. For fuck's sake, they knew who he was. He practically lived in this bar when in Rome.

He removed his sunglasses and fixed the idiot with his glare. "Are you new? Because you clearly don't fuckin' know who I am. You have three seconds to let me pass."

"Sir—"

Sal appeared, like a muscular suit-clad fairy to wave his magic wand and open doors that shouldn't have been closed.

"Angel, what are you doing here?" he grouched. "What the hell happened to your face?"

What had gotten into everyone? He sidestepped the doorman. "I'm trying to get inside. What the fuck? Why am I still standing out here like a fucking tourist, Sal?"

"Easy..." He opened the door, finally. "Just a misunderstanding. Get in here."

He entered and saw the reason for the security. Giancarlo had the capos visiting, meaning the bar was closed to the public. Important caporegimes ran various branches of the Battaglia operations. Vitari recognized them all and almost miss-stepped over his freewheeling emotions. These men were the old guard, second only to Sal's father, Toni. This was not the time to lose his shit. One of the men, known as Slider, reported on the state of the guns they were trading with the Mano Nera cartel in the U.S.

Vitari maneuvered behind the bar, poured himself a drink and one for Sal, seeing as the barman was AWOL, and settled down to listen in. Once he'd returned to Italy as a boy, he'd learned all about the inner workings of the Battaglia from these men.

These meetings were tight. He'd only been present at three before.

Interesting that Sal was here, and Vitari hadn't even known it was happening.

Sal's father, Toni, sat at Giancarlo's side, ever the underboss, angling for the top spot.

How would that work when Giancarlo retired?

Although, with the way shit was going, it was highly unlikely Vitari would be alive to see it.

He scanned the faces. All old-blood men, generations of Battaglia, dons of their own specializations. Someone here coordinated the trafficking side of the business. Someone here knew they were selling children into sex slavery, and they did it with Giancarlo's explicit awareness.

Fuck, it was all so messed up.

During a quiet moment, Sal leaned over and said, "Tried to call you. Where have you been, fra?"

Vitari gestured at the bruises on his face. "The DeSica picked me up."

"Fuck—"

"Right. Fuckers. They tossed me back once they figured out who I was."

"We'll deal with that," Sal grumbled.

Vitari downed the remaining vodka and poured another. He couldn't afford to drink himself into a hole with everything going on—he needed his wits about him—but what he really wanted to do was pick up the bottle and throw it across the room. He wanted to scream at his father like a child and blame him for everything—for Stanmore, for his mother, for Francis leaving him.

He just needed a few more glasses of vodka to numb it all.

He'd been a fool to think any of it had mattered.

Francis had always been meant for more.

His ditching Vitari didn't change anything.

Vitari was still going to ruin Giancarlo for Sasha, if only because his father deserved it. Not much felt right in his life, and now Francis was gone, there was even less. But ruining Giancarlo was the right thing to do.

His ears pricked at hearing "Caracas," the Venezuelan capital city where the Stanmore girl's sister had reached out to him and had gotten a bullet between her eyes for her trouble. The man talking now was a cruel Spaniard, his attractive face aged by the sun—Santiago Garcia. Vitari hadn't paid much attention to him in the past. He'd only seem him on the few occasions the capos met up. He spoke of product, which could mean anything. Gold, drugs, guns, or people. It all came out of Venezuela.

Vitari listened and noted the locations of crossings, usually by plane, then boat. The product was offloaded and split up, then disguised among legitimate entry points into European countries. These handpicked examples of product fetched five figures.

The product was people.

Santiago ran the people smuggling business.

Vitari studied Santiago's face, committing it to memory. He needed an in, a weak point, some way of applying pressure so he could manipulate Santiago. And he knew how to get it.

The meeting wound down, the capos left, and the public were allowed into the bar. Vitari was pushed down the list of people waiting to speak with Giancarlo, but that gave him time to gather everything he needed.

It was only when the club was near closing that Giancarlo invited him to ride along in his car on the return journey to the villa. Vitari sat in the back alongside his father, waiting for him to speak first. The car rumbled, and a slideshow of nighttime Rome passed by their car windows.

"Business is good," Giancarlo said. "Venezuela is once again producing." The side-eye left Vitari in no doubt that was a reference to his fuckup.

"Santiago is skimming profits," Vitari said.

Giancarlo looked over, surprise very clear on his face. It wasn't often Vitari was able to surprise him. His heart thumped. He had to follow this through now and hope he was wading into territory he knew more about than Giancarlo.

"Santiago is loyal," Giancarlo said. "Just rumors."

Vitari pulled his phone from his jacket, opened the various pictures—sent to him by Carolina Diaz just two hours before, right after the capo meeting—and handed the phone over to Giancarlo. "Those images show Santiago taking payment for private sales. He takes what he calls the best product and sells them on the black market, stealing from the Battaglia."

"These are just images." He handed the phone back, steely eyes cold. "They prove nothing."

He'd figured Giancarlo would want more than Vitari's word and some inconclusive photos. "Then put me on him. I'll check he's running all profits through the business."

"You want to observe Santiago?"

"If he's not selling product for himself, then he'll have nothing to hide."

"Why now?"

Vitari paused, even though he had his next words all worked out in his head. Everything was calculated. Nothing could be left to chance. He needed this to work. He needed his father believing in him. "I've been off my game lately. I want a chance to earn back the trust I've lost."

"You assaulted a bishop."

Vitari winced.

"This is unacceptable. Each mistake you make reflects upon me, upon the business. And you have been making many."

"I know, I'm sorry. Some things from my past got back inside my head, but that's over with." He twisted in the seat and held his father's gaze. "Allow me to prove myself. I won't let you down. You said I could be more, and I want that. I want to be worthy. Let me start with this."

"Santiago's business is sensitive. It requires subtlety and discretion."

Vitari hadn't been discreet since meeting a priest. It had all begun with a superyacht exploding and hadn't ended with the collapse of the gold mining operation. For someone who was calm, Francis sure attracted chaos. But Vitari wasn't thinking about Francis. He *couldn't* think about him.

"Who beat you?" Giancarlo asked, referring to the bruises on Vitari's face.

"The DeSica picked me up. I dealt with it."

"Sasha?" Shadows gathered on Giancarlo's scowling face. "What did they want?"

"Nothing, just to rough me up. They didn't know who I was."

"No, Sasha knew it was you. The fact he picked you up at all says much. He believes me weak... Yes, go with Santiago. It will get you out of Rome. There is a shipment of product next week. Find me this evidence of his theft, if there is any." Giancarlo studied Vitari under the light shifting through the car windows. "Do not let me down again."

He said it like a threat, as though this might be Vitari's last chance to prove his loyalty.

"What of the priest, Vitari?"

"The priest is nothing. It's over." There was no point in hiding the fact he'd had a relationship with Francis that went beyond the photographic evidence Giancarlo had of the hand job in a Spanish villa. His father was no fool. And this was the truth. It *was* over.

Giancarlo narrowed his eyes.

The car swept up the villa driveway, toward the house in all its blazing mansion-like glory. Vitari likely wouldn't get another chance like this to sit with Giancarlo. He took his father's hand and raised it to his lips. "Forgive me, Father. I will make up for my mistakes." *Forgive me, Father, for I have sinned.*

Giancarlo nodded. "I look forward to it. Join me in my study, Vitari."

He trailed along behind Giancarlo, nodding to the staff they passed. Giancarlo seemed to be in good spirits, probably due to a successful meeting with the capos. Vitari wasn't feeling too bad himself. Half of that was the vodka and the rest was *not* thinking about Francis.

Giancarlo's office was airy and cool, thanks to the open windows and refreshing night air swept in by the ceiling fan. Giancarlo removed his jacket and fixed them drinks from the decanter. He removed a cigar from the tin the American priest had given him, snipped off the end and lit it, then sat behind his desk and offered Vitari the seat beside him.

"We all make mistakes, Vitari," he said. "I've made many, especially at your age. We are much alike."

Vitari bit his tongue to keep from asking if he was like his mother too. He was supposed to have moved on from all that. Tonight was about the future. Looking forward. Not back. A future with Giancarlo behind bars, and Vitari likely in a shallow grave somewhere.

Fuck, he didn't want to die.

But he wasn't thinking about that.

"Boss, Toni has arrived," one of staff said, poking their head around the door.

Giancarlo nodded, signaling he'd be there soon. As the door clicked closed, his heavy gaze settled on Vitari. "Wait here..." He rose and left the room.

The computer was still on. Unguarded. Not locked.

Vitari waited a few moments, listening hard for his father's retreating footfalls, then dashed behind the desk. He clicked on the search icon in the top right-hand corner of the computer's screen and typed in *Stefania Angelini*. A mosaic of files popped up, one after the other, photos, documents, and JPEG images. Vitari didn't have long. He needed something solid, something he could show the world. The information on screen was both too much and not enough. He didn't have time to go through it all.

He searched for *Stanmore*.

One document came up.

An Excel file.

Vitari highlighted it with the mouse arrow, then hesitated. If he opened it, it would show in the file history, and he didn't know how to delete that. Fuck it. He was already *all in*. He double-clicked it. The file was old, dated ten years ago, and listed bank transactions both in and out of a registered charity's bank accounts: Stanmore Recuperation House. The left-most column listed names, then the deposits, as well as numbers that resembled serial numbers.

Those numbers were the kids, Vitari knew it. Somewhere, there would be a file with those numbers linking them to the names of the Stanmore children.

He clicked, dragged the transaction file to emails, attached the file, and sent it to his own email address, then deleted it from the Sent items, closed everything down, and dropped back into the seat. Fuck, fuck, fuck...

Giancarlo returned. "I have to go. We will do this again when you return. I expect not to hear a word of you until that return. Discreet, Vitari. Understand?"

"Yes. I won't let you down again, you have my word."

"Good." He hesitated, as though he might say more, then remembered his computer and moved around the desk to shut it down. "You may go, son."

"Good night, Father." He headed out of the door, just catching the sound of Giancarlo's soft *good night* in return.

CHAPTER TWENTY-ONE

Francis's return to his duties at Westminster, London, was uneventful. Life tick-tocked on, one day at a time. It should have been enough, helping the people who came to him, rejoicing at weddings, holy communions, and baptisms, and consoling families during funerals. This was what he'd vowed to do, what he'd given his life in service for.

He spoke with Father Hawker on the phone several times, seeking guidance. He certainly couldn't ask Archbishop Montague—who had at least been avoiding him since the assassination attempt. Father Hawker didn't mention what he called *the incident* from Francis's past. They talked around it, but even without sharing the details, it was enough to know he had a friend in the church.

The monotony was good, he told himself. Routine was healthy. Loneliness was... normal. Father Hawker had tried to explain how they could never be lonely with God. But Francis had found God to be rather one-sided lately.

Still, life went on. The near miss across his temple left a faint pale scar and the circular patch of bubbled skin on his palm had healed, leaving the area numb. He stroked it often during prayer to remind himself that sometimes the hardest thing a person ever had to do was walk away.

"We rejoice in our sufferings, knowing that suffering produces endurance, and endurance produces character, and character produces hope, and hope does not put us to shame, because God's love has been poured into our hearts through the Holy Spirit who has been given to us."

He'd said those words during a service earlier in the day, said them a hundred times before, but this day they struck a chord. He'd had hope once. But somewhere along the way, he'd lost it.

Would he ever find hope again, or had he walked away from that too?

"Father Scott?"

"Yes?" He looked up from reading Psalms, startled by the archbishop's arrival into his office.

Montague stayed near the door, as though sensing Francis needed space. Dressed casually in his normal civilian clothing, a V-neck sweater and slacks, he'd rarely appeared friendlier.

"Did you not hear me knock?" he asked.

"Uh, no, I was just reading."

"I'm retiring for the evening, and I have a casserole in the slow cooker. Deacon Strong is joining me. Won't you join us? The evenings are drawing in and I'm sure you don't relish the thought of another evening alone in your apartment."

It was just a casual offer between colleagues, nothing more. Francis had been expecting some kind of peace-making olive branch for weeks now, since their return from

Rome. But the archbishop had been withdrawn, busying himself with his duties and staying far away from Francis.

Deacon Strong was nice enough, still finding his feet and learning the ways and rituals of cathedral life. The offer of dinner was a kind one.

Francis swallowed. "I had planned to go over my notes for a wedding at the end of the week."

"Bring them with you." Montague beamed. "We'll all go over them together. Strong could use the practice. You can't tell me you're looking forward to returning to a cold apartment either. And when was the last time you had a hot meal? No, I insist. Join us. I always make too much. I'll see you in twenty minutes." He'd turned and left the office in a few strides.

Francis could have said no, but Montague would manufacture another reason to ensure it happened, and it would continue day in, day out, until Francis agreed. It would be better to get it over with.

He'd go, they'd eat, and Francis would leave the deacon and archbishop as soon as it was polite to do so. Montague had been aloof, disinterested even. This dinner was nothing more than he'd said, a reason not to be alone, and he was right, Francis had no wish to return to his cold, quiet apartment for another night of loneliness.

He finished up, tidied the office, and left for the archbishop's apartment. As all the residential buildings were part of the converted chancery, next door to the cathedral courtyard, he didn't have far to walk.

Some lighthearted jazz played from behind the apartment door. Francis knocked.

"Come in!"

Inside, the delicious aroma of hot casserole brightened his mood. Perhaps this hadn't been so terrible an idea.

Francis followed the sound of clanging pots to find Montague in the small kitchen amidst wafts of steam from the slow cooker. Three plates awaited their servings.

"Perfect timing. Deacon Strong will be here soon," Montague said with a smile.

"May I help?"

"Oh, thank you, yes. It's been a while since I entertained and there's more to think about than I recall, or I'm simply getting old and have forgotten how to cook for more than one." He laughed.

Francis fussed with plates, then laid the table in the dining room, trying not to think about how horribly familiar the evening was becoming—a dinner at Montague's place, leading to intimate moments afterward, to Montague leading him by the hand to his bedroom.

He pushed the old memories away. It wouldn't matter; soon Deacon Strong would arrive, and they'd discuss his studies and work like the three professionals they were.

"How is Father Hawker? You speak with him regularly, yes?" Montague asked, arriving with two loaded plates.

"Occasionally, yes. Why?"

"I have some concerns. Please do sit. Now, where's the wine?"

"Oh, Strong's plate, let me fetch—"

"Oh, no need." Montague laughed again. "He's not coming." He placed a bottle of red wine on the table and two glasses.

"He's not?" Francis asked, frozen half out of the chair.

"No, he called a moment ago. While you were setting the table. An emergency. He was very apologetic." Montague poured the wine.

"Oh." It was... plausible.

"So, Father Hawker," Montague continued, filling his own glass. "How does he seem to you?"

"I uh..." Francis sat and automatically thanked Montague for the wine as he handed his out. "He seems fine."

"Do you speak at length?"

"At length? I... Sometimes, I suppose. He was my mentor—"

"I was your mentor. But go on."

No, you were the man who groomed me into having sex with you when I was too young to know what sex was. Francis's mind abandoned him, going blank. "I'm sorry, I lost my trail of thought. What did you ask?"

Montague sat and smiled and appeared to be the perfect host. "Do eat. It will get cold otherwise."

Alone. With Archbishop Montague. For dinner. He'd lost his appetite but succeeded in poking and prodding the food around the plate. It shouldn't have been like this. He was a grown man, and Montague no longer had power over him.

Yet, he did. Inexplicably. And it wasn't just that Francis had vowed to obey him, although that was surely a part of the tangled mess in his head.

"What do you speak about, you and Father Hawker?" Montague pressed on.

Francis's thoughts swam, as though detached from the rest of him. He didn't want to panic, but he felt it rising. "Oh, not much, daily events, any troubles we might have."

"Does he take your confession?" Montague asked, cutting at a piece of potato as though disinterested in the answer.

Francis picked up the wine and took a generous gulp. Bitter. Like this evening. "Yes, he does." Taking confession for colleagues was normal for priests. Why did Montague care so much about Father Hawker?

Montague smiled and placed the piece of potato between his pale lips. A dribble of gravy dripped down his chin.

Francis was done here. The quicker he could get out of the door, the better. "You know, I think I should probably go. I have a busy day tomorrow—"

"Oh, don't be silly. You only just arrived. And you've hardly touched your food."

Francis glowered. "Well, it's not quite the same without Deacon Strong, is it? If he was coming at all."

Montague stopped chewing and straightened. His flinty eyes narrowed. "What are you implying?"

What if Francis was wrong? What if this whole evening was exactly as it appeared to be, just an innocent dinner? What if Francis was the problem, bringing his past into the present for no reason? "I'm sorry," Francis found himself saying. He could almost hear Vitari chastising him for that, telling him he had nothing to apologize for.

"I am the one who is sorry," Montague said, sweeping his tongue around his teeth, then sitting back. "For the past."

Francis froze. His heart thumped against his ribs. No, he didn't want to talk about the past or bring any of that into the room with them now.

"My behavior was... terrible. I apologize for all of it. You were right. I was in a position of authority and I had no right to assume things of you at that age. It was wrong of me. And I am very sorry, Francis."

Was he sorry? The words appeared to be genuine, but they'd been said almost flippantly.

"I... Well... I'm not like that... anymore," he added, sipping his wine.

So, he'd just stopped molesting boys after getting away with it for years? That seemed unlikely. But Francis *wanted* to believe him, if only it meant nobody else had suffered after Francis.

What was he supposed to say? Thank you? You're forgiven? Was that what Montague was looking for, forgiveness?

"I wanted to er..." Montague poked a fingernail at the tablecloth. "I wanted to ask about someone you may know, actually."

Francis sipped his wine. He didn't drink before meeting Vitari. Now he wondered if he might be able to nip down to the local store after leaving the dinner and buy a bottle of something strong and potent so he could drown in it when he got home.

"An Italian man, in fact."

Francis lifted his gaze.

"I believe his name is Angelini. Vitari Angelini. Do you happen to know him?"

Was this a trick? Did he already know Francis knew Vitari very well indeed? Was this a test? Why was he asking now? "I uh... I'm not sure."

"He was very adamant about getting into your room at the hospital after that terrible moment in St Peter's."

Francis leaned back in the chair as several snippets of that day fell into place.

Montague had been attacked in the hospital ward's reception area, and now Montague was asking after Vitari by name? He suddenly knew *who* had assaulted Montague. God, no wonder the archbishop had been hiding himself away. He was lucky to be alive. Although Francis—quite terribly—wished he wasn't. No, that wasn't true. He didn't wish the man dead.

Maybe a little.

Or a lot.

Maybe he wished Vitari had punched him into the ground for everything Montague had done to him, in the past.

"I don't think... I know him, no." Blood rushed through his ears. "Who is he?" He drank more wine, hiding any expression that might give him away.

"He rather viciously attacked me. Apparently, he has connections with the Mafia. Can you imagine? A man like that attacking me in broad daylight. Terrible. But, well, with your recent... *bad luck*, I wondered if you might have met him?"

Francis pulled a vague face and shrugged. "I wouldn't know... They didn't really use real names around me. It doesn't sound familiar."

"It's just you may have met him before, you see," Montague went on, and this time when Francis glanced over, Montague stared into his eyes. "From your past."

"Oh?" Francis's heart hammered so hard it would surely break through a rib at any moment.

"Never mind. I'm sure it was just a freak accident."

Yes, Vitari had slipped and his fist had fallen onto Montague's face. Repeatedly.

Francis smiled into his wine. Vitari had told him he'd cut Montague's balls off. He would have too. Vitari unleashed was as vicious as a wolf. He wouldn't stop there either. Not after what Montague had done to him. He'd torture him, and while it was wrong to think such things, Francis could imagine his screams.

And here Francis was, having dinner with Vitari's abuser.

Disgust fermented the wine in his gut.

This was a betrayal of both their pasts. He should never have come.

And if Francis believed Montague when he said it was over, then he was a fool. He'd absolutely lied to get Francis here this evening. Deacon Strong had probably never been invited.

Francis studied the aging man across the table. Montague knew what he'd done, and he'd felt the sting of Vitari's vengeance. Montague had power, he had connections, but were those connections strong enough to control L' Angelo della Morte? Clearly not, as Vitari had beaten him in broad daylight and still walked free.

Fear touched his gaze.

Good, he should be afraid.

Francis drank the last drop of wine and set the glass down. "Thank you for dinner. I should be going."

"Very well. If you really want to, I suppose I'll finish the wine alone?"

What did he think would happen? That Francis would stay, and they'd talk, and what? Would it be just like old times? To think Francis had once believed he loved this man, that what they had was *normal*. That Montague had loved him back. Nothing about their past had come from *love*.

"I know one thing," Francis said, stroking his finger down the stem of the empty glass. "I wouldn't want to cross any of the men who kidnapped me. They are cruel, ruthless, and vicious. They kill without hesitation. Perhaps this Vitari mistook you for one of his enemies? If that's the case, you're lucky to be alive, Archbishop."

Montague's thin smile twitched. "A mistake, yes. I'm sure that's what it was. Well, good night Francis."

Finally, the awful dinner was over and Francis was free to leave. He pushed his chair back and stood. The room spun—how much wine had he had? He reached for the table to steady himself, almost missing it altogether. This wasn't right. He glanced at Montague, at his blank, unsurprised expression. No concern, no alarm. Just waiting...

Francis's heart thumped in his head. "Did you... drug me?"

He chuckled. "Don't be so dramatic, Francis. Just too much wine, I think. Don't you?"

"No, that's not... what... this is." He'd been drugged. He was sure of it. One glass of wine wouldn't make the room spin. And spin it did. The walls slid, the floor tilted, a pounding began in his head.

"Now, then—" Montague said from in front of him, reaching out to him. He'd moved too fast—this didn't feel real.

Francis backpedaled but got tangled in the chair legs and fell, tumbling to the floor on his hands and knees. No... This couldn't happen. He had to get up, to get away... "You did this," he slurred. Panic made him shiver. *God, help me.*

Montague crouched in front of him. "It's all right. Relax."

"Why... doing this?"

"Because you're mine and will always be mine."

The shadows throbbed, creeping closer with every beat of his heart. No, he couldn't pass out. He couldn't be with this man and be vulnerable again. It couldn't happen. He didn't want this.

He tried to reach for his phone in his pocket and got his

fingers on it, but it slipped away and clattered to the floor. He was falling, falling but not moving...

"It's perfectly all right, Francis. You're safe. I'll never hurt you." Montague's dry, thick finger scraped down Francis's cheek, and it was the last thing he felt before the shadows washed in and carried him away.

Francis woke with a jolt, heart racing, his body on high alert but his head slow to catch up.

He lay on a couch in an unfamiliar front room with a heavy brown blanket draped over him. His thoughts were jagged and broken. Then one came at him, like an arrow out of the dark: this was Montague's apartment.

He lurched from the couch and stumbled against a nearby chair. His head thumped, his chest too, and his lungs burned, desperate for air he couldn't seem to inhale. He just needed a few seconds to think.

Last night, the dinner, the wine...

"God, no."

Did Montague *touch* him?

Nausea made his head spin even more. He dropped into the chair, closed his eyes, and concentrated on breathing. Breath by breath, his heart slowed and the room sharpened into focus.

His body didn't ache, he didn't feel... *touched*. But he still felt used on the inside, tricked, made to feel stupid and small all over again.

And the bastard *had* drugged him!

Where was Montague now?

Francis pushed to his feet, swayed, swallowed, and willed his body to shake off the grogginess. The archbishop was even more wretched then he'd believed, and nothing had changed. He was still a foul, controlling pervert. "Montague? Are you here?"

Nobody replied.

If Montague wasn't here, then Francis had free run of his apartment. This might be the only time he'd be alone within its walls, because he wasn't ever returning.

The photograph of the Stanmore boys Montague had stolen from Francis? He had to find it.

He hurried from the living area, passing the dining room—the table had been cleared of last night's meal. God, what had he drugged him with? Some kind of date-rape drug? Why do that if he hadn't touched him? Power, probably. Or a warning.

He couldn't think about that. He needed to find the photograph, leave, and be done with this whole sickening incident.

Pushing open the bedroom door, he scanned the room. The bed was made, and thankfully, empty. Had he found Montague sleeping he might have considered taking one of those pillows and holding it... No, he couldn't think it. Where would the archbishop put something important like that photo? He'd want it nearby, somewhere he could admire Francis's younger self. The idea of Montague fondling the picture churned Francis's insides all over.

He opened the bedside drawer, and there it was, crinkled and folded, tucked next to a pocketbook of Psalms with an embossed gold cross on the front.

Francis snatched the picture back and slammed the drawer closed. A vicious, horrible urge to do something vindictive swelled within him, like cut up his sheets or trash the room.

But he swallowed the rage. It was better to do nothing and just leave. He had the photo.

One thing was certain. Francis could no longer keep quiet. If he said nothing, then Montague's abuse might escalate. Francis couldn't live like this, forever looking over his shoulder.

Archbishop Charles Montague was dangerous.

Francis slumped against the wall to catch his breath and glanced at the photo. Since it was all folded and creased, he glimpsed a column on the back, sketched in pencil that he hadn't noticed before. It had been too faded and dusty. Montague must have brushed it clean. The column held fifteen numbers... for fifteen boys. Were those numbers significant?

He wasn't supposed to investigate Stanmore. It was supposed to be over, in the past, buried, for everyone's sake.

But the photo and Montague's actions made it clear: there was no forgetting Stanmore.

Francis glanced at his left hand, at the cigar burn scar. He couldn't pretend to be a good person, and he certainly was not a good priest. But the one thing he could do, the one thing he needed to do, was bring all those responsible for the Stanmore atrocities to justice. Whatever shape that justice took.

Beginning with Montague.

He hurried from the apartment, returned home, stripped, and showered under scorching hot water, then dressed for work. If he saw Montague, he'd remain quiet, for now.

Using his phone, he took pictures of the printed photograph, including the numbers on the back. At least now he'd have a copy if Montague stole it again. Then he dialed

Father Hawker's number and left a message for him to call as a matter of urgency about *the incident.*

He'd tell Father Hawker everything. It was time.

The church would take Francis and the archbishop off active duties while the claims were investigated. A small victory, but hopefully the first of many. Montague shouldn't have been allowed to continue in a position of power all these years. And that was perhaps Francis's fault, for not acting sooner. An error he'd fix today.

Francis entered the cathedral's admin building. Phones rang and people chatted behind doors. Montague's office door was closed too, at the end of the hall. Francis hesitated outside his own office, staring at Montague's closed door as though he could see through it, at the man sitting behind his desk. He should march in there and tell him he had no right to do what he'd done. Confronting Montague couldn't be more difficult than the things Francis had done in Venezuela.

But if he raged at him, the Archbishop would use his loss of control against him. No, he had to think and be smart.

Montague's door opened and a smiling blond-haired boy said goodbye to Montague, then closed the door behind him and hurried down the hallway. "Father," he greeted, passing Francis.

"Good morning," Francis mumbled.

He wasn't any older than Francis had been when Montague had seduced him, on the cusp of puberty, blue eyed and full of dreams.

Rage bubbled up inside him.

He'd drugged Francis last night, then invited that innocent boy into his office this morning?

No. Enough was enough. It ended now.

Francis marched down the hall and flung open Montague's office door. Montague looked up from behind his desk. Francis slammed the door behind him. He didn't say anything—had a thousand things he wanted to yell, but none of them made it past the lump in his throat. He'd killed a man in Venezuela. Shot him in the head. Why couldn't he scream at Montague? Why wouldn't the words come?

"I have some bad news, Francis. You may want to sit," Montague said, folding his hands on his desktop.

He didn't want to sit. He wanted to demand why he'd been drugged, he wanted to know what Montague had done to him while he'd been unconscious, but he also wanted to leave. He knew he had to stay though, for that boy's sake, for all the boys Montague had touched. For the boy Vitari had been before this man and the others had ruined him.

"You should get your affairs in order." Francis lifted his chin. "I will be reporting what you did to the police."

Montague breathed in and leaned back in his creaking chair. "What is it you think I did, Francis?"

"No! I will not let you gaslight me. You drugged me, Charles."

He didn't seem startled, or afraid. Just stared back at Francis, so calm. "You drank a little too much wine."

Francis slammed his hands down on the desk, rattling the pot of pens, and locked his glare on Montague's blank face. "Do not make the mistake in thinking me weak. You have no idea what I'm capable of. I'm not a naïve kid who thinks you're a fucking superhero. Not anymore. I know what you did, and I know you're still doing it, and I will fucking ruin you." Montague's eyes widened. "Do I know Vitari Angelini? Yes, I know Vitari. He has another name. L' Angelo della Morte. I see from your eyes you know what that means. I *know* what you did to him, and I know that when he meets you again, he will rain vengeance down upon you, Charles—"

"Francis—"

"You are a sick excuse for a man who should not be a part of the church and should never be left alone with a child—"

"Francis, you need to calm down—"

Francis yanked the picture from his pocket and slammed it down. "All of them dead, apart from me. Because I'm protected? Because you want to fuck me? Is that it? Did the others threaten to expose Stanmore too, is that why you had them killed? But not me, because you think you control me?"

Montague barked a laugh. "This is insanity! Calm yourself, Francis!"

"What's insanity is that you sit there and you laugh, as though nobody can touch you."

"Father Hawker is dead."

Francis's runaway thoughts stuttered. He wasn't sure he'd heard him right. "Don't..." No, it couldn't be true. His head spun, and all the rage drained away.

"Terrible, truly. I'm so sorry. I know you were close."

No, it couldn't be true. "You're lying."

Montague pulled a dismissive frown and reached for a folded newspaper on his desk. He slid it toward Francis.

Local Priest Found Dead at Home.

Francis gasped and dropped into the chair. Father Hawker...?

He reached for the newspaper with trembling fingers and read the first few paragraphs. Father Hawker had been found at the bottom of the stairs in his house. All signs pointed toward an accident, although the police had yet to release an official report due to recent events surrounding St Mary's, including Francis's kidnapping.

They'd killed him.

Montague had been asking after Father Hawker. But that was just last night. Newspapers weren't that fast. Father Hawker had died two days ago, just a day after Francis had last spoken with him. Montague had *known*. "You did this."

The archbishop laughed. "It clearly says it was an accident."

It took all of Francis's restraint not to leap across the desk and wrap his hands around his neck. Shock and disgust tangled inside him, making him sick.

"You need rest, Francis. Come now, have you learned nothing from all this?" Archbishop Montague leaned forward and looked at him as though he was just a caring, concerned friend. "People die around you, Francis. There are even rumors you killed a man. Now, I obviously do not believe that, but the assassination attempt on your life makes it clear you are embroiled with some very bad people. People like this Mr. Angelini. You need to think very carefully about your future. I sponsored you, mentored you. I even had you ordained early. You owe me a great deal, and it's time you obeyed me."

God, he was going to throw up, or faint, or lose his mind altogether. "I won't be bullied by you. Not anymore. I'm going to expose everything you've done. I don't care about my future."

Montague sighed. "If you were to accuse me of certain things, I'm afraid it will not reflect well on you, as a jilted lover."

"Jilted?!" he spluttered. "I am no such thing!"

"Dear Francis, I have the photographs to prove it.

While I would prefer our relationship is kept out of the public gaze, I will release some photographs taken of you last night, clearly in my bed. A scandal, of course, which is why I'm sure you'd rather I don't reveal those photographs."

Francis laughed. It was that or cry, and he couldn't give Montague the satisfaction of seeing his tears. The man was insane. He had to be. "You took photos of me *in your bed?*"

"As insurance, should you become difficult," he said, matter-of-factly.

"Do you hear yourself?" Francis closed his eyes and swallowed his anger. It didn't matter. What were a few photos compared to everything Francis knew Montague had done? But he still didn't have any solid evidence. Everything was his word against Montague's.

This was never going to reach a courtroom. Not with the power Montague had.

So that left him no choice.

He didn't need evidence. He knew what had been done to him and to Vitari.

Francis wasn't going to report any of this to the police. No.

He'd buy a gun.

And he'd shoot Montague between the eyes, just like he had Luca. Then it would be over.

"There's no need to make this difficult, is there, Francis?" Montague said, so reasonable.

Francis sighed and opened his eyes. There was more than one way to find justice. He'd been going about this all wrong. "It's not me you should worry about, archbishop." He smiled. "L' Angelo della Morte will be coming for you." Francis stood and held Montague's glare. "I'd start praying now, if I were you."

CHAPTER TWENTY-TWO

It was a good thing Francis had ripped Vitari's heart out, because if he'd had any feeling left during the last few weeks, he'd have been buried under the weight of them.

The *product* of human beings began in South America, taken from parents who believed they were paying for their kids to have a better life in Europe. From there, they were shipped, trucked, separated, smuggled, and finally sold into domestic slavery, which more often than not included anything their new owners wanted to do to them. Some didn't survive the journey over, and knowing where they ended up, he also knew some didn't survive long at their destinations either.

And all these years, he'd looked the other way. Just as Francis had said.

He'd *known* it happened. But he'd never seen it with his own eyes. Now he had their innocent fucking faces keeping him awake at night.

There had been this one kid. No more than nine years old. That kid, destined for London, had stared at Vitari, daring him to hurt him. Nine years old, and he was ready to burn the world. Vitari admired that, but the kid would soon have that fire beaten out of him.

Vitari couldn't close his eyes without seeing him. Without seeing himself.

Santiago chinked his glass with Vitari's. "To another shipment."

Vitari smiled and downed the tasteless drink. The club around them was too loud, too bright, too full of people, just the way Santiago liked it. When he wasn't working, he thrived on chaos and women and flashing cash. This job wasn't a loss, though. Santiago was trading a few of the *hot products,* as he called them, on the side. Sometimes after he'd sampled them first. Exactly as the Spanish cop, Catalina Diaz, had said. Santiago was screwing the product and screwing the Battaglia.

There was a special place in Hell for people who stuck their dicks where they weren't wanted.

It had taken a while to figure out how to kill the bastard without Giancarlo knowing he'd been the one to pull the trigger, but he was on track—just so long as everything went to plan this evening.

He checked his watch.

Just gone midnight.

"Look—" Santiago showed him his phone screen and the vast sums of money. "—and that is why your father trusts me. I keep the product flowing, si? There's a skill to it. All these moving parts. Making sure they come together and split off at the right time, in the right places."

Vitari shifted on the barstool, sitting up to pretend he was interested. "Can I see that again?"

Santiago, more than happy to flex his wealth, unlocked the phone and handed it over. It wasn't the euro amounts Vitari was interested in, but the column of numbers next to them. "These numbers, what do they mean?"

"Codes, for the product. So we can track them. We can't use names, right?"

He'd seen numbers like it on the Stanmore transaction document he'd emailed from Giancarlo's computer. "Track them, how?"

"The letters are locations, then the numbers. Months, years, when the product was sold. The last letters indicate—"

"You number each person you sell?" Like fucking cattle? "How long has this operation been going on?"

"Over a decade. Slick, like a well-oiled machine."

He'd been right. The numbers were people. "Do you know anything about Stanmore?"

"Stanmore?" Santiago frowned. "I don't—"

The phone rang in Vitari's hand. A name he didn't recognize flashed on-screen. He handed the phone back and watched as Santiago wandered to the other end of the bar to answer the call, not wanting Vitari to hear. He wouldn't have heard much over the thumping music anyway.

Santiago hadn't appeared to know Stanmore, but the names and numbers, it all looked too familiar to be coincidence.

Vitari checked his watch. Twelve-fifteen.

It was time to get things moving. Santiago wrapped up his call, and with a sour face, he returned to Vitari's side.

"We need to go." He downed his drink in a few generous gulps, and checking over his shoulder, he ushered Vitari from the bar, toward a side door. "Let's get out of here."

Vitari shoved open a fire escape door and entered a back corridor. The thumping music became muffled through thick walls, leaving a new headache behind.

"What's going on?" Vitari asked. "Who called?"

"I had a suspicion something was wrong with the shipment... I moved the drop site. And I was right. Border patrol were there, waiting to pick up the product. We got a fucking rat."

"You moved the drop site?" Shit. He'd been banking on the boat landing at the same location as always. He needed those kids to be found. If that kid with the angry eyes wasn't intercepted now, he'd drop off the radar, and Vitari knew all too well what happened to kids who slipped through the cracks. "Where's the new drop site? We should be there, check it's running smoothly."

Santiago stopped him in the middle of the corridor. Some of the club staff shoved by them. Santiago studied Vitari a moment, eyes narrowing. He couldn't know Vitari had tipped off the cops. Vitari was Giancarlo's son, above reproach. To accuse Vitari of being the rat would be insane.

"A few miles southwest," Santiago said. "Wait here." He left Vitari in the corridor, disappearing back into the club.

"Fuck." Vitari pulled his phone from his pocket and tapped out a quick message. *Drop is southwest. Find them.* He needed this to work for the sake of his own goddamned soul. This shit was why he didn't get involved, why he always looked the other way. His heart couldn't take it if those kids vanished. If he failed them.

Santiago swaggered back through the door. "We're clear. Just asked the staff. No cops yet. But this whole thing stinks. Let's get outside, discuss the next move."

Vitari slipped his phone into his pocket and fell into

step alongside him. It was fine. Diaz would find the kids, they'd get the happy ending he'd been denied.

He checked his watch.

Fuck. He was almost out of time. They *really* needed to be outside.

"You got somewhere to be, *An-hel?*" Santiago smirked.

Someone already held the back fire door open, drawing on a vape and blowing mint-scented smoke into the air. Vitari passed through, out onto the street. The evening was cooler than of late, but still hot for the time of year. Vitari shrugged on his jacket. "No. Nowhere to be. Thinking I might head to another bar. You wanna walk—"

Santiago snorted and stepped around in front of Vitari, blocking his retreat. "Why me, huh?"

"Huh?"

Santiago's shoulders were up, his jaw set.

The hair on the nape of Vitari's neck tingled.

"Why did you pick me to fuck over?"

Ah. He knew Vitari was onto his side hustle. But that was fine, it was almost over. "What the hell are you talking about?" He glanced down the street. A few drunken couples stumbled along the sidewalk, but it was late, and the clubs were winding down. Not many people were outside. Few witnesses for what was about to happen.

"Give me your phone," Santiago said.

"What?" Vitari snorted.

"Give me your fuckin' phone, Angel." Santiago held out his hand.

"What for?"

"Back there, right after I told you the drop had moved, you sent a message to someone." Santiago lunged, shoving Vitari, rocking him backwards. "Give me your phone, hijo de puta."

"Get the fuck off me."

Just a few seconds more...

Santiago slammed into him, driving him against the wall. "You piece of shit." He scrunched Vitari's shirt in his fists. "It was you," he sneered in his face. "You told the cops, you motherfucker!"

Vitari laughed, half out of nerves and half bullshit. "What the fuck are you talking about? I didn't tell them shit."

"My operation was fine until *you* showed up. My driver vanishes—you fuckin' stole my last shipment. You think you're untouchable, Angel? Your father knows. It's why he sent you to me. He trusts me more than he trusts you."

Wait. No. That couldn't be true. "Don't blame your shit on me." Vitari shoved at his chest, trying to pry him off. "You're selling product on the side!"

"Si, I am. But I'm not a snitch!" Santiago swung a fast right hook that landed like the lash of a whip across Vitari's jaw. He reeled from the shock. "Your father will kill you, you dumb fuck!"

Not if he was already dead.

A black SUV roared up the street.

Blinding headlights blasted over them. Fuck, this was it. Santiago had him in his fists again, rattling him, accusing him of ratting him out, of stealing his product. Time slowed. Vitari watched that black SUV bear down.

The passenger window rolled down.

A semi-automatic assault rifle appeared.

Vitari closed his eyes.

"You are a traitor to your own blood, your own family!" Santiago yelled in his face. "You're dead!

Staccato gunshots rained. Brick dust exploded. Rounds peppered the wall. Santiago convulsed. Blood splashed

Vitari's face. A round struck his arm, jerking him back. Then another punched into him—high in the chest, shocking the air from his lungs. He gasped, hit.

Santiago had hold of him, dragging him down onto the sidewalk. His mouth opened and closed, silently begging for help. The SUV's tires screeched, and the screaming started.

Vitari gasped, trying to fill his lungs, but something was wrong. The air wouldn't come. He groped at his chest.

Fuck.

Why couldn't he breathe?

He wheezed, choking.

Santiago fell onto his side, his eyes open, the life fading right out of them, just like his blood spilling across asphalt.

Vitari—on his knees—clawed at his chest, at the hole in his shirt.

He was underwater, drowning.

He slumped onto a hand. *Breathe. Just fucking breathe.*

Francis...

He just wished...

He'd told Francis...

He loved him.

CHAPTER TWENTY-THREE

It had been almost a month since he'd watched Vitari leave. Every day he'd hoped for a call, even knowing he'd pushed him away.

But weeks had gone by, and Vitari hadn't called. Vitari hadn't even fought for them, so maybe it wasn't meant to be, maybe Francis had just been a good fuck.

He knew he shouldn't want to hear his voice, knew that his calling would drag him back into Vitari's world, but he craved it too. Craved him. And ever since Montague had drugged him, he'd dreamed of having Vitari with him so he might feel safe. And maybe they'd deal with Montague like they'd dealt with Luca...

The call from an international number came at the end of a busy day, and Francis's heart lurched to see it.

But the caller wasn't Vitari.

"I'm sorry, Padre," Catalina Diaz began. "There was a shooting outside La Cabana club in southern Murcia."

His heart knew what she was going to say before she'd said the words. He'd always known this call would come. But he hadn't expected it to be so soon.

"Vitari Angelini and another man, Santiago Garcia, were killed at the scene."

Francis smothered his gasp with a hand and dropped into his office chair.

Killed...

All thought and emotion vanished. Silence consumed his mind and body. Diaz was still talking, something about a trafficking operation and how Vitari had been instrumental in saving children. But the words faded behind a roaring in his head, coming at him like a freight train.

"Father?"

"He's... dead?" Francis whispered, too afraid to ask aloud.

"Lo lamento, I am sorry."

The last time he'd seen Vitari, he'd forced him away. He'd told him... he hadn't meant anything, when the opposite had been true. Vitari had meant *everything*. Vitari was Francis's heart, the reason it beat at all. And now he was gone.

He could see him now, leaning against the rail outside the Basilica—half smiling with his shades hiding his beautiful eyes—moments before Francis had broken his heart.

A sob lodged in his throat. Why had he done such a thing?

"Were you close, Father?"

He couldn't answer. The words wouldn't come. *I love him.* But he'd never told him. Never told anyone. And now he was gone.

"Oh God..." He ended the call and stared at the office door. Outside, staff milled around, shoes clopped on the old wooden floors, phones rang, drawer cabinets rumbled open and closed. Life went on.

He couldn't be here. If he didn't move, he might shatter.

He drifted from his office, as though half outside his own body, and left the administration building, left the cathedral grounds. He walked through Westminster, walked without seeing the people, the cars, without feeling the rain or hearing London drum and rumble. He moved like a ghost, until finding himself back at his apartment, in the cold and the dark. So very alone. He grabbed a bottle of whiskey he'd bought in a moment of weakness, but never opened, and poured two glasses.

Drink?

I don't drink alcohol.

Of course not, you wouldn't want to dirty up your halo.

He smiled at the memory of his first real conversation with Vitari on a luxury yacht that had later been blown to tiny pieces and took a sip, then chinked the glasses together. "To surviving, amore mio." He'd looked up the Italian words. He knew what it meant when Vitari had spoken them to him. *My love.*

He could see him smiling now, hear his accented voice taunting, teasing, laughing at him. *Padre Blanco.* That smile, that vibrancy, the way his eyes flashed with mischief, and how he loved life, loved living right to its very edges. He recalled too, how kind and gentle Vitari had been with the smuggled people he'd taken to the farmhouse.

Francis had believed God's love would be enough. But it wasn't.

They hadn't had long enough. They'd had no time at all.

Was their love so wrong a thing that God had sought to punish them because of it?

"And then there was one." Francis raised the glass and drank.

He couldn't do this alone. He couldn't be the hero when there was nobody good left to save.

He sat back, eyes burning, and let the tears fall.

Vitari had died saving people. He'd died doing what Francis had *told* him to do.

He downed the whiskey, glared at the glass, and snarled at his own selfishness. Rage bubbled up inside. He shouldn't have tried to change Vitari. He should have let him go earlier, should have let him have his life. But no, Francis had tried to save him, and in doing so, he'd killed him. The one man, one soul, he'd truly loved.

He flung the glass at the wall and unleashed a shout, then sobbed in the chair, wrecked. "Why... God, why?" He clutched at his chest, where his heart scorched his soul. The agony of grief consumed him. "Take me, take me..."

Where was God when Vitari had suffered as a boy? Where was God when he'd tried to do the right thing and been gunned down for it?

Why did Francis still live?

He'd never been worthy, and never would be.

Vitari had deserved so much more.

His tears dried. He had none left to shed.

Empty. Cold. He slumped against his desk.

He knew how this ended, knew what had to be done.

The path ahead was clear.

Vitari had died doing good, so then it seemed fitting, poetic even, that Francis would end his own life with sin.

Francis applied for a month's leave from his duties for emotional reasons. The entire Westminster staff wished him well, gave him cards and flowers, told him he just needed to take some time since the awful ordeal at the Vatican and the kidnapping before that.

But he didn't need time.

He needed a gun.

Vitari had guns around him most of the time. In Italy, in Spain, in Venezuela. But not in the UK. Francis had become so accustomed to seeing them, he hadn't considered how difficult it would be to find one. There were gun dealers in the UK, but a quick Google search revealed he needed a police check, background check, and a reason to have one, such as shooting foxes. Francis had none of those things.

But there *were* guns in England. The illegal kind.

His only option was to name-drop his way into finding an *underground* supplier. Which meant finding where, in London, being known to the Battaglia might grease some palms.

It was easier to focus on this task than to think about anything else in his life. Get a gun. That was all the thought he allowed. And pray. Pray for Vitari's soul, in the hope God had accepted his redemption. Pray for all the souls of the children ruined by Stanmore. Pray that Francis could follow this through... so no more children had to suffer.

Killing Montague wasn't the morally correct thing, but it was the *right* thing.

A few false starts in some unsavory areas of London got him no more than some strange glances. He assumed he was still protected and therefore unlikely to get attacked. Although, apparently that protection didn't extend to some of the more desperate criminals, one of whom cornered him after leaving a bar and stole his wallet at knifepoint. But he wasn't perturbed.

Over several days, he put the word out in various criminally associated bars that he wanted to buy a weapon, but after a week all he'd managed to collect was hangovers. Vitari would have laughed at him. *You can't buy a gun in London, Padre Blanco.* He'd have flashed his smile, then kissed Francis on the neck, and everything would have turned out just fine. Because it always had with Vitari.

He missed him.

Missed him so much that he didn't know who he was anymore, didn't know what he stood for.

He drank too much cheap whiskey and fell into bed when his head spun, and hated himself for that too.

But nothing mattered anymore, just getting a gun.

"What the fuck do you want a gun for, Padre Blanco?"

The man who'd sidled up to him at the bar wore a hooded sweater with some kind of Japanese writing on the front. He wore the hood down and seemed to be eyeing Francis both with suspicion and intrigue. He wasn't old, perhaps around Francis's age. The way he carried himself, with absolute confidence, he didn't fear anyone in the bar.

"I think that's my business." Francis pretended his heart hadn't just leaped into his throat. He'd been daydreaming, waiting for the night to pass him by in a blur just like all the others. But this man's approach had startled him back into the moment. "Can you help?"

"Maybe." He roamed his gaze all over Francis. "I know you. You're the Battaglia's priest."

Was he their priest? He didn't work for them. Certainly not now Vitari was gone. But it wouldn't hurt to lean into that assumption, if it got him what he wanted. "I am. Who are you?"

"The man who can answer your prayers."

Francis didn't much care for the way this stranger was eyeing him. "Do you have a name?"

He offered his hand. "Neo." Francis shook Neo's hand, for the sake of politeness, and found it firm. "Five grand," Neo said.

"Five thousand pounds?"

"Cash. It's a bargain."

Oh. He had that much in his account. He might be able to do this, to own a gun. "Will it be... Will it be small?"

"'Small'?" Neo snorted and leaned back against the bar. "You don't know much about guns, Padre? Tell me what you want it for and I'll get you the right weapon."

Francis peered into his drink, at the slosh of golden whiskey. "What do most people want guns for?"

"You're not most people though. And right now, there are three other men in this bar watching you. Lots of people are interested in why a priest wants a gun. And others want to know why *you* want a gun."

Francis glanced over his shoulder but couldn't see anyone looking his way through the writhing, dancing bodies. Was he really being watched?

He'd tried to keep his head down. He hadn't worn the collar. He'd even grown the stubble of a golden beard in the hope it might disguise him some. Apparently not.

"I'll get you five thousand cash," Francis said.

"I'm going to assume you don't want a semi-automatic rifle. Which is good, as those are fuckin' difficult to get into the UK. I can get you a handgun and some rounds."

That would be perfect.

This was happening.

He was getting a gun.

"Will it be... traceable?"

Neo arched an eyebrow. "I'm offended you'd think I'd be so unprofessional. The gun will be clean. Once you've used it, toss it. It won't come back on you, or me. And if you mention me at all, I'll deny everything. You know not to fuck with the Battaglia, right, Padre?"

"Yes." Francis swallowed too much whiskey and coughed. "Then you are Battaglia," he wheezed. "Why are you helping me?"

"Let's just say my employer has an interest in letting this play out."

Giancarlo knew what Francis was doing and wasn't stopping it? Did he grieve for his son? Did he know what Montague had done to Vitari, and that was why he'd sent Neo here? It seemed likely, *if* Giancarlo cared, but he'd been prepared to kill Vitari himself to keep the Stanmore secrets a secret. It was too late to care now.

With Montague gone, Francis would be the only one left who knew about Stanmore. The last remaining thorn in Giancarlo's side. And without Montague's protection, the Mafia don would try to kill him.

"Good man," Neo said, shaking hands again. "Meet me back here in two nights."

He nodded and watched Neo flick his hood up and disappear into the crowd.

This decision would be the end of Francis. His final sin among many.

He'd killed once, to save Vitari. And he'd kill again, to end Montague.

Soon, he'd see Vitari again in Hell.

It was always going to end this way.

CHAPTER TWENTY-FOUR

Vitari

"You well?" Sasha asked, entering the bedroom. His bulky presence shrank the saferoom around them.

Vitari pushed upright from the bed and stretched his left arm, rolling the ache from bruised muscles. "Yeah, I think so."

Wearing a ballistics vest hadn't stopped multiple rounds from punching him. But he preferred the bruises over a bleeding hole in his chest.

"Congratulations, Vitari Angelini is a dead man," Sasha said, pulling a chair out from the nearby desk and spinning it around to sit in front of Vitari.

"It won't fool them for long." Giancarlo would become suspicious as soon as the morgue refused to release the body. He had a few days to get out of Italy before the shit hit the fan.

"Long enough."

Vitari reached into his pocket and handed over the phone. "It's all on there. Trafficking routes, documents, names, dates. Everything I could get."

Sasha's dark eyes widened with respect. "Enough to ruin your father."

Vitari sniffed and rested his elbows on his knees. "Yeah."

Sasha opened the phone with a swipe of his thumb and browsed the images. "This is good."

"You'll need to secure the witnesses. Once the Battaglia know there's been a leak, they'll send people like me to scorch the earth. They'll burn it all down so there's nobody left to testify."

"I know how it works." He dropped the phone into his pocket and brought out the USB drive Vitari had given him as insurance. "This is yours."

Vitari looked at it pinched between Sasha's fingers, then up into the man's eyes. Sasha had seen the images. He'd seen Vitari at his most vulnerable. Vitari snatched it back. "Grazie." He turned his face away and swallowed his pounding heart. "You're not going to use it?"

"The trafficking operation is enough for the authorities to prosecute. With Giancarlo arrested, the Battaglia will be in freefall."

And the DeSica would rise. "You'll have to act fast. Give them time to breathe, and they'll regroup. Antonio—Little Toni—watch him. He's sharper than he looks."

"Toni is the underboss. Da." Sasha nodded. "You prove very helpful, Angel."

Once Giancarlo was arrested, and the Battaglia fell, people were going to die. People he knew well, people he'd grown up alongside. But that wasn't Vitari's fault. All he'd done was expose the worst part of the business. What happened next was out of his hands.

He'd hide out in Panama until the dust settled, get himself a new name, new life.

His only regret was Francis.

He probably didn't yet know Vitari had been declared dead. Maybe wouldn't even care when he found out... It wasn't as though Vitari was going to live a long fucking life into retirement. This way Francis got to live unmolested by the Battaglia. Montague, however, was another problem, and one he'd hoped Sasha would deal with. But it seemed even the DeSica boss didn't have the stomach for Stanmore.

Once the heat died, Vitari would track down Montague and put a bullet between his eyes.

For now though, he had to lay low.

"You are brave and fearless, Angel." Sasha stood and peered down at him.

Vitari chuckled. He didn't know about fearless. This whole fucking plan terrified him. The fact he was sitting in the same room as the DeSica boss, his whole world in ashes, about to betray his family—it terrified him. The future terrified him. Being alone terrified him. It always had. But he was alive. And that was all he dared hope for.

"We make good team." Sasha grinned. "Shame I cannot trust you."

"Then we're even, as there's no way I'd ever trust you."

Sasha laughed. "And that is why you are alive, Vitari Angelini. Go live your life somewhere far away, as your mother wanted."

Vitari's smile froze and his heart turned to ice. "What did you say?"

Sasha waved his question away, like shooing a fly. "You are free to go."

"No, wait." He stood, wincing around a riot of bruises in his chest. "You knew my mother? Sasha, wait!"

Sasha stopped in the doorway, with his guards outside. He faced Vitari. "Let sleeping dogs lie... That is the expression, yes?"

"How do you know Stefania Angelini?" His thoughts spun. How would the DeSica boss know about Stefania?

"You told me her name." He shrugged. "Of no consequence."

No, it was more than that. He could see it in the man's eyes and the way he held Vitari's stare, as though willing him not to ask. If he'd known Vitari's mother, had he always known about Stanmore and Montague? Had he tricked Vitari into revealing all *he* knew? "You never intended to do anything about Stanmore, did you?"

Sasha's smile faded, leaving his hard, haggard face blank and difficult to read. "Goodbye, Angel. For your sake, I hope never to see you again."

"Wait, tell me—" Vitari followed him out of the room, but the guards raised their rifles. Vitari stopped and lifted his arms. "Easy, easy."

Sasha was already gone, and outside the safehouse a car engine rumbled. Vitari backed into the room. "Fuck." He didn't have time to pursue what Sasha knew about his mother and Stanmore. The clock was ticking. He had to get out of Italy.

He grabbed his blood-stained jacket, turned toward the door, but paused. Someone had placed a crucifix high up on the wall. He'd stared at it over the last few days, while he'd healed, and kept his head down.

"We're done. I don't want to see you again."

"So you're just going to walk away, after everything?"

"It's because of everything that I have to."

It didn't matter how much Vitari wanted to reach out, Francis didn't want him. Vitari had ruined his life.

This was a good thing. A clean break.

Vitari Angelini was dead.

As he always should have been.

And Francis was free.

CHAPTER TWENTY-FIVE

He had the gun.

A 9mm 1911, or so Neo had told him. He'd also demonstrated how to use it.

But now the gun was real and in Francis's hands, he wasn't sure he could go through with it. Killing Luca had been a spur of the moment desperate reaction to terrible circumstances. He'd had no choice. But buying a gun and shooting Archbishop Montague was premeditated murder.

It had seemed like a good solution, like the only solution. But now that Francis sat in his office, with the door locked, the gun in his hand, he doubted himself.

There was no coming back from cold-blooded murder.

He was already well on his way to Hell, his soul damned long ago. But what if everything Montague had said was true? What if all of this was in Francis's head? He had been the one to tempt him. People made mistakes. What if Montague had just made a mistake? A terrible mistake, but a mistake nonetheless. What actual evidence did he have that Montague was still a monster?

None.

The archbishop had even protected him from the Battaglia.

Had grief curdled his mind? Was *he* making a terrible mistake?

He couldn't do it.

He placed the gun in the desk drawer, buried it under papers, and locked the drawer. It was safer in the office than at his apartment. He could argue he hadn't been the one to put the gun in his desk, if it was ever found. But denying he had one if it was found at home would be more difficult.

Francis spent the rest of the day working on menial office admin that required little thought. Still on vacation, he should have stayed at home and finished off the whiskey, but he didn't want to impair his judgment.

The noise in adjacent offices faded as the staff left for the night, until it became so quiet that he was surely alone. The old building sighed around him. Central heating pipes ticked and hummed. It was a good quiet, a peaceful quiet.

He opened the photos folder on his phone and looked at the photo of the Stanmore boys. All of the boys gone, all but him.

"The sword of the wicked shall enter their own heart, and their bows shall be broken." Vengeance should be left to God. But if God had cared at all, Montague never would have touched Vitari. He would not be alive to hurt others.

A door slammed.

It was late. His office and the corridor outside it were dark. He'd been alone in the building, he'd been sure.

The sound of shoes on floorboards passed by his door

and faded. He knew that gait like he knew the sound of his own heartbeat. Archbishop Montague had just left.

Keeping the light off, Francis unlocked his door and peeked into the corridor. A light glowed from within Montague's office. He'd be returning. Francis had no wish to be alone in the building with him, but if he'd left the door unlocked, now was the perfect opportunity to get inside and search for incriminating evidence. Evidence that would properly ruin the man. No bloodshed. No murder. A different kind of smoking gun. Ruining him had to be better than killing him.

Francis hurried down the corridor, opened Montague's office door, and slipped inside.

A blond-haired boy looked up from a chair beside Montague's large desk. "Oh!" It was the choir boy who Francis had seen leaving some weeks ago. Francis blinked. "I was uh... just... visiting..."

Something was wrong.

The boy—wide-eyed and red-faced—shrank back.

"It's all right, I won't hurt you." Francis held out a hand. Something had happened, something that had this boy racked with shame and guilt and confusion. "My name is Father Scott. Did..." Francis swallowed to keep his voice from cracking. "Did he do something to you?"

The boy shook his head but bit his lip.

"What's your name?"

"Toby."

"Toby, listen... I know this is difficult, but I need you to be truthful with me." Francis scooted around the desk and knelt in front of Toby. The lad was all sandy-colored hair and freckles, just as Francis had been at that age. "It's important you're honest. Did he do things to you, things that made you uncomfortable?"

Toby chewed on his lip.

"You won't be in trouble."

He nodded.

Sickness burned the back of Francis's throat, or perhaps it was rage bubbling up from his soul. "Oh, I'm sorry, Toby..." Toby blinked, probably only half understanding what was happening. "All right, listen. What he's doing is wrong, but it's not your fault. It's important you know that. Whatever he's told you, you are not to blame." Francis offered his hand. "Come with me. I'll take you home."

"Francis!" Montague snapped. "What are you doing in here?"

If there had been any doubt, Toby's terrified gasp confirmed it. How dare Charles Montague continue to manipulate young, innocent children. Toby clutched at Francis's hand, so scared.

"It's all right," Francis told him, then straightened and turned to face Montague while protecting Toby behind him. Anger heated Montague's face and flushed his neck. The white band of his priest's collar stood out starkly compared to his black sweater. Even to Francis's adult eyes, his air of authority made him seem all-powerful. "You will immediately hand yourself into the police or by God I will report you."

Indignation hardened Montague's eyes. "Get out of my office at once. This does not concern you."

"I've stood by long enough." Francis stepped forward. "You will never touch another child—"

Montague's backhand scorched Francis's face, shocking his mind blank, but rage washed back in. "Toby, can you please leave the archbishop and I," Francis said with his glare fixed on Montague. Toby didn't need to see what came next.

"Toby, stay," Montague ordered. "There's no reason to leave. Francis is the one who is leaving, aren't you, Francis."

Toby scooted around Francis and lunged toward the door.

Montague made a grab for the boy.

Francis had been that boy once. And there was no way he was going to allow Montague to control Toby's life like he had Francis's. Francis shoved at Montague, pushing him back. Montague reeled, startled, but as Francis pinned Montague to the wall by his sweater, the sound of Toby's shoes hitting the timber boards confirmed he'd escaped.

Montague eyed him coolly. "You should know by now not to threaten me, Francis. It will not end well for you."

The laugh that fell out of Francis didn't sound sane. "I don't care." He dropped Montague and took a step back. "I'm done with you, and the church. All of it. It's not about me, it's about that boy!"

"What's gotten into you? Look at you." Montague straightened his clothes with a sharp tug. "You haven't been taking care of yourself, Francis. You're pale, and you've been drinking..." He stepped forward. "Let me help you."

Francis stepped back. "What are you doing?"

"Trying to help. You've always needed my help. You wouldn't be here without me."

"Well, that's true enough. I'd be dead, like the others. Did you think he was dead? Did you think you were safe?"

Montague frowned. "What are you talking about?"

"Vitari? The boy you raped in Stanmore's back room? All these years, did you think you'd gotten away with it? Until you saw him in the hospital, until he attacked you?"

Realization crossed Montague's face. "This is about *him*? He's dead, and you're upset? That troubled boy should have died long ago, Francis. This is God's will."

How dare he bring God into his own twisted desires. "God had no hand in the disgusting things you've done."

"Oh stop!" Montague barked. "You think you're some enlightened pillar of goodness? You *wanted* to be touched," he snarled. "You begged me for it, and you liked it, just like *he* liked it. He looked at me with his pretty eyes, and he wanted it."

Fury tried to choke Francis, made his voice thin. "None of us *wanted* it."

"You can't do anything. You can't tell anyone. I will expose everything you've done," he snapped. "I have the photographs of you and that Vitari boy *together*, sucking each other's cocks."

"Oh God." Giancarlo had given him the pictures? Why? What hold could Montague have over the Battaglia don to make him risk his own son?

"I'm more powerful than you can imagine, Francis. Nobody can touch me. Certainly not you. You should get down on your fucking knees where you always belonged and worship me." He straightened, shoulders back, and glared at Francis with a self-satisfied smirk. "I'm going to pray for your soul in the cathedral. Do what you will, but you can't stop me, because I own you. You are mine, you were always mine. Bought and paid for from that boys' home. Be grateful I care, because if I hadn't, then you'd have been one of those whores in the back room, spreading their legs for money."

He strode from the office.

Francis, stunned numb, stared after him. His ears rang as though an explosion had blasted in his head.

Montague was right. Nobody could touch him. And nobody cared.

But Francis did.

He dashed into his office, unlocked the drawer, grabbed the gun, and slotted the magazine in place with a foreboding click, just like Neo had shown him.

For Vitari. For all the boys, past and future. He was ending Montague's abuse tonight.

He hurried from the administration building, across the foggy courtyard, and into the cathedral. The huge door clanged as he opened it, ringing through the cavernous space. And there was Montague, kneeling in front of the altar at the end of the cathedral's grand nave. Enormous arches framed the aisle. All the pews were empty.

At this late hour, nobody else was here.

Just Montague and Francis. And God.

Montague peered over his shoulder.

"Stay there!" Francis raised the gun and strode down the aisle. "If you move, God help me, I will shoot."

"F-Francis." Montague climbed to his feet and glared defiantly. "What nonsense is this? A gun?" he scoffed. "Where on God's Earth did you get a gun?"

"Shut up. Listen—You will listen!" He made it all the way down the aisle but stopped at the end of the pews, still several strides from Montague. "Someone should have done this years ago."

Montague heaved in a great sigh, but his eyes turned steely with intent. "Francis, you aren't going to murder an innocent man in front of God."

"Did you just say 'innocent'? Is that what you think you are?" He kept the gun raised, kept Montague in his sights. He just had to pull the trigger. It was loaded and cocked. Just pull the trigger and end the nightmare.

"You are a disturbed young man, I see that now." Montague raised his hands. "I believed I could help you, believed God would help you, but I fear you are beyond help. You were always difficult."

"This is *not* my fault!" His shout filled the vast arches and domes high above them. The candles on nearby candelabras flickered.

Just pull the trigger. It was easy. He'd done it before. Why couldn't he do it now?

His face was wet; from tears or sweat, he wasn't sure. He was furious, not sad, so why was he crying? He wanted this man to die for everything he'd done, for the weekends he'd taken Francis into his bed, for raping Vitari, for making Vitari think that was all he was good for.

His hand trembled, and his aim was skewed. Why couldn't he pull the trigger? Why was he so weak? "God, give me strength to deliver your vengeance."

"Vengeance is God's work, Francis. Not yours. Put down the gun." Montague stepped closer.

Francis backed up. "Stay there! Stop! I will do it! I've killed before!"

Montague stopped, his face sympathetic. "My boy, let me help you."

A sob fell from Francis. His mouth twisted around a grimace. "I am *not* your boy."

"Oh, but you are. I loved you when nobody else would. Your parents gave you up. That's why you were in that place. I took you in. I saved you, Francis."

"No, you ruined me!"

"There were worse places to be sold to, worse people to own you. I was always kind, I always gave you what you wanted. I guided you into God's hands. Pray with me—" Montague stepped forward again, hands coming closer, arms open, as though to embrace him.

And even now, there was some small part of Francis

that *wanted* to go to him. Francis lurched back. His finger greased the trigger, slick with sweat. He had to do this. There was nothing left to live for, no going back. He was broken, but in this, he'd finally do something good. "I hated myself for so long," he said with a sob. "But you were wrong, it wasn't my fault."

"I'm sure you're right, just put the gun down and we'll talk about it."

"I can't. I have to do this."

"Francis, whatever happened, whatever you've done, you can be redeemed. But not for this. Never for this. Your soul will go to Hell."

He hiccupped a laugh. "I'm already there."

"I know you think you loved the Italian, and your heart is hurting. I see that. I forgive you. Come to me. Come to God. He will heal us both."

The mention of Vitari almost brought him to his knees. The tears came freely now. "You don't know what love is! He was everything, and he tried, even after what was done to him—what you did to him!" Francis jerked the gun, and Montague stilled. "He deserved *more*, and you and those men took it from him!"

"Those men? You don't know what you're talking about."

"Stanmore! I'm talking about Stanmore. Your charity, and the vulnerable you were supposed to care for. It was all a con, just a way for you to sell sex with children."

Darkness filled Montague's glare. "Perhaps I should have let Giancarlo kill you."

"Perhaps you should have. Then all your secrets would be dead and buried like all the other boys."

"I protected you."

"I don't want your protection. The cost is too high."

"Kill me, and you will no longer be protected. Giancarlo will come for you."

"I know that!" God, it hurt. But he had to do this, he had to pull the trigger.

"You don't want to die for this, Francis."

"I do... I do want to die. I can't... I can't go on like this. It has to end. I have to end it." He jerked the gun up. "What do you have on Giancarlo, why does he do as you say? Is he part of Stanmore, like you?"

Montague sighed hard, his shoulders heavy. Did he see now, how he faced death?

"Give me your confession. Unburden the sins from your soul, Charles."

"She was a good girl, Stefania. A good young woman. Giancarlo loved her, but they were not wed, and when she became pregnant, her father refused to bless them with marriage. A strict Vatican family would never allow a babe with such a man. They sent her here, to me in England, where the sin could be hidden. I helped her, truly. The babe, Vitari, was beautiful from the day he was born. And she loved him. She took him home, to Italy. To Rome. I... told her father." Montague paused and wet his lips. "The Russian, Sasha Zhukov, killed her. Gunned her down on Giancarlo's front lawn as she played with her son. He took her son, he took Vitari, and put him in Stanmore."

No, that... Francis's thoughts tumbled. "*Sasha* put Vitari in Stanmore?"

But he'd claimed not to know about Stanmore. He'd asked them about it at gunpoint as though all of it was new information.

"It was by chance I found Vitari there. I didn't know who he was. I was there for the boys, and he had the most beautiful eyes. So like his mother's... I just wanted a piece of her, just a moment, and he was there... I don't... I tried to help him for her. I sponsored Stanmore, tried to watch out for the boys, for you. Sasha did not know me, but he learned of my interest in Stanmore. He threatened me, warned me to stay away from Stanmore. I reached out to Giancarlo—told him I'd found Stefania's boy—and I suppose he eventually got Vitari out. I didn't know he was saved. I thought... I thought he died there, or was sold on—"

But how could that be? "The Russian was behind Stanmore?"

"Yes. He trades in children, even today. Although, as you know, Stanmore is long gone. But it began there."

Francis lowered the gun as all the pieces tumbled into place. "Then Giancarlo lost them both to Sasha? His son and the woman he loved? Vitari and Stefania?"

Francis had thought Giancarlo had been behind everything—Stanmore, all of it. But all this time, the secret Giancarlo had kept was how Sasha had killed his love and taken his child? It wasn't guilt silencing the Battaglia don. It was shame.

It explained Giancarlo's hatred of the DeSica, of Sasha.

The young woman who had come to Francis in St Mary's church—months ago now—the woman the DeSica assassins had killed and left in the churchyard. She'd been a DeSica prostitute. They'd silenced her to stop her telling Francis everything. The DeSica men had been there to *stop her,* and to find out what Francis knew about Stanmore. And Sasha had held him and Vitari at gunpoint to find out all they knew, and to secure the evidence. It had never been about destroying Giancarlo. Sasha was cutting off loose ends, perhaps triggered by Francis's impending lawsuit.

But none of that mattered in this moment. Knowing who was behind Stanmore did not absolve Montague's sins.

Francis's tears had dried. He raised the gun.

Montague raised his hands too. "Giancarlo owes me for caring for Stefania when he could not. For seeing his son into the world, for telling him his son had been found. He is in debt to me."

"A son you later abused."

"It wasn't like that, I just... He was always so beautiful. I needed... him."

"He was a child! God, you make me sick." His aim steadied on Montague's forehead.

"Francis, wait! Everything I did, I did for love!"

"Love?" Francis's heart shattered anew. "You don't know what love is!"

"You think you loved him?" Montague snarled. "How can you love a man? It is forbidden by God!"

"God knows love, and it is not your twisted idea of it." The more he talked, the easier this became. Francis applied pressure to the trigger. He'd killed before. It hadn't been hard. Not really. Just pull the trigger.

"Francis, I am begging you, don't do this. I love you. I will get help, I promise." His words slithered their way around Francis's conviction, undermining it like waves around a sandcastle. "Please, I beg you. I am sorry for what I did. I never meant to hurt you. I will find help. I'll change. I'll admit everything. Please... don't condemn your soul for me... I am not worth it."

Oh God, why did he have to say those things, and why did Francis believe him?

"You'll get help?"

"Yes, tomorrow, right away." He went down to his knees and sobbed. "I beg you, please, Francis. I will admit to it all. I will tell the police. Everything! Please, Francis. Please."

"He's lying," a smooth Italian voice said, a voice Francis

couldn't be hearing, a voice from beyond the grave.

Francis spun.

Vitari Angelini leaned against the pew at the far end of the nave, as though he had every right to be there and wasn't a phantom risen from death. He couldn't be real. It wasn't possible. The cathedral spun. His heart thumped in his ears. Francis stumbled against a pew. "Vitari?"

Montague bolted from the altar, along the front pew, heading for the west entrance.

Francis jerked the gun up. "Stop!" His finger slipped, jerked the trigger. The gun kicked, the round flew, and a piece of stone chipped off the pillar beside Montague's head.

Montague froze and whimpered, then prayed.

Vitari's warmth coiled around Francis first, and then he was there, beside him, his fingers easing into his, taking the weight of the gun from his hand. "You don't want to do this," he whispered, his words cool against Francis's ear.

Relief freed his heart, his soul.

He really didn't want to do this. And Vitari was here, he was alive. He was real.

Vitari stepped up to the altar and aimed the gun at Montague's back. "Turn around."

Montague raised his hands and slowly turned. He trembled, eyes wide with fear. "Vitari—I knew your mother! We were friends. I cared for her!"

Vitari's top lip curled. "You're right, Francis doesn't need to condemn his soul for a piece of shit like you." Vitari started walking closer. One step, two. "But I'm already damned."

"Wait—" Francis blurted.

Vitari pulled the trigger. The gun jumped. The boom blasted through the cathedral. The archbishop's head jerked. The impact flung him backward. He fell with a heavy thump and lay sprawled on the floor, twitching, his fading nerves trying to make him move even with the back of his head blown out.

The grand arches shifted sideways; Francis's drumming heart grew louder. *Oh God.* It was too much. He slid down the side of the pew, his legs too weak to hold him. Vitari was here. He'd killed Montague.

Vitari was here...

"We need to ditch the gun." Vitari casually wiped the weapon on his shirt and tucked it against his lower back, hidden under his jacket. He glanced over, spotted Francis, and knelt in front of him. Alive. So alive. Francis couldn't look away. If he did, Vitari might vanish again. His dark hair was a little unruly, escaping its styling. But his face was the same, his dark eyes so entrancing that Francis must be dreaming.

"How are you here?" Francis reached up and touched his face, to feel his skin and know he was real. His fingertips skimmed a bristle of rough whiskers. "Is this a miracle?"

Vitari's grin slid sideways. "Come on, Padre. It's time to go."

"I don't understand."

"Francis, look at me." Warm hands clamped Francis's face. "We need to go right now."

"Go... where?"

"Anywhere that isn't here." He grabbed Francis's arms and heaved him to his feet. "It would be helpful if you hold yourself together while we get out of this."

Get out of it? Vitari was here, and he'd just killed Archbishop Montague with the gun Francis had bought. There was no getting out of this.

"Oh God. You killed him," Francis muttered, stumbling

along beside Vitari.

"You're welcome."

"I didn't... He wasn't—"

"If you're about to tell me he didn't deserve it, I'll leave you here." He smiled as he said it.

No, don't leave me. Francis couldn't think; his thoughts took an age to come, as though his body and brain moved through syrup. Shock, it was shock. He wasn't sure if any of this was real. But it felt real. The foggy night air outside the cathedral was cold and wet on his face. Vitari's grip was right there, on his arm, solid, firm, and real.

They hurried through the courtyard, through the barriers stopping traffic from entering the cathedral grounds, and there was Vitari's car, parked on the curb.

His chest tightened; his heart squeezed. He braced against the roof of the car, trying to breathe, as Vitari opened the door. He couldn't do this. He couldn't keep running from his sins. He should stay; he should face justice for what he'd done. "I can't—"

"Francis," Vitari warned.

"I can't go with you."

Vitari straightened by the open passenger door, no longer smiling. "You don't have a choice, Padre."

"I just killed a man."

"No, I did." Vitari squared up to him, forcing Francis to straighten and look him in the eyes. "Get in the car."

He loved Vitari, he loved him so much that his whole soul screamed to go with him, but they couldn't keep running from their mistakes.

Vitari's eyes widened. He was surely going to say something about Francis not thinking clearly. But instead, he took a step closer, banishing the distance between them. His fingers skimmed up Francis's face, sliding into his hair, and then Vitari's mouth ghosted over Francis's, there but not, real but distant. Asking... Asking what? Francis parted his lips and breathed him inside. His hands found Vitari's waist, his body filled with feeling and warmth, coming back to life after being empty for so long. It wasn't even a kiss, not yet, just a tease of the lips, breaths shared, heart to heart.

He should never have pushed Vitari away, should never have hurt him.

Francis ran his hand up Vitari's back, skimming the gun, then splayed his fingers between his shoulders and nudged Vitari's lips apart with his tongue, seeking everything he didn't deserve, asking for the love of a man who would ruin him in all the best ways.

Vitari smiled against his lips, pulling back just enough to peer into his eyes. "There you are, amore mio."

My love.

Yes, Francis would go with him. He'd go with him to the ends of the earth.

"Angel!" A voice came out of the dark.

Vitari twisted around, blocking Francis from the approaching hooded figure.

The figure dropped his hood. Neo. The Battaglia man who had sold Francis the gun. What was he doing here?

The flash of a knife caught the diffused glow from the streetlight.

"Thought you were dead, fra," Neo said.

Francis dropped his gaze down Vitari's back, to where the gun was wedged between his back and his belt, asking to be taken, to be used a second time, as though Vitari's being here were fate, as though God had given Francis the things he needed in the darkest of times.

God had brought Vitari back to him.

And this time, Francis would do anything to save him.

CHAPTER TWENTY-SIX

Vitari

"Neo, why are you here?"

How had Neo known this would be where Vitari was? Vitari hadn't even known he was coming until the last moment, when he'd told the pilot of the light plane to detour to an airstrip outside central London.

"Not for you, yet here you are, a dead man walking." Neo gestured with flair, and the knife flashed.

He wasn't here for Vitari. Then Neo was here for Francis? To kill him?

"There were rumors you were a cocksucker, but I didn't believe it," Neo said, stopping in front of him. "You fucking the priest, Angel?"

This was ridiculous. Neo wasn't going to kill him. Regardless of what Vitari had done, Neo wouldn't act without Giancarlo's permission. Vitari snorted a laugh. "Back off, Neo. Francis is above your pay grade."

"That's where you're wrong. I don't work for Don Giancarlo." Neo brandished the knife, bringing it closer. "Sasha thanks you for all your help in bringing down Giancarlo. Now all he needs is for you to die."

Vitari's smile faded. He raised his hands. "You're DeSica."

"Yeah, Ricky almost gave me away, so he had to swing off a bridge. You understand?"

"You didn't shoot up a DeSica bar, did you?" But Vitari had checked. Neo's story had been legitimate. It was the whole reason Giancarlo had let him in.

"I did that, to get in with you." He smirked. "And it was too fuckin' easy. Enemy of my enemy, right?"

Except, Neo was no friend. Enemy of their enemy was still an enemy. Vitari tasted betrayal. The DeSica had no honor, no sense of loyalty, of family. Sasha had used him. "You gunned down your own people?"

"Sasha's orders. Worked, didn't it?"

"Then you're the assassin who tried to take out Francis in St Peter's."

"Fuck no, not me. We still don't know who's bankrolling that hit. Doesn't matter. You two loose ends are both about to die."

The hard press of the gun shifted against Vitari's back, then its weight vanished. Vitari breathed in and lifted his chin. He hadn't killed the archbishop so Francis could turn around and kill this DeSica nobody.

"I *helped* Sasha. I gave him everything he wanted."

"And he's grateful. This isn't personal. Just business. You understand." Neo lunged. The knife slashed.

Vitari jerked back, stumbling into Francis, pinning him against the car. Neo was *fast*. Vitari lunged and threw a right hook at Neo's cheek. His knuckles struck, whipping his head back. Neo grunted, reeled, and slashed the knife up, almost nicking Vitari's chin, and Vitari thrust his forehead into Neo's nose. Blood spurted, and Neo cried out. Vitari slammed a punch into the man's middle, doubling him over, then brought his knee up, smacking Neo's already bloody nose. Neo screeched, roared, and with murder in his eyes, he charged.

The gun boomed by Vitari's right ear.

Boom!

Vitari jerked from the deafening blast. *No, Francis...*

Neo teetered, then stumbled over the curb and fell to the sidewalk. But he wasn't dead. Blood stained his shirt's left shoulder. Vitari pinned Neo's wrist to the ground under his shoe, crushing it, and Neo dropped the knife.

"Your fucking priest shot me!" Neo screeched.

"Yeah." Vitari kicked the knife away. "He's good at that."

Francis loomed at Vitari's right, gun pointed down at Neo, vengeance ablaze in his fierce hazel eyes. Fuck, like this he was more of an avenging angel than Vitari would ever be. And hot as Hell. Vitari reached for him and pushed his arm down. "Not today, Padre," he said, taking the gun for a second time.

Francis choked out a gasp now he was free of the weapon. Later, when he'd calmed down, this would probably all be Vitari's fault. And he'd gladly shoulder the blame. But for now, they needed to get out of London.

"You're dead, both of you!" Neo screeched. "If Sasha doesn't kill you, Giancarlo will! You're fucked!"

Vitari guided Francis back to the car and sat him inside. Francis looked up, big eyes full of sorrow and regret. Maybe even shame. He shouldn't feel any of those things. He should be fucking proud.

"There won't be a hole deep enough to hide in!" Neo yelled, then swore some more as he tried to stand.

Vitari closed the door and faced Neo. He still had the gun, and he was tempted. What was another murder on the streets of London? "You really want to die tonight, huh?" He approached Neo and peered down.

They both knew, if Vitari chose, Neo would be dead. "Sasha can send a thousand men for Francis. I will kill every single one of them." Vitari crouched. "If he wants a mountain of DeSica corpses, tell him to send his assassins. And when there are no more men left, when I have killed them all, I will come for *him*."

Neo bared his teeth. "You can't fight the DeSica and the Battaglia, you can't fight the whole fucking Mafia, Angel."

"For Francis, I can."

Disgust crossed Neo's face, almost earning him a bullet in the head, but Vitari needed to get his message back to Sasha. He needed them all to listen. Francis was off-fuck-ing-limits. He was protected by the Angelo della Morte. And that was no idle threat.

He left the Battaglia traitor writhing in his own blood, wiped the gun down, and tossed it into a nearby drain, then climbed behind the wheel of the rental.

As Vitari pulled the car away, Francis twisted in the seat, staring back. "You're just going to leave him there?"

"He's someone else's problem now."

Francis watched Neo's reflection shrink in the side mirror, then when they turned a corner, he slumped in the seat, pale but bright-eyed. His freckles were dark on his skin. He looked... different, from the last time Vitari had seen him outside the Basilica. Thinner, rougher, with a shimmer of a golden beard and tired, haunted eyes. More haunted than before.

He should never have let Francis push him away. That kiss... That kiss moments ago had been the truth. Whatever Francis had said about it being over was bullshit. Nobody kissed as though they were handing over their soul if they didn't mean it.

Vitari was so fucking relieved he'd detoured to London on a whim. He hadn't even been sure he'd find Francis at Westminster Cathedral, but he'd suspected he'd return to London after *everything*. He'd had to try, one last time, to ask him to run away with him.

They were meant to be together.

And Vitari would fight the whole world to save him.

CHAPTER TWENTY-SEVEN

Vitari

They boarded the light plane from London to an airstrip in Spain, and from Spain, Vitari used old contacts to hitch a ride on a cargo plane to Panama. He joked about it not being five-star luxury travel, and that Francis should be used to roughing it with him by now. But Francis merely smiled and withdrew into himself.

It was a lot. Francis had clearly believed Vitari had been dead, and then to have him walk back into his life and execute his mentor right in front of him...

He needed space. Even as it killed Vitari not to wrap him in his arms and tell him how he'd done all of this *for him.* He wanted to tell him he loved him in Italian, in a thousand different ways, wanted to kiss him stupid, to fuck him hard, then love him slow. But he couldn't do any of that while Francis was hurting.

So he stayed quiet too and went over in his mind all the revelations he'd heard Montague spew to Francis after

Vitari, upon hearing their raised voices, had snuck into the cathedral.

He'd heard half of their argument from the shadows and didn't want to believe most of it. Sasha was behind Stanmore? Montague must have been lying to try to save his own skin.

Once they landed in Panama City, Vitari paid cash for a rusted old Jeep and drove Francis to the forgotten waterside town of Gamboa. Only there, surrounded by monumental palms and rainforest, did Francis begin to relax. He even cracked a smile at some of the more exotic birds cawing from the canopy they drove under.

He hadn't once asked where they were going, or where they were. Vitari might have thought that a good thing, but Francis made good complicated.

Vitari pulled the Jeep up outside what would be their home for the next few weeks—a timber-slatted casa on steel stilts, hidden by jungle, that resembled a storage barn from the rear.

He climbed the outside steps to the second floor and unlocked the door, exposing a smart, functional interior with broad beams arched above and a vast wall of glass overlooking the jungle. The distant waters at the mouth of the infamous Panama Canal drew Francis toward the glass.

Vitari heard his sigh, as though he'd finally relaxed. He'd figured Padre Blanco would prefer distant jungles, making this house perfect. For a little while.

"You all right here while I get some supplies?"

He didn't move.

"Francis?"

"Huh?"

Vitari joined him at the window. Their ghostlike reflections shimmered in the jungle. They'd left their lives several thousand miles away, but somehow, it was all still here in the room with them. Vitari felt it too. As though it was far from over. "Francis, are you all right?"

"Yeah," he replied, too quickly, adding a shy, fake smile.

"I'm going to get groceries. Relax, okay? We're safe here."

Francis nodded, but his eyes had gotten brighter and his smile twitched like a dying thing.

The last thing Vitari wanted to do was leave him, but they needed supplies. He planned to hunker down here, where nobody was going to find them, and then figure out their next move.

He took the Jeep back into the local village and bought groceries, then returned to the house on stilts and unloaded the Jeep.

Francis was sitting on the couch, just a few feet from the window where he'd left him.

"Coffee?" Vitari asked, after packing everything away and Francis had still not acknowledged him.

"You got anything stronger?"

"But you don't drink?" Vitari quipped, but Francis looked away, not in the mood for jokes.

Vitari fixed them both the Panama equivalent of whisky and sauntered into the living area. He handed Francis his.

"Thanks." He smiled and peered into his glass.

The distance between them had grown painful, and it was worse now than ever before. Vitari didn't know how to fix this. Maybe Francis just needed more time, or maybe the problem was Vitari? What if Francis hadn't wanted the archbishop to die? What if he didn't want to be here? What if he had meant to push Vitari away?

Jesus, everything was fucked up. Vitari considered sitting next to him, talking to him, but what would he say?

He sipped his drink, still standing, feeling lost. And he hadn't even allowed himself to think about the enormous fucking mistake he'd possibly made in helping Sasha.

"Oh God," Francis whined. He covered his eyes and almost dropped his drink.

Vitari plucked the glass free, set both down on the coffee table, and watched Francis come apart right in front of him. He sobbed, and sobbed hard, as though every shudder came from his soul.

Fuck. He really was hurting.

Vitari sat next to him and hauled him close, almost into his lap. "Shh." The sobs racked him so hard they shuddered through Vitari, making his own heart ache.

"I thought you were gone," Francis wheezed.

Vitari clutched Francis's head close to his chest and squeezed his eyes closed. He hadn't meant to hurt him. Not like this. He should have gotten word to him somehow, some way, to let him know it was all fake.

"Catalina told me you were dead."

"Mi spiace, ti chiedo scusa dal profondo del mio cuore ."

"I was going to kill him! I found him—There was a boy —I knew what he was doing—" Words fell out of him in a rush.

Vitari let him talk, despite most of what he said making no sense. But the hurt in every word was real, the agony Vitari had caused him. Why the fuck had Francis pushed him away? "I'm sorry." But he knew why he'd done it. For the same reason Vitari had killed Montague. To keep him safe.

"You pulled the trigger, but I killed him." Francis pulled back. Tears glistened on his face. Vitari dried them. Francis was so beautiful, even like this, puffy-eyed and distraught.

"It doesn't matter who killed him, he had it coming. He deserved it."

"It matters, Vitari." He blinked wet lashes, and a few more tears escaped. "I don't want to be like this."

"You are... You are everything. Don't let one sick fuck ruin you. Don't let him win. You're worth a thousand of him. More. Sono mortificato, scusami. I'm sorry I left you. I thought... It doesn't matter. Listen, we're here. You and me. We're going to be all right." He couldn't read Francis's face, only that he was in pain, and Vitari wanted to save him over and over again, until his real smile returned. Until he scowled at Vitari, in that way he did, with comedic disapproval that made Vitari laugh.

He kissed him. He needed to make the hurt go away, and he could show him more than his words could tell him.

Francis kissed him back, but even that felt wrong, as though Vitari had forced all of this on him. Vitari eased back and bumped forehead-to-forehead. "Please, don't lose who you are, not for him, not for me. Be brilliant, Francis. Be you. None of this was your fault."

"Then why does everything hurt?"

Vitari swallowed and kissed him again, kissed the tears off his face and tasted them on his lips, wishing he could kiss away that hurt. Francis kissed him back, opening himself up. His wet tears dampened Vitari's face too, and as the kiss deepened, this would be how they healed, together. "Amore mio, potrai mai perdonarmi?" Vitari asked between kisses. *Please forgive me.*

Francis's tongue thrust in, taking more. His mouth and hands became desperate. He climbed into Vitari's lap, easing him back in the couch, and rocked, kissing each breath away. It was grief, Vitari sensed that. Grief for his old life, grief for Montague, and perhaps grief for what he believed to be the loss of his own soul. He tore at Vitari's shirt, and Vitari swept his hands up Francis's back, relishing how his body trembled under his touch. God, when he was raw and desperate like this, he set Vitari ablaze, made him wild and mad to taste him, feel him.

He swept Francis's sweater over his head, then swooped in and suckled a pert nipple as Francis rocked in his lap. He could see how Francis's dick stretched his trousers, and he wanted nothing more than to go down on him, but Francis was driving this, he needed it, needed the control of a life he thought had spiraled out of control.

Vitari grasped at this hair, sucked on his neck, bit down, and sighed at the delicious sound of Francis's moans. His cock throbbed, trapped in his tight trousers. He wanted to fuck him into the couch, fuck him until he forgot who he was, forgot who they both were.

Francis yanked Vitari's head up and slammed a kiss on his lips, swept his tongue in, attacking. "I don't know... what I... want," he said breathlessly, between kisses.

That was Vitari's cue. He clutched Francis close, picked him up, twisted, and dropped him on his back, then tore at his trousers, freeing his flushed dick. Vitari went down on him, sliding him in, over his tongue.

Francis's fingers twisted in his hair. "God, yes!" He bucked, thrusting down Vitari's throat. Vitari gagged, gasped free, then licked down his shaft and tongued his balls, gently sucking them between his lips.

"I can't... I need you. Fuck me, Vitari." He lifted his head and snarled, "Fuck me *hard*."

The demand in Francis's voice tore out the rest of Vitari's restraint. He scooped him up, flipped him onto his hands and knees, and yanked his trousers down to expose his peachy ass. "You have the finest fuckin' ass I've ever seen."

"You goin' to fuck it or talk about it?"

"Oh, Padre." Vitari grinned and gave his ass a slap.

Francis flung his head back and gasped, in no mood to go slow. And that suited Vitari just fine. He freed his dick from his pants, spat into his hand, and slicked Francis's hole. It wasn't enough lube, but there was no way he was leaving Francis with his ass in the air to go find some. He spread his cheeks with one hand, and with the other, guided his cock down his crack, mixing pre-cum and saliva together, greasing things up, then pushed inside his tight hole. Exquisite pleasure set Vitari's fuckin' nerves on fire, then Francis's moans got in on the act, and Vitari slid deeper, killing himself to go slow.

"I'm so hard, I'm going to come," Francis growled.

Growled.

Vitari gritted his teeth, willing his own urges to calm the fuck down. "Not yet, cuore mio."

"Take me. God now, Vitari, fuck me."

He wanted it to last, wanted to feel every inch slide around him, but Francis getting all demanding was messing with Vitari's control. Francis wanted to be fucked, then he was going to get fucked. Vitari plunged in, balls deep, thighs to ass. Francis arched, and Vitari lost himself in the feel of tight muscle clutching his cock. He grasped Francis's thighs, holding on as he relentlessly pumped his dick so fast that any chance of holding back or savoring the ripples of plea-sure was long gone.

Francis's grunts, his panting, his whole body twitching and bucking under Vitari, how his body gave with every thrust—it was too much.

"Yes, yes... Oh... I'm... *Fuck.*"

Francis always swore when he was about to come, or kill someone. Vitari could feel the release in his body, in how his ass clenched, hear it in his stuttered breaths and the quickening of his all-over tremors. Pleasure crested to a blinding point, and with Francis crying out, Vitari came too, shuddering and pumping his load deep into Francis. He clutched his hips, trying to touch his fucking soul.

Neither of them had lasted long, but his orgasm might have been the most blinding he'd ever experienced. He drew Francis's naked, slick back against his chest, wishing they were both naked so he could feel every single one of Francis's tremors skin-on-skin.

There would be time for that, time for so much more. He wrapped his arms around him and kissed his salty shoulder, proving he could be gentle—*wanting* to be gentle, especially after that brutal fucking.

"Never leave me again," Francis said, panting, and when he threw his glare over his shoulder, there was so much righteous fire in his eyes that Vitari wondered if Francis had the power to incite God's wrath.

Vitari grinned and Francis's glare softened. "You're so fucking hot when you're furious."

He frowned. "I'm serious."

"So am I."

He twisted out of his arms, then winced as Vitari's dick slid free. A sensitive burn sizzled through him too. They were both going to be feeling that railing for a while. Francis continued to glare, as though furious, but an angry Francis was a whole lot better than a sobbing Francis.

"Whisky?" Vitari offered, sensing he was about to get his ass handed to him, and not in a good way. He'd listen to Francis yell all night if it meant it helped him find a way out of his grief.

Francis scowled at that too, and yanked his trousers back up, fixing the fly. "You should have told me you were alive."

"There wasn't time—"

"How did you do it?"

"Bulletproof vest. Still hurt, though."

"Oh, *it hurt?*"

And here it came. Vitari tucked his dick away, regaining some measure of composure, then grabbed his drink and slumped back into the couch with it. "Have at it, Padre."

"You could have told me, Vitari!"

"You told me to fuck off. So I did."

"I didn't... That wasn't what I said..." Francis huffed and tried to comb his fingers through his hair, but Vitari had made a mess of it during their frantic fuck, and now he was angry at that too. So angry his little freckles stood out on his red face.

"You said we were over."

"Yes, but..." He raised his hand for some reason and stared at his palm. "You weren't supposed to die," he whispered.

He'd been keeping his hands clasped together since they'd left England, as though hiding something. And then Vitari saw it, the little ring of pink scar tissue.

A burn.

"The fuck—" Cold rage burned through him. Vitari grabbed his hand. "Who did that?"

"Oh, that I..." He tried to tug his hand back but Vitari held on.

"Don't lie to me."

Francis closed his eyes. "I met your father."

"*He* did this? He fucking burned you?!" At the Basilica,

that day Francis had told him it was over, his hand had been bandaged. "Why didn't you tell me?"

"Because." Francis snatched his hand back. "He threatened to hurt you if I continued looking into Stanmore, your mother, all of that. He said to let it go, or he'd kill you. And so, that's what I did. I let you go. You were supposed to be safe... But now that doesn't make much sense, if Sasha is behind Stanmore and your mother's murder, wouldn't Giancarlo *want* to expose him? Did you hear what Montague said in the cathedral, about you, about Sasha shooting your mother?"

"It's all lies. Montague was bullshitting you to buy time." Vitari didn't care about Stanmore right then. His father had fucking *burned* Francis. He'd hated him before, but he hated him even more now.

"You heard what he said though, about your mother, about Sasha taking you to England?"

"Yeah..." He didn't remember any of it. He'd been too young. "If that had happened, Giancarlo would have told me."

"But it explains your father's hatred of the DeSica."

"Francis, leave it." Vitari slumped back in the couch. "I'm not listening to Montague's desperate ranting. Besides, my father had documents on Stanmore, he had photographs. The way the trafficking operations were being run were too similar to Stanmore. He had to be involved. He was complicit in all of it."

Francis hesitated, then said softly, "Just because he knew, it doesn't make him a part of it. What if he was investigating, gathering evidence, like we were?"

"My father burned your hand. He trafficked Venezuelan kids. He's threatened to kill you, and me. He sent me to St Mary's to watch you, and probably kill you. Why are you taking his side?"

"I'm not saying he's good, just that... What if your mother *was* killed by Sasha, what if Stanmore was Sasha's enterprise all along? What actual evidence do we have that Giancarlo is linked to Stanmore, other than him getting you out of there? Do you have anything solid, anything at all you can point to that shows Giancarlo was complicit in what was going on there?"

Vitari didn't need evidence. He *knew*. Giancarlo had to be involved, because if he wasn't, then the alternative didn't bear thinking about. "If Sasha is behind it all, then I just handed my mother's killer everything he needs to destroy my father, and probably the Battaglia too."

"What?" Francis asked. "What have you done?"

"I've given him everything on the trafficking operations. The routes, the sources, the capos. Handed him a gold mine of information to bring my father down. If Sasha hasn't already told the authorities, he will soon. Giancarlo is over, and Montague was lying, because if he wasn't, Francis, I've just betrayed my family in the worst possible way." Vitari clamped his mouth shut and breathed hard through his nose. He refused to believe Montague. The archbishop was *evil*. Everything he said was lies.

"Oh. No, you're probably right. Of course. I... It doesn't matter. It's over now, anyway."

But it did fucking matter, because ever since Montague had said those words, accusing Sasha of killing Vitari's mother, Vitari had gone over all the pieces of the past in his mind, all his fragments of memories. The DeSica feud, his father's warning not to go near Francis and the past, his rush to get Vitari out of Rome the moment he'd heard Sasha had picked Vitari up.

And the fear in his father's eyes.

Giancarlo's love for Stefania, no photos displayed of either of them, because he couldn't bear the agony of grief.

The hidden documents and images, collected—not for blackmail—but for proof.

He'd saved Vitari from Stanmore, he'd gotten him out— that was a fact. Perhaps the *only* fact that mattered.

"Fuck." No, he couldn't think it. It couldn't be like that. And Montague was not going to stick the knife in his heart from beyond the fucking grave. It was all in the past. "I need a shower."

CHAPTER TWENTY-EIGHT

Francis

Everything was... a lot. Every time he tried to grapple with events of the past two days, the scenes replayed too fast in his head. The choir boy, Montague, the revelations about Sasha, and then Vitari... alive. Back from the dead. The gun —the archbishop dead on the floor.

Francis's chest tightened, choking him.

And now here, in another country, somewhere in South America. Again.

If he thought too long about it, all the thoughts piled on top of him, trying to smother him, so he didn't think, he just... breathed, and tried to hold himself together.

Sex had helped. Furious, desperate sex. It was probably wrong, to want that, but he'd needed it and Vitari had been willing. *So willing.*

His ass burned, making him shift on the couch.

Had Francis used Vitari? No, he'd needed him, needed to feel him, to know he was real and here and alive, and

Vitari had satisfied those needs, as desperate to feel as Francis had been. Although, it had left Francis uncomfortably sticky.

The sounds of the shower shut off, so Francis ventured downstairs. The house had been designed with the bedrooms on the ground floor, to make the most of the jungle views from the living room. But it meant the downstairs was dark, and Francis could feel the walls closing in again. He preferred the bright, open upstairs, overlooking a whole different jungle world, one as far away from Westminster as was possible on God's Earth.

Francis knocked on the bathroom door. "Can I shower?"

"Sure," Vitari said.

Francis pushed open the door and found Vitari towel drying his hair, a second towel tucked around his waist, leaving his tanned chest gleaming wet. The razor wire tattoo encircled his wrist, dark against his skin.

With the numbness creeping back in, Francis stripped off his already loose trousers, tugged off his pants and socks, and stepped into the shower. Hot water rushed over him, cleaning the sin from his skin, but not his soul. He'd gotten used to it there.

Vitari left, which was probably for the best. After finishing in the shower, Francis wrapped himself in a fresh towel and emerged from the bathroom to find Vitari splayed on the bed, head propped on a hand, wholly naked, stopping Francis in the doorway. He was glorious, slim, but with enough muscle to throw a punch. Francis had once compared him to some kind of flashy men's magazine model, but now he resembled a pornographic poster, all laid bare. His cock began to stiffen under Francis's gaze.

"Goodness me." Francis looked away, and Vitari chuckled.

"Blushing, Padre, after demanding I fuck you in the ass?"

How could Vitari lay there so effortlessly confident in his attractiveness? Compared to him, Francis was all skinny limbs and pale skin. He didn't do naked displays like the one Vitari was giving him now.

"Come sit by me," Vitari purred, then lay back and interlocked his hands behind his head. "We don't have to do anything."

"Your cock says otherwise."

Vitari's mouth fought with a smile. "I know it's hard, but ignore my cock."

Francis arched an eyebrow at the double entendre, took a breath, and dropped his towel.

Vitari's smirk vanished, and his expression turned serious as he admired Francis's naked body. "Il mio cuore è tuo."

Smiling, Francis climbed onto the bed. "What did you just say?" He lay with his head propped on a hand, facing Vitari. With just a few inches between them, Vitari's heat warmed him through. His own cock began to harden, but he didn't feel shame. Not like he would have before.

Vitari's flashy smile returned. "You're going to make me say it?"

"You *just* said it. Say it again in English. Otherwise, it's not fair."

"Fine, Padre. *My heart belongs to you.*"

Francis's own heart did a little hiccup behind his ribs. He tried not to smile and failed. "Really?"

Rolling his eyes, Vitari curled an arm around Francis's

waist and pulled him down, and now they were chest to chest, naked and hot and tangled together.

Vitari nudged his mouth, seeking a kiss, but Francis pulled back. "It sounds better in Italian."

"Voglio passare tutta la vita con te," Vitari teased, then poked Francis's ribs.

Francis laughed, brushing his hand away. "Tell me what you said!"

"Vuoi stare per sempre con me?" Vitari tickled him, fingers digging in and skimming in an unfair fight.

Francis barked and writhed. "Stop! Oh God. *Please.* Don't. It's not fair."

"Stop? But your cock likes Italian. See?"

Francis snorted and hooked his leg around Vitari's, then trapped his hands between them. "Yes, that part of me is very fond of Italian." He nudged noses but pulled back when Vitari tried to capture a kiss again. "What does sempre mean?"

"Always." His dark lashes flicked up. "Forever."

He thought he might know what Vitari was telling him in Italian. That maybe this was more than just a passing fling, more than just two desperate men clinging to something in their messy lives. That maybe this was... love? The words were on Francis's lips, right there, almost spoken, but he couldn't say it. What if he was wrong? What if Vitari was just saying these things out of guilt for hurting him?

Francis touched Vitari's face and flicked a wayward lock of dark hair from over his eye. To think of him as gone, that he'd never see him again, it had broken something inside Francis, and whatever it was, it wasn't yet fixed. He was so damn scared of this, of them, of their past, of everything. Scared to lose him again.

"Hey." Vitari tipped his chin up. "We're safe here."

"Are we?"

"For a while." Vitari tucked him close, and Francis burrowed against his chest, snuggling in. The warmth of his skin, the soft touch of his velvety hairs, his smell, soapy from the shower and so very masculine. Francis let his thoughts drift, letting the worst of the memories float away—most of them. A stubborn one persisted. A gun shot, and watching Montague fall.

"Do you regret killing him?" Francis asked.

"Not for a second." Vitari met his gaze. "I'd raise him from the dead to fucking kill him again, only slower."

Yet, Francis hadn't been able to pull the trigger, even after knowing all the things Montague had done.

"My only regret is I didn't have time to cut his balls off like I promised," Vitari added.

Francis circled a finger around Vitari's nipple and skipped it down, over his abs. Vitari was a true avenging angel, a man of fury and retribution. "He sent upon them His burning anger, fury and indignation, a band of destroying angels."

Vitari arched an eyebrow. "Are you quoting a Bible verse?"

He'd thought him dead, but in his hour of need, Vitari had returned. It felt like God's work, as though He'd known Francis had been about to fall. "Will you really leave a mountain of corpses if they come for us?"

Vitari blinked up at the ceiling. "They won't find us."

That hadn't been an answer. But Francis already knew Vitari didn't make idle threats. L' Angelo della Morte had a reputation for a reason. And this avenging angel was the man he loved.

They fell silent, tucked close, and after a while, Vitari's breathing slowed. Francis looked up to find his lips slightly parted and his eyes closed, lashes fluttering from dreams.

This was good. Better than good. It was perfect. But even on the other side of the world, it wasn't yet over. The chaos they'd left behind would find them again.

They couldn't run from the past.

He extracted himself from Vitari's limbs, tucked a towel around his waist, and collected his phone from his bundle of clothes. There was no Wi-Fi, and the battery was on red, but he had one bar of signal. Enough to make a call. He headed upstairs, stared through the window at the swaying palms and distant river, and dialed.

The line clicked and rang.

"Chi é?" Giancarlo's low growl rumbled.

Francis glanced at the back landing, where the open stairwell descended to the bedrooms. Vitari would never allow this. He'd be furious, if he learned of what Francis had done.

But it was the right thing. Because Montague hadn't lied. Sasha had been behind Stanmore.

Francis loved Vitari with all his heart and soul. He'd do anything to protect him, to save him. Even go against his wishes.

"It's Father Scott. I don't have long. Please, listen. Vitari is alive, and I fear he may have made a terrible mistake."

Vitari and Francis's adventure concludes in the finale, Save Me, Forgive Me #3. Out now.

ABOUT THE AUTHOR

Rainbow Award winner A. Nash (Ariana Nash) writes LGBTQ+ fantasy and contemporary novels full of morally challenging characters, action, betrayal, and steamy love between two (or more) men.

Sign up to her newsletter and get a free ebook here: https://www.subscribepage.com/silk-steel

ALSO BY ARIANA NASH

Sign up to Ariana's newsletter so you don't miss all the news.

www.ariananashbooks.com

***

Shadows of London

(Five book urban fantasy series)

A sexy assassin, a billionaire boss with secrets, and magic bubbling up through the streets of London. All in a days work for artifact agent, John "Dom" Domenici.

Start the Shadows of London series with Twisted Pretty Things